THE *Last* KNIGHT

KNIGHT PUBLISHING BOOK 3

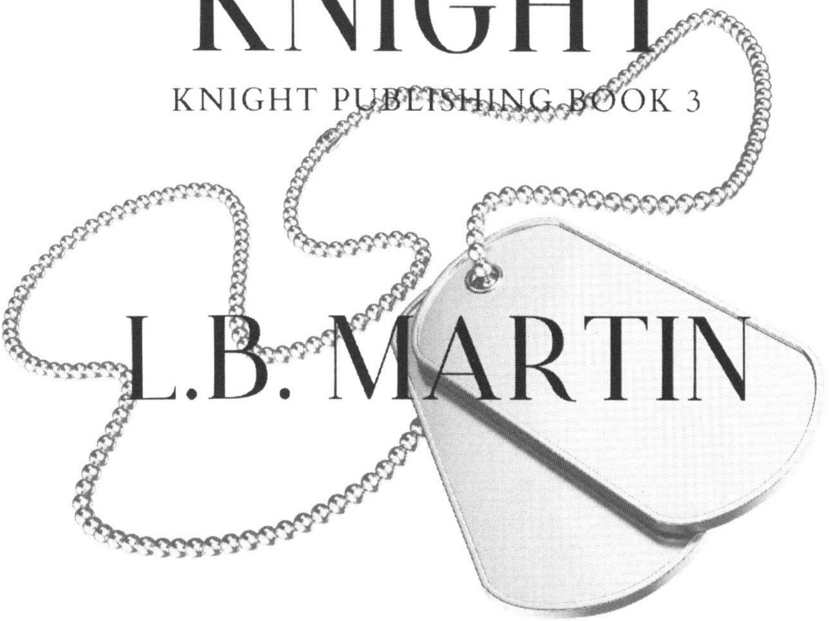

L.B. MARTIN

Copyright

Brantley Greenwald is affiliated with L.B. Martin.

This book was edited by Terry Hooker, Blue Dahlia Publishing House, LLC

Cover Art by Taylor Dawn, SWEET 15 DESIGNS,LLC

Ebook & Paperback: Danvers Designs

ISBN: 9798325563348

Dedication

To my husband, my own American hero, my rock in the deadliest storms, and my knight. May we always stand side by side, our hearts entwined like ivy on a castle wall. And when life's battles rage, know that I'll fight alongside you, armor-clad and resolute. For you are my hero, my sanctuary, my forever knight.

To everyone, don't give up, your knight is coming. Keep believing, keep fighting, and keep your heart open to the possibility of better days ahead.

Content Warnings

Some scenes in this novel may be extremely upsetting, therefore, reader discretion is advised.

This book contains references to themes of mental illness in the form of PTSD, survivor's guilt, anxiety attacks, depression, and suicidal thoughts/attempt. There are descriptions of death on page (military), a car accident on page and depictions from September 11, 2001.

Some sexual scenes involve BDSM, spankings, breath play, praise kink, breeding kink, bondage, orgasm denial, forced orgasms, anal, and blindfolds. This novel is a complete work of fiction and should not be used as a BDSM resource.

Always practice safe sex and remember consent is key. After that have fun you naughty vixens!!

"Our struggles may only seem as a walk in the park for some- one's ordinary eyes, but it's our shadows that understand the perils of our inner battles."

-Lyon FC

PLAYLIST

- *Out of the woods – Taylor Swift*
- *Enchanted – Taylor Swift*
- *Through Glass – Stone Sour*
- *Don't Blame Me – Taylor Swift*
- *A Thousand Years – Christina Perri*
- *Broken – Jonah Kagen*
- *Lonely – Machine Gun Kelly*
- *Coming Home – Skylar Grey*
- *Bad Things – Machine Gun Kelly*
- *But Daddy I Love Him – Taylor Swift*
- *Knife – Bad Wolves*
- *Aphrodite – Sam Short*
- *Beautiful Things – Benson Boone*
- *Snuff – Slipknot*
- *Broken (feat. Amy Lee) – Seether*
- *Let The World Burn – Chris Grey*
- *Slayer – Bryce Savage*
- *Brother – Kodaline*
- *Sister – Dave Matthews Band*
- *Lean On Me – Bill Withers*
- *Everlong – Foo Fighters*
- *Set Fire To Rain – Adele*
- *Like A Drug – Bryce Savage*
- *The Alchemy – Taylor Swift*
- *Thinking Out Loud – Ed Sheeran*
- *Lover – Taylor Swift*
- *The Bolter – Taylor Swift*
- *All Of Me – John Legend*
- *Lovely – Billie Eilish & Khalid*
- *Twin Flame – Machine Gun Kelly*
- *How Did It End – Taylor Swift*
- *Heal – Tom Odell*

Prologue

Samuel

Forever is a word for memories, not people.

Nighttime is suddenly illuminated with bright flashes as enemy gunfire rains down. The unbearable smell of blood and gunpowder engulfs me, leaving my senses tainted with a bitter aftertaste. Every muscle in my body locks up, and I hesitate. Crucial seconds tick by that I could have been returning fire. Maybe then he wouldn't have died. Maybe then he wouldn't have bled out in my arms screaming for me to take care of his sister.

It is supposed to be a simple enough mission for our men. Get in, make the connection, and get out. It all is going according to plan, until it isn't. Matthew and I are in the second of three Humvees heading back to the FOB, Forwarding Operating Base. It is a night mission in Afghanistan and our security detail are escorting us back.

Bullets begin spraying down on us as we pass through a small city. Although our armored Humvees can see some action, they can't withstand the amount they are receiving. We have no other choice but to stop, making a perimeter around ourselves to return fire. This is my first experience in combat since joining the Army. While everyone is piling out of the vehicles, I hang back. For just a moment I sit there frozen in place with my military training running through my mind. Orders are being thrown out, with a deep breath I steady my mind, grab my M4 and join my team. Bullets are showering down on us from every direction. I take a few enemies down before I hear the screaming behind me. John goes down in a blur. Matthew, our combat medic, rushes to his side. He is bleeding from the lower leg where the bullet shattered his bone. Matt pulls John into the back of the vehicle and begins bandaging the wound. He administers an IV then goes around to the side of the truck to pull him in further. As I turn the corner following Matt, a rogue bullet flies at the side of his neck. Time stands still as I watch my best friend collapse to the ground. I drop my weapon and crawl through the rubble to where he has fallen. It is so dark, the only light is the flickers of gunfire from overhead. His wound shows itself to me in spurts of light, each time looking worse as the blood pools out.

"Matt, can you hear me? You're going to be okay. I just need to put pressure on your neck," I yell down at him. Arterial spray covers me as I try to apply pressure. I know this is a substantial wound, but I am doing everything in my power to keep my best friend alive.

"Take care," he gasps for air as he tries to get the words out.

"Shut the hell up, Matt. You aren't going anywhere." I don't want him to waste his strength, but he is a determined asshole and he is going to say what he needs to.

"Take care of Marcy." He grabs my face in his hands. "Take care of my sister, man!" The pleading in his tone sends chills through my body. Before I can respond, I see the life leave his eyes. He's gone. Here

one moment, gone the next. His hands fall to the side as I sit there clutching his body to mine.

"Matthew, you bastard, wake up! Don't you leave me. Don't you fucking leave me!" I shout as tears mix with his blood cascade down my face.

"Marcy needs you not me!" I plead but it's too late.

This isn't how it is supposed to go. I should have been shielding him as he worked. As I begin spiraling into the abyss, hands grab me, hoisting me to my feet. The chaos around me springs to life again. I pull Matt to my chest trying to lift him into the Humvee. I can't leave him here. We are brothers for life, through this one and the next. Finally shouts ring out that the perimeter is secured and relief floods my body. A ranger comes to my aid lifting Matt into the vehicle. We pile into the trucks making our way back to camp.

The scene of Matt collapsing to the ground plays over and over in my mind as I stare at his cold lifeless body. The ride is a quiet one as we let sink in the fact that we are returning with one less soul than we had before.

I wake to a cold sweat covering my body and tears streaming down my face. The dream sits in the foreground of my mind like a tidal wave ready to wreak havoc on all that comes before it. I scrub my hands down my face to loosen the tension that's built up. It's always the same dream. Always about Matthew. I am plagued by the vision of seeing my best friend die in my arms over and over.

I check the time on my phone, seeing it's the middle of the night. *Of course it is. I can't fucking take this.* These dreams have haunted me since that night. I know I won't be able to sleep again so I throw the blankets off me to get out of the bed. The only thing that quells the night terrors is to either drink until I black out or work out until my muscles are screaming in pain. Tonight, I choose the latter. Maybe I'll end up on a bender too. Who knows? Heading down to the gym I get to work removing the memories from my mind.

As the sun rises, I'm sweating my ass off and trying to catch my breath. Grabbing a towel from the rack, I wipe away the terrors that haunt me in the night. The darkness fades from view and I'm rewarded with a clear head, hopefully lasting the rest of the day.

One

Marcy

"Marcy, you are a force to be reckoned with. Thank you for all you did to help Stormy and me." As I drive through the city Sebastian's voice fills the car from the speakers. A smile spreads across my face knowing that all the hours I spent diffusing the situation paid off. That's why I got into public relations. I wanted to help protect people from the nasty press that is always present in big cities.

I remember being bombarded when my parents' died, and how helpless I felt. Being the daughter of a politician made the press go wild wherever I went. Microphones and cameras were shoved into my face, making life miserable for me. Now, I help those that go through similar situations while also helping clients like Miles and Sebastian Knight who find trouble at every turn. Since they are my biggest clients, I guess I can't complain and it's because of them that my business took off. Somehow I landed the wealthiest clients in New York City. After that, more people followed suit.

"Seriously, you don't have to keep thanking me. I was doing my job," I insist.

"Well, you did it spectacularly. So," there's a pause and I know by now that Sebastian has some crazy idea up his sleeve. He's definitely the brother most prone to provoke the press, and me for that matter. I sigh and wait for him to finish. "Miles and I were talking and we know your birthday is coming up so we wanted to throw you a little party as a thanks for all you do for us." He asks me this every year but I always decline.

Every year, the calendar slyly nudges me towards a date that holds a special place in my heart. It's my birthday, an event I've always shared with my partner in crime, my brother Matthew. Once I hit eighteen, the wild parties morphed into more subdued celebrations. Our unique bond, unfazed by our nine-year age gap, was a comical twist of fate that had us blowing out candles together. Matthew's joy for our mutual birthday was infectious, dubbing me his 'best-ever birthday present'. My mind drifts to thoughts of him and I together and my throat clogs with emotion.

"You don't need to do that, Sebastian," I assert. They all know the pain that surrounds me on that day.

"Please let us do this for you. Stormy and Lizzie are itching to plan it. And before you say no just consider this. It's been a crazy year for all of us and we could use an excuse to celebrate." I pull into the parking garage for my apartment building, always a plus in the city, shift the car into park and sit for a moment, thinking about the proposition. Matthew died while he was serving in the military. He's been gone for eighteen years, our day continues to be difficult to get through for me. Sitting here in the car, I contemplate what I should do. Maybe it's time to face this day head on. Maybe it could be used as a remembrance.

"Are you still there?" Sebastian asks.

"Yes, sorry. I'm here. I was just thinking. Could we maybe include Matthew and let it be a celebration of life? It doesn't have to be a big party..." I emphasize.

"Yes! That sounds perfect. Let us take care of everything." I sigh, nodding my head even though he can't see me.

"Stormy and Lizzie are going to be thrilled. Is there anything special you want?"

"I don't think so. This is all a little overwhelming. How about tell me when and where and I'll be there," I manage.

Sebastian chuckles into the phone making me feel somewhat better about this. He and Miles have really grown on me over the years since I have been working for them. They are my top clients but they are almost family to me.

"I can definitely do that," Sebastian replies.

"Thanks for wanting to do this for me. Let me know if I need to do anything." Sebastian laughs again, warming my heart.

"You most definitely don't need to do anything. I will call you with the details," he responds.

"Okay. I'm home and I need to get some groceries inside," I reply.

"Great. Talk soon." Sebastian hangs up and I'm left wondering if I made the right decision. Opening the door, I get out of the car, grab the groceries and make my way up to my apartment.

I barrel through the door clutching the thousand bags I carried because I didn't want to make a second trip. Dropping them onto the counter, I slink into a chair at the table rubbing my hands where the bags have dug into them. I don't know why I always do this to myself but I think it can be attributed to laziness.

After putting the groceries away, I sip on a large glass of Pinot Noir while I draw a hot, soothing bath. I'm exhausted from always putting on a strong mask when deep inside I want to crumble. Everyone expects a brave face and that's what I give them. I only get to allow the veil to drop when I'm in the safety of my home. I try to think back to the last time I was truly happy and it always involves Matthew. It's been eighteen years, not a day goes by that I don't feel like I may die without him

My mind needs to float away on a sea of bubbles and bath salts for a while. With relaxing music playing, I slip into the tub letting my head rest on the edge. My eyes fall closed, the only images I see are my brother and I together. I miss him with every fiber of my being. Tears begin to trail down my cheeks as I think back to one of the last times we were together.

Matthew was home for two weeks before he'd been scheduled to be deployed to Afghanistan. I was sixteen at the time and skipped more classes during that time than through my whole academic career. I wasn't going to sit in class when I could be spending extra time with him before he left. Matt was more than my brother, he was my best friend. Of course we bickered like siblings but we would come back together stronger.

One day in particular, our parents left for work early believing Matt would get me to school on time. Only he had different plans for the day.

"Get up, sleepyhead," Matthew croons in my ear as he jostles my bed. I groan, rolling over and putting a pillow over my head.

"Five more minutes," I plead. Matt grabs the pillow and tosses it to the side.

"Nope. Mom and dad are gone so we're getting out of here. Now get up and get dressed, sunshine." He yanks the covers from me as he leaves the room laughing. Turning over, I look at my clock knowing I should be getting ready for school but instead I'm going to blindly follow my brother into whatever crazy plans he has arranged for us today.

Giddy excitement courses through me as I jump up from the bed wondering what plans Matt has made. I go through my morning routine, only I don't dress in my school uniform. Barreling down the stairs, I head to the kitchen to see Sam leaning against the counter.

"Don't mind Sam coming with us, do you?" Matthew asks over his steaming cup of coffee.

Butterflies erupt in my stomach and my cheeks flame when I look up at my brother's best friend. He is the epitome of tall, dark and handsome with his strong, masculine jaw and chiseled cheekbones. Those gorgeous hazel eyes look over to where I'm standing as a faint smile ghosts his lips. I've had a crush on him since I can remember. He's been my brother's best friend since kindergarten and has always come to the house to hang out. My crush for him has only grown stronger over the past few years.

"S-sure," I manage to get out. Sam will be spending the entire day with us? Could this day get any better? Matt slides a to go cup of coffee across the counter for me as he gulps down the rest of his. The boys talk about their upcoming deployment as I add sugar and creamer to my coffee. I can't help but to listen to their plans, getting a sinking feeling in my stomach. My mind drifts off down a rabbit hole of worst-case scenarios involving my brother in battle.

"Ready?" He questions, grabbing his coat from the hanger jolting me back to the present. They both look over their shoulders at me waiting for my reply.

"Uh, yeah. Let's go." I grab my mug and follow behind.

We spend the day sailing around Manhattan. That's the surprise Matthew had in store for me. He knows how much I love being on the open water. There's an unparallel liberation in standing on the deck, eyes closed, wind sweeping through my hair. All of my worries seem to fly from my mind as we glide through the open waters.

Matthew takes a seat beside me casting a shadow over my face. Cracking my eyes open, I look up to him.

"I was thinking that when I get back we can go see The Phantom of the Opera together. It will give us something to look forward to while I'm overseas," he mentions as he looks out at the sea.

"That sounds perfect, Matty, but what I will most look forward to is you being back here. I wish you didn't have to go, but I understand." I sit up as he pulls me closer.

"I don't want to leave you. I think that's been the hardest part about all of this. I hate to leave you here alone," he admits.

"I won't be alone. I have mom and dad and Jenny." Matt slings his arm around my shoulders looking down at me.

"You know what I mean. It's always been you and me," he says. I nod, knowing he's right. I'm going to miss him more than words can say.

"Just promise that you will come back to me." I hold out my pinkie for him to take in his.

"I will always be with you, sunshine." He uses his old nickname for me. Samuel even started to use the name for me sometimes. I can't

remember a time that he didn't call me his sunshine. He always tells me that I am his light whenever I ask him why he calls me that.

I knew he wouldn't promise something that is out of his control but I wish just this once he would. I need some reassurance that he will come back to me. I think that's what terrifies me the most, not knowing if he will make it back. I don't know what I would do. I close my eyes as tears begin forming. I don't want him to see me cry. It would gut him and that's the last thing I want to do. I am incredibly proud that he is fighting for our country. I just wish it didn't come with so much uncertainty. I know Matt must sense how my mood has changed because he takes my chin in his hand and brings my face up to look at him.

"Marcy, I didn't mean to make you cry. I will do whatever it takes to come back to you." He wipes away a rogue tear as I nod my head.

"I know you will. I love you, Matty," I whisper into his shoulder.

"I love you, sunshine." He kisses my forehead and we sit in silence looking out over the water. I can't help the feeling of dread in my stomach but I won't waste the time we have left together dwelling on a what if. I want to cherish these times I have with him.

As I open my eyes, tears run down my cheeks. I'm no longer sailing with Matthew. I'm alone in my bathroom, drinking wine and clinging to memories before they melt away. I take a large gulp hoping it wipes away the pain in my mind. The talk of a birthday celebration has stirred all these old memories that I've tried to keep at bay. Maybe it was wrong of me to agree to a party. *How will I get through the night?* With lots of wine, I imagine. Setting my glass down, I submerge my head under the water needing to drown out the heartache.

Two

Samuel

Racing down the street in my royal blue Subaru WRX STI, I blare music loud so I can drown out the silence. "Gasoline" by *I Prevail* roars through the speakers, the lyrics evoke a range of emotions and memories. A surge of energy blasts throughout the car. Before the light changes to red, I quickly turn into the parking garage of Knight Publishing Company, my tires screeching as I come to a stop. Miles and Sebastian have been inviting me to hang out with them and my excuses were starting to run thin. So when they invited me for lunch, I knew I needed to attend. They're the only family I have left. I tend to isolate myself since retiring from the military. That's why I started a cyber security company. It's easier to isolate myself behind a computer screen because I only need to deal with people virtually.

Pressing the elevator button, the doors seal off, directing me towards their floor. I haven't been here since my uncle died, leaving the company to his sons. They wanted to bring me on board to work with them, allowing my company to be subsumed by theirs.

However, I didn't see myself dressing up every day and going to work. I like the comfort of my home too much.

The doors spring open and the receptionist area comes into view. An energetic blonde woman at the desk looks up and smiles.

"How can I help you?" she asks, sitting up straighter in her chair and jutting out her chest for me to notice.

"I'm here for Miles and Sebastian. I'm Samuel Knight." I see the recognition flash in her eyes as a blush creeps up her cheeks.

"I'm sorry, sir. I'll let them know you're here." She continues to blush as she picks up the phone. "Mr. Knight, Mr. Samuel Knight is here for you. Yes sir, I will send him back." The receptionist places the phone back in its carriage and looks up at me with a faint smile.

"You can head back to their offices," she replies as she motions to the hallway.

"Thank you." I pass her desk and round the corner to two large office doors. I see the name plates on the doors and decide to knock on Miles'.

"Come in." Opening the door, I see Miles and Sebastian sitting around the desk.

"Sammy, long time no see! How've you been, man? Glad you could make it." Miles jumps up from behind his desk and comes to greet me with a hug. He's always been the more affectionate cousin.

"It's been too long, cousin." Sebastian is next in line, giving me a pat on the back. I return the gesture before he backs away.

"It has been a while. I've been pretty good. Thanks for the invite," I reply as I look around the newly furnished office.

"Yeah, yeah. Of course. Let's get out of here, I'm starving," Miles says as he opens the door for us to step out.

"Meredith, we will be out for a while. Make sure to take any messages because we don't want to be interrupted." Before she can reply, he's turned away and heading for the elevators.

"Do you mind driving? Seb and I have a meeting across town after lunch."

"Not at all. You know I love any chance to get behind the wheel." Sebastian and Miles nod along with me. We are a family with expensive tastes, especially when it comes to cars, so of course we use any excuse to bring them out to play.

Once we arrive at the restaurant, Sebastian requests a secluded corner for us to sit in. We order and Miles raises his glass. "To being Kinghts. Family first. Always."

"Cheers." Sebastian and I speak in unison as we clink our glasses together.

"So, Sam, how is business in cyber security?" Sebastian questions.

"It's actually going very well. I've had to hire several more employees since the new year to compensate for a handful of more contracts we've received," I announce as I sip my drink.

"Great. I heard someone mention your company the other day and I was pleased with the traction it's getting," Miles comments.

"How is KPC doing?" I query.

"We've expanded into parts of Europe. We're hoping to become an international name by 2025," Sebastian answers.

"Wow, I hadn't realized. Uncle Ben would be proud of the both of you." They both nod their head solemnly.

"We wanted to make sure his company flourished with us at the helm," Miles interjects.

Our meals come quickly and we dive right in, talking and carrying on about our lives. Both Miles and Sebastian have settled down. That's not something I think will ever be in the cards for me, but I find myself yearning to have that connection with a woman. Well, not just *any* woman, but a special one. The only problem with that is I keep people at arm's length, never fully letting them get close to me. The military fucked up my mind and even with the therapy visits, I may be a lost cause.

Sebastian clears his throat, wiping his mouth on the napkin and placing it back in his lap.

"We are planning a little celebration for Marcy Hillary; remember the PR rep you told us about?" Hearing her name makes my head snap up. Of course I remember her. If only they knew to what extent. How could I ever forget the red headed vixen that plagues my mind daily? I nod so Sebastian will continue.

"She has done so much for us over the years and we want to show our appreciation. Marcy is an exceptionally bright woman, now with her own firm, Big Apple PR," Sebastian explains. Yes, I know all about her company. She decided to start her own firm right out of college and when she struggled, I worked tirelessly under the radar to make sure it was a success for her. It was the least I could do.

Hearing Marcy's name uttered from another man's mouth, even my happily married cousin, ignites something deep within me. Matthew always adored his sister and that's why it was his dying wish for me to make sure she was taken care of. A pit in my stomach forms when I think about those last words Matt spoke to me. I haven't taken care of her like I should have. I haven't been present in her life. I have been on the sidelines watching at a distance for when she needed help. Although she doesn't know it, I have been a presence in her life long before I returned to the states.

It was too hard to face her after everything that happened to Matt, but I still had a promise to uphold. I've blamed myself for his death since that day. In my opinion, those few seconds I hesitated could have been the difference between life of death for Matthew.

"Sammy, where'd you go?" Sebastian muses with a concerned look on his face.

"Sorry about that. You were talking about Marcy?" I try to push the topic away from me and back on what they were talking about.

"Yes, we are throwing a birthday party for her and we would love it if you could make it. If I remember correctly, you served in the military with her brother? Anyways, since they shared the same birthday, we were thinking of a celebration of life in remembrance of him but also a birthday party for her. Are you interested?" Both of my cousins look at me with something similar to pleading in their eyes.

"Yes, I knew the Hillary family very well and I went overseas with Matthew." I can't deny that I've wanted to approach her in person but I figured it was always best to hide in the shadows. I'm unbelievably proud of her for accomplishing so much after she lost her brother and then her parents as well. I know the toll that can take on a person.

Would she even recognize me? Would she even want to see me? I can't deny the temptation to see her gorgeous long curly red hair and her sultry green eyes up close again. She could make any man fall to their knees.

The last time we spoke was at her brother's funeral and I couldn't believe the agonizingly stunning woman she had become. She had grown up so much since we went overseas. Her young, deliciously curvy, eighteen-year-old body had me thinking things any grown man shouldn't. I knew she was too young for me and I was still in the military at the time but fuck, if I didn't want to make her mine. I was only on leave for a week before I was expected to be back in uniform. That still didn't deter my thoughts of her, both good and bad. A lapse in judgment had us both suffering the consequences.

"Great! I knew we hadn't mistaken the connection. Will you be able to attend? It's this Saturday at eight on The rooftop of Hotel Chantelle. Lizzie and Stormy are taking care of everything." The question looms in the air as my cousins look to me for an answer. This isn't my usual scene, but I can't help but to be intrigued at the thought of being that close to her.

"Sure. I'll be there." The words are out of my mouth before I have time to think of an excuse not to attend.

"Perfect. Would you like us to send you a car so you can relax and enjoy the evening?" I think about their offer and I can't deny the appeal. It's been so long since I let loose and enjoyed an evening out.

"Actually, yes. That would be excellent. Thank you both for the invite." I down the rest of my whiskey and wipe the corners of my mouth. Since we have finished our meals, there isn't much more of a reason to hang around unless they have something else they want to run by me.

"I will make the arrangements and send you the details."

My phone pings in my jacket pocket. As I retrieve it I see that there has been a breach in one of my client's security. This matter has to be taken care of immediately. Unfortunately, I can only do so much from my phone before I need my computer and software in front of me.

"Forgive me. I need to get this," I apologize to my cousins, motioning to my phone. "Thank you for the lunch. It was great to catch up and I look forward to the party." Rising from our seats, we embrace and then I'm on my way out of the restaurant.

Jumping into my car, I connect my phone and call my second in charge.

"Philip, where are we on the Worthington's breach?" Pulling out onto the street I speed to the other side of the city where my condo is.

"I'm localizing the main threat and trying to isolate the spread. I really need your algorithm on this. This hacker seems to actually know what they're doing," Philip replies.

"I'll be at my computer in ten. Make sure to hold off any other threat until I can log in." Ending the call, I switch lanes back and forth in order to get to my condo faster.

Once I pull in, I jump from the car and jog to my private elevator. Time comes to a standstill while I wait to reach the top floor. Flashes of Marcy spring into my mind, reminding me that I will be seeing her at the end of the week. Nerves, both good and bad, shoot through my body causing me to need a serious distraction once I reach my home. It's a good thing I can drown myself in work for the next couple hours or I might sit fantasizing about my best friend's little sister.

Three

Marcy

I lie there for a moment listening to my alarm, a wave of exhaustion washes over me. I extend my arm, moving it slowly toward the device. With a sense of resignation, I delicately press the button, silencing its incessant noise, bringing a moment of quiet reprieve. Glancing at the window, I see the sun streaming in. It's time to get up, but the urge to lay here longer overwhelms me. I stayed up late last night looking through old memories of Matthew and me in a scrapbook. He's been on my mind a lot lately. As our birthday approaches, I'm missing him even more.

After swinging my legs over the bed and stretching, I get up and head to the shower so I can get to work on time. The bathroom fills with steam as I step in. The hot water washes over me, further waking me up. I bathe quickly, dry off and dress for the day. Coming back to the bathroom, I free my hair from the towel and watch as it cascades in wet ringlets all around. A chuckle bubbles up from my chest seeing the sight in the mirror.

"Whoa, that's going to take some effort!" Chuckling, I shake my head, reaching for the hairdryer. "Time to tame this wild mane,"

I declare to the mirror. With a playful grin, I lavish my hair with everything but the kitchen sink, then bend over to run my fingers through the tangled adventure.

Once my hair finishes drying, I'm pleased with the result and move on to my makeup. Embracing the au natural aesthetic today, I keep it light letting my freckles shine through.

The familiar hum from the kitchen as the coffee pot comes alive is a testament to the reliable alarm I've set. Its awakening stirs a sense of comfort and routine in my morning. Giving myself a last once-over in the mirror, I make my way to the kitchen, drawn by the irresistible call of my much-anticipated caffeine fix.

Preparing a take-away mug of coffee, I gather my essentials - purse and phone, before stepping out of my apartment. The crisp fall air sends a shiver down my spine, a stark reminder that I should have brought a jacket. My lack of foresight in checking the morning weather forecast has left me in a chilly predicament. Contemplating a dash back home, I suddenly recall - there's a cozy sweater stashed away in my car.

The drive to my office is uneventful, which makes my mind wander back to the upcoming party I will be attending. A smile crosses my face thinking of the celebration for Matthew. This party will be good for me, I think. I need to get out from under the dark cloud that persists over my head and step into the sun again.

Taylor Swift comes on the radio so I turn it up and sing along like I am in a concert the rest of the way to work. Once I pull into the parking garage, I'm pumped and ready for a day of kicking ass, after making sure my mask is in place.

Walking through the main lobby, I smile and acknowledge a few employees as I make my way to the bank of elevators. Sarah walks up beside me after I press the button to go up.

"Hey, girl. How are you this morning?" I ask looking over..

"Today has already been eventful and," she checks her watch and looks back at me, "it's only 9am," she replies with a pinched expression.

As the doors open, we step through and press the number to our floor. Sarah, in a display of her having upped her corporate game, clinched a promotion and is now my partner-in-crime at the firm. Her office was moved to my floor at the top of the building, making it easy to slip into each other's offices during the day. She recently returned to work from her honeymoon. She had a whirlwind romance with a local military man that works in security. They got caught in a snowstorm, and well, the rest is a frosty fairy tale.

"What happened this morning?" I question as we ride the elevator.

"Travis was up all night working on a surveillance camera for a client and forgot to make sure I was awake before he headed into the office. From there I ran over a nail on the way to work and pulled over with a huge gash in my tire. Obviously, not the best start to a day." She palms her forehead and grimaces.

"Wow, sorry for all that. At least it's Friday. Do you have any special plans this weekend?" I question as we exit the elevator.

"I'm not sure. Travis mentioned going out this weekend to dinner and a show. Although he hates going out, he does it for me. You know he's content with being a homebody." Sarah shrugs her shoulders as she walks toward her office.

"Oh, well, the Knight brothers have planned a little get together this weekend to celebrate my brother's and my birthday if you and Travis would like to come," I mention before she steps into her office.

"That sounds great, I'll ask Trav, although I'm sure he won't want to come. I can persuade him though." She chuckles with a wink.

"Nice. I'll text you the details," I reply, leaving her office and heading toward mine. Once I round the corner, Nora is there waiting for me with a stack of paperwork. My heart sinks at the sight – I had hoped for a peaceful Friday, but who was I kidding? Fridays are typically hectic, rivaling the pace of Mondays. To be honest, all my days seem to be packed with activity lately.

"Hello, Miss Hillary, I have several updates for you and some contracts that need your review." As she makes her way in, she settles down on the opposite side of my desk, carefully positioning the documents before her.

Nora is my right-hand woman. I hired her soon after I started this company and she has been with me ever since. I don't know what I would do without her. She is a wearer of many hats and I'm thankful for her to be by my side.

"Thanks, Nora. You know I've asked you a million times to call me Marcy," I declare, casually removing my sweater and placing it on the back of my chair. "How was your night out?"

"I know, I know. Marcy. There, I said it!" she giggles. "It was great, actually. Ally and I went to Club Vibe. Thanks for the tickets by the way. We danced and drank entirely way too much but it was a magical anniversary night. Somehow I drug my ass in here this morning," Nora laughs, comfortably receding into her chair. I sink into my seat, booting up my computer and drawing the paperwork closer.

"Aw, I'm so happy for you. Do you think she will pop the question soon?" I ask. A few years back, I had the privilege of meeting Nora's partner during the hush-hush phase of their relationship. Both Nora and Ally, trapped in abusive marriages, found solace in each other's company. Their bond became their sanctuary, their beacon of hope. Eventually I encouraged her to file for divorce and secure a much-needed restraining order against her husband.

When the dust settled, Ally followed suit, and their love story became a cherished tale. It's rare to witness a love as profound as that between Nora and Ally. It's heartening to realize that genuine love persists in this world, fostering hope that I may discover mine someday.

"I'm not sure. I drop hints all the time like what kind of ring I would want and perfect places for destination weddings. I think she really wants to surprise me." Nora shrugs but her cute cheeks flame red. I decide on a subject change to get the work day going or else we could sit here all day and talk about her perfect love life.

I smile at her quirkiness. "You know, I haven't been out in forever but I'm glad you all had a good time. I had a quiet night at home but I still feel like I'm dragging this morning." After taking a large gulp of coffee, I log into my computer and pull up the emails that I need to go through. Nora filters my emails so I only get the ones that truly need my attention. She's always a life saver.

Nora stretches her hands over her head and rises from her seat. "I'm going to go make a cup of coffee. Do you need anything?" she asks.

"No, I brought coffee with me today. Thank you though." I gesture to my mug. "Oh, I almost forgot. Miles and Sebastian Knight are putting together this little birthday thing for me this weekend and I would love it if you and Ally could be there. I need more people there that I'm comfortable with. I don't want to get overwhelmed."

"Absolutely. We don't have plans and I know Ally would love that. Message me the info and I'll send it on to her to make sure. Yay! I can't wait! We are going to get you so drunk. Drunk Marcy is the best!" Nora lets out a giggle as she opens my door.

"I don't know about all that but it should be fun. Sarah and Travis will be there as well if she can convince him." Shrugging my shoulders I glance down to my computer and pull up an important email.

"Right. Well, I'll leave you to work. Let me know if you want me to order lunch for you today or if you are going out." Nora leaves my office as I pull out my phone to put on some music. It helps to keep me on task.

Lunchtime rolls around and I'm right in the middle of paperwork. It's strewn all across my desk with no ending in sight. With a heavy sigh, I lean back and look at the mess in front of me. I need to get out of here to get my head back on straight. My eyes are starting to cross from all the documents sitting before me. I jump up from my chair, grabbing my sweater and purse and head out the door.

"I'm taking a lunch break. Hold my calls for an hour or so. Do you want anything?" I question.

"No ma'am, ," she answers .

"Alright then, I'll be back soon." Making my way to the elevators, the sound of my phone breaks the silence. I rummage through my purse swiftly and finally hold it in my hand. Sebastian is calling.

"Please don't tell me you or Miles have gotten into more trouble." I chuckle.

"Not this time. I was calling to tell you the details of the party this weekend. Stormy and Lizzie have everything settled. Be on the rooftop of Hotel Chantelle, Saturday at eight p.m.," he says.

"Wow, they sure got to work, didn't they?" I ask. Now that I hear the details, my nerves begin to flutter.

"Yeah, well, they wanted to make this special for you. I think the girls already went out shopping to get outfits and everything. You know how they go all out." Sebastian laughs and I do as well. I can see them using this as an excuse to buy a bunch of new clothes. I wish they would have included me on their little shopping trip because I have no idea what I'm going to wear to this thing.

"We invited my cousin, Samuel, as well because he knew your brother. I told you that I would introduce you to him one day but it seems like you may already know him. Anyways, I'm getting another call. We will see you this weekend." Sebastian hangs up before I can ask anymore questions about this mystery Samuel. The first thing that comes to mind is Matthew's very best friend Samuel. The Samuel that I was in love with for most of my childhood and teenage life. It can't be the same. *Right?* The name Samuel is common, I tell myself but I think my subconscious flutters at the thoughts of 'what if'.

I walk to the deli around the corner and order the same sandwich I always do, as if on autopilot. With the name mentioned I can't help but think about that handsome boy I once knew. I wonder what he is doing now. Is he still in the Army? I haven't heard anything about him since I saw him at my brother's funeral. He was only on leave long enough to put his friend in the ground then he was gone again. I felt like I lost both of them after that. Even though we weren't close in age, they would take me with them to hang out all the time before they left for the military. I felt like part of the group and I was thankful that Matthew always wanted to include me in his plans and that Sam didn't mind.

The waitress serves me as I slip into a seat next to a bank of windows. I always sit here so I can see the people walking by. My appetite seems to have dwindled since Sebastian uttered the name Samuel. I don't know if it's the same man I once knew but for some reason I hope it is. I peck at my sandwich then decide to pull out my phone and look Samuel up to see if he has any social media. As I type in Samuel Knight, I freeze realizing that I knew his last name all along and I didn't put two and two together. *What are the fucking odds?* I never once, in all the years working for Miles and Sebastian, made the connection with Sam. *How could I have missed this?* When I type his name into Google, an image of him surfaces on my display. The years have added a layer of sternness that wasn't present earlier, yet undeniably, this is the same boy who I thought I would marry one day. The thought sounds preposterous now.

My mouth becomes dry as I stare down at my phone. It's the captivating hazel eyes reflecting from the screen, the ones I've often dreamt of, that cause a ripple of excitement within me. I can see his war riddled face but it somehow makes him even more stunning than he was before. My finger runs over the screen as if it was really him. In an instant all those feelings from long ago come screaming back to the surface. I thought I had moved past him but apparently I'm still just as smitten as I once was.

"Mom, I don't have time to take Marcy to lessons today. I've got to get this essay finished for Psychology," Matt replies into the phone. My heart drops because I look forward to this day every week. Sam is sitting in front of me at the table where we have been working on homework. Not that I can get much done with Sam this close. I keep sneaking glances when I know he isn't looking.

"Yeah, she'll just have to miss this week. Sorry, mom." I feel like I could cry so I tuck my face into my folded arms resting on the table.

"Hey, man. I don't mind taking her," Sam mentions. My flushed face swoops up to look at him. He shoots me a wink and I think I instantly melt into a puddle on the floor.

Matt moves the phone from his ear. "Are you sure?" he asks. Sam nods as he flips his books closed. "Thanks. I owe you one." Matt slaps him on the back then starts talking to mom again. I'm going to be in Sam's car with just him. This is too much for my teenage heart to handle. I think it might burst at any moment.

"Mom, Sam just said he would take her."

"Yeah, I'll tell him."

"Okay. We love you too." Matt hangs up then looks over Sam again.

"Thanks for doing this. You know how much she loves going."

"It's not a problem. Besides, I'm already done with my essay." His eyes lock on mine. "Are you ready?" Am I? Yes, I got dressed when I got home from school.

"Yep," I muster. Jenny is going to have a cow when I tell her about this tomorrow.

Sam stands from the table and starts to walk off then stops and looks back at me.

"Are you coming, princess?" He quirks his brow at me and a nervous giggle bubbles out of me.

"Yeah, oh, yeah. I am. Totally." I cringe at my stupid response. I swear he melts my brain cells when he's this close to me. 'I'm smart, I promise.' is what I want to say.

"Heh, well let's get a move on." He gestures behind him toward the front door. I jump up, nearly knocking my books to the ground. Matt looks up shaking his head at me and chuckles.

"Maybe you need to wear that helmet all the time. You're clumsy, sunshine." He loves driving me crazy but I love him. He's not just my brother, he's my best friend. I stick my tongue out at him and follow behind Sam. Sometimes I feel like Matty knows I have a crush on his best friend but how could he? I definitely haven't told him and I keep cool, for the most part.

We drive out of the city heading toward the stables where I have horseback riding lessons. I've been doing this for years but continue because I love riding out into nature exploring different trails. Since I began jumping lessons, I've been even more eager to attend. I love to feel the rising excitement right before we jump an obstacle.

Sam turns the music down pulling my attention back inside the car. "So, how are your lessons going? I haven't been out here to watch in a while."

"Oh, um, I began jumping higher obstacles with Rocky." I pick at a piece of invisible lint on my pants trying not to act too eager that he seems interested.

"That's really cool. You've come a long way since you began. I remember those alligator tears from your first lesson." He chuckles as he turns down the dirt road I travel every week.

"Ha, Ha. Very funny. That horse was huge in my defense and I had never done it before. I was scared I would fall to my death or something." I pull my black velvet helmet up to my lap.

"Seriously though, I'm impressed you kept up with it this long. I figured you would bail like the piano, guitar and singing lessons." My eyes shoot over in his direction allowing me to see the smirk on his face.

"Okay, one, I can't believe you remember all those. Two, I'm pretty sure old Mrs. Fenderson purposely gave me the sheet music meant for advanced students. Three, no amount of lessons can make my singing better. Come to find out, there isn't a musical bone in my body. That's why my concerts are alone in the shower." As the words slip from my lips, I instantly want to reel them back in. Facepalm. How embarrassing to spill that tidbit.

Sam's laughter roars through the car as he cuts the engine looking over at me.

"Is that what that screeching is that I hear sometimes? I thought there was a dying cat outside. I even went looking for it once." He wiggles his eyebrows at me as I roll my eyes but I can't help laughing along with him. I really do suck at singing.

"I've got to get to my lessons, smarty pants." I begin opening my door but Sam puts his hand on my arm to stop me.

"Be careful out there today." The sincerity in his eyes makes my belly do a flip. I can't help but notice the spark of electricity where he grabbed my arm.

"I will be. Plus I have this." I knocked hard on the black velvet helmet in my lap. He nods, though still looking unconvinced. "Come out and watch and I'll prove to you that I know what I'm doing."

"Did you think I was going to sit in here the whole time and let you out of my sight?" His words give me chills but then he ruffles my hair like Matty does and the moment is lost.

"Besides, your mom would kill me if I let anything happen to you, princess." The butterflies in my stomach have now been devoured by dinosaurs. A sigh escapes my lips and I nod turning to get out of the car. Will he ever see me the way I see him? Maybe...I don't know...maybe I should start looking at boys my own age. The thought feels like a punch to the gut but I smile up to him before I sprint off to pull Rocky from his stall.

"At least I have you, right boy?" I scratch his chestnut muzzle as he nods his head to me as if he understands my problems. Throwing on his halter, I lead him from the stall as the moments from the car wash away into the here and now. I can't think about the love of my life when all I'll ever be is 'Matt's baby sister'.

Sebastian said Sam is going to be at the party so I need to be ready. Pushing my plate aside, I decide to take a break from work for the rest of the day and indulge in some retail therapy. I need to look jaw droppingly gorgeous tomorrow and I can't do that with anything I already own. I'm all grown up now. This once ugly duckling transformed into a swan and it is time that he sees me, really *sees* me.

Four

Samuel

It's Saturday afternoon, as I effortlessly navigate the gym, my thoughts are elsewhere. They're with Marcy and the daunting reality that I'll be seeing her tonight. I was tempted to cancel on Miles and Sebastian, but I knew my deceit would be transparent. The raw truth is, I'm unnerved at the thought of being near her again. The reason for my fear is unclear, whether it's guilt for somewhat breaking my promise to her brother or the undeniable pull of attraction I have towards her. Whatever it is, I need to get my ass in gear.

As the rhythm from my headphones shifts to a calmer tempo, I know it's time to begin the wind down. My body is protesting, having been driven beyond its limits in this workout, yet it kept moving, as if on autopilot, while my mind wandered elsewhere.

Switching off the machine, I reach for my towel, dabbing away the sweat from my face and neck. A wave of fatigue washes over me, providing the exact relief I was seeking. The weight of responsibilities, worries, and expectations—dissolving. I toss the towel in the bin and head to the shower. I step in, a torrent of comforting hot water washes over my aching body. I stand for a moment basking in the feel of the water sliding over me. Scrubbing my hands down my face, I wash up and get out.

Draping a towel about my waist while I study the mirror's reflection over the bathroom counter, my eyes trace the countless faded scars and healed battle wounds. The scar above my eyebrow—the result of a daring leap. The one on my knuckles—the aftermath of a fight for justice. And the one normally hidden beneath my sleeve—the battle against inner demons. They've witnessed tears shed in solitude, laughter shared with friends, and the quiet determination that carried me through sleepless nights. The scars are a testament to the trials of years past, a silent narration of my transformation. I've evolved; I'm not the man I used to be. My transformation into the person I am today is deeply rooted in my experiences with the Army. The blend of enriching encounters and rigorous challenges has sculpted my character.

When I think back over my time in the military, it's always clouded over by the death of Matthew. Running my hands through my hair, I head into my closet to get dressed. I don't want to sit around and think about him, especially not when I have a party to get ready for. One that will bring me face to face with his sister.

The sound of my phone ringing from the bed grabs my attention, pausing my thoughts about tonight. Sebastian's name appears on the screen and I know why he's calling.

"Hey man," I answer as I walk over to the bank of windows in my bedroom.

"Sam! I just wanted to make sure we will be seeing you tonight, man," Sebastian booms over the phone.

"Heh, I figured you would be calling to check up on me." I roll my eyes because he can't see me.

"Well I hate to tell ya but you have a history of not showing up. Miles and I want you here with us," he states, joking aside.

"Yeah I'll be there. I was about to get dressed when you called." I walk over to the wet bar in my room to pour a glass of whiskey. I need something to take the nerves away. I do better when I'm on my own in the comfort of my penthouse. Unless, I'm out following *her*. She makes me yearn for things that aren't possible. Even with that knowledge, I can't keep away from her. I need my daily dose of her. She's like a drug and I'm an addict.

"Good, good. See you tonight." Sebastian ends the call, leaving me alone with my thoughts. I place my phone on the bed, my fingers curling tightly around my drink. As I savor its warmth, I find my worries fading away. Whiskey has become one of my constant companions. I wish it wasn't, but here we are. I head back to the closet to dress in something appropriate for a birthday party that I'm sure will be the talk of the town. The Knights, renowned for their extravagance, have been this way since our childhood. With a resigned sigh, I ruffle my still damp hair and select a pair of slacks, accompanied by a shirt and tie.

My mind wanders back to *her*. She's a magnet and my brain can't resist the pull. I question, not for the first time, if her brother implied more when he asked me to look after her, but that's an answer I'll never know. I drive myself mad thinking of what he really wanted from me. An overwhelming sense of regret washes over me. I know I shouldn't have left her alone all these years. I helped her from afar but the guilt of not physically being there for her haunts me, especially since she doesn't have any family left.

Before I returned to the states, I found out about the accident that took her parents' lives. I was physically ill, knowing that she had been alone in the world all this time.

I hired a P.I. to track her down a few years before I got back to the states so that I could learn more about the woman she grew into. I didn't plan on becoming obsessed with her every move. I admit that I tried to break the connection many times, but I felt compelled to look after her, like a crazy guardian angel. I even went so far as to threaten potential suitors of hers. No one could ever be good enough for her. I'd told her once that *boys* didn't deserve her. She needs someone worthy of her. I smile at the memory from long ago.

Even with everything I've done to assist Marcy, I still feel as though I've disappointed Matthew. Even if I knew what he meant when he told me to take care of her, the guilt of him dying in my arms has kept me from initiating anything with her. He should have been the one that came back from war, not me. Survivors' guilt is a real and ever-present cloud hanging over my head. I down the rest of my whiskey then place the glass back on the bar debating on refilling it. Alcohol numbs the pain and memories. It keeps me going on most days.

Matthew would probably argue that I haven't been caring for myself, yet I've been giving it my all. Unfortunately, the VA doesn't consistently provide aid to those in need, regardless of their circumstances. I'm basically a soldier left to my own devices. A twinge of anger rises when I think about the soldiers that need more help than me and aren't getting it. An idea sparks in my mind growing brighter and brighter. I jog to my computer to write it all down before I forget.

An overwhelming need to help those soldiers rises in my chest. With the resources I have available at my fingertips, I can come up with a way to help those soldiers that get out of the military and don't receive the help they deserve. I want to be there for them instead of letting them fall into the cracks as I did.

Once in my office, I login to my computer and begin putting together a proposal that I can pitch to different agencies in order to get the right professionals involved. My fingers fly across the keyboard explaining my personal situation and mental condition when I got back to the states and how it's so similar to many others. I have comrades that couldn't handle civilian life and so they took their own. It doesn't get easier to attend these funerals that could have been avoided. I haven't been this excited about a project in a long time and I think I have what it takes to get it off the ground. To be honest, being a Knight opens many doors for me as well. Miles and Sebastian are bound to want to back this passion project because they have seen firsthand the toll the military can take on a person. Men and women are suffering and I have the means to do something about it. I know I can't help everyone but if I can help someone, that means more to me than anything at this point.

I finish my statement using examples and first-person accounts of the mental state I was in and still struggle with since becoming a civilian. The writing process was actually cathartic because I got out all the emotions that clog my mind every day. After shedding a few tears over the specifics surrounding Matthew's death, I breathe a sigh of relief. It filters through my body and I feel as though a weight has been lifted from me. Of course I will still continue to have mental problems but I think I tackled a huge milestone with putting it into writing.

Once I got started, it was like word vomit and I couldn't have stopped it if I tried. My fingers play over the keyboard explaining specific hardships I face to this day. Once I take a step back and look at the document I'm stunned that all this came out of me. I knew I kept things close to my heart but I never knew that this was all bottled up inside me, waiting for the right conditions to explode. I need to send this to my therapist since she has been urging me to write about my experiences. She said getting them out onto paper would aid in personal growth and emotional healing. I have to admit that she was onto something.

I glance at my watch and realize my driver has probably been waiting for a while since the party is about to begin. I spent so much time in front of the computer coming up with this plan for fellow soldiers to get the help they so desperately need that time ran away from me. Rubbing the tears from the corner of my eyes, I save my project and run out of my office toward the front door. Grabbing my jacket off the hook, I head out and down the elevator. There is a lightness to my step that wasn't there before. As I descend the floors, I can't help but think about this new project and all the possibilities that could arise from it.

"Mr. Knight, good evening. I was beginning to worry," Thomas explains as he opens the door for me.

"Thank you. I'm sorry to keep you waiting. I lost track of time." I slide into the plush Bently, remembering a time when this was the norm.

"Not to worry. It's good to see you, sir." He closes the door then rounds the car to his door. Thomas pulls out into the city traffic heading toward the venue.

For the first time, I'm not dreading this event but excited about what tonight can hold. Getting that shit out of my head cleared a way for new possibilities to grow.

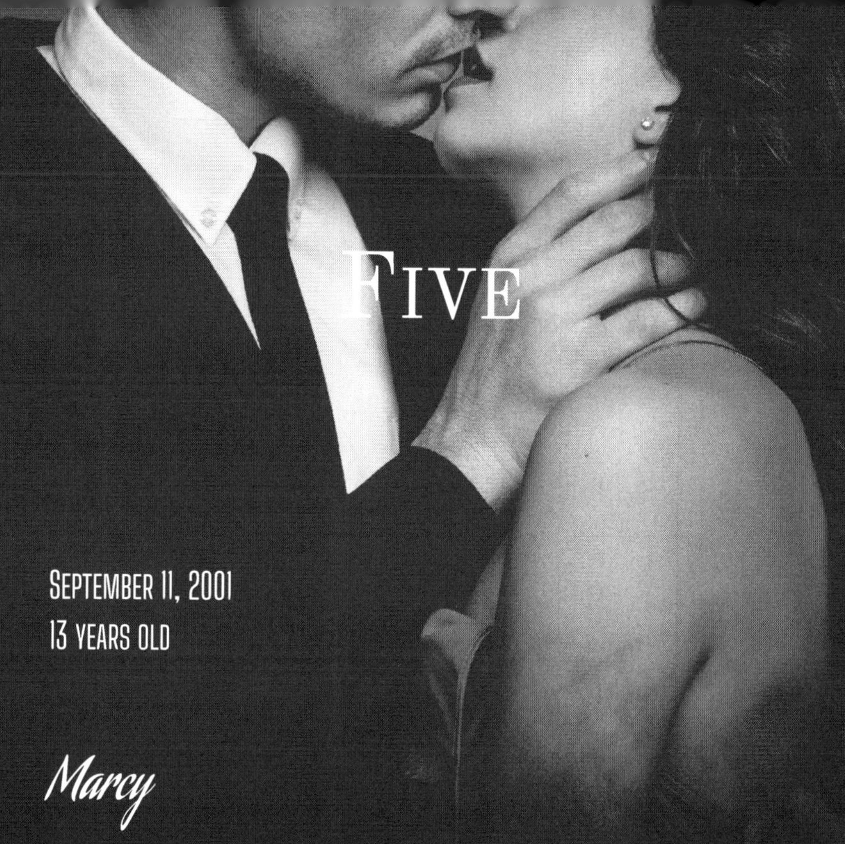

Five

SEPTEMBER 11, 2001
13 YEARS OLD

Marcy

It started out like every other Tuesday since the beginning of eighth grade. Matt, my brother, and Sam, his best friend, dropped me off at school while on their way to classes at a local community college. There was no way to know the horrors that awaited the United States.

As I make my way through the crowded halls, Jenny walks up beside me telling me about the latest scoop with her ex-boyfriend, Ben.

"He called me over and over last night. My mom finally told him to stop calling the house. I don't know why he would think I would answer after seeing him with Anna at the dance on Saturday." Jenny sighs looking down at her books. She's trying to come off as indifferent but I know how much it hurt her to see him kissing someone else.

"Listen, he knows he messed up by losing you and now he's trying to get you back. Keep ignoring him. He will get the message eventually." I give her a little bump with my shoulder.

"You're right. I'm not interested in his excuses. I need to focus on school anyway. Especially this class." She gestures as we enter Advanced English. We take our seats next to each other while taking out our notebooks. The rest of the class files in along with Mrs. Hammond. "Did Matt and Sam drop you off this morning?" she asks.

"Yep." Is all I respond.

"Did he notice you dressed up for him? I know you. This isn't your usual style." Jenny smiles as she looks me over.

My cheeks heat as I ignore Jenny by opening The Great Gatsby to the chapter we are covering today in class.

"Marcy, he'll notice you eventually. He would be a fool not to." I look up at her. "Trust me. Eventually your age won't be such a problem." She smiles as I nod my head. Before I can comment, Mrs. Hammond instructs us to open our books and leads us in a discussion that lasts through class.

As we are waiting for the bell to dismiss us from class, an alert comes over the intercom for all teachers to turn on the TVs in their classrooms. Everyone looks around wondering what's going on. When the TV comes to life, we see a plane crashing into one of the World Trade Centers in Lower Manhattan. Both have been hit at this point and dozens of alerts fly across the screen for people to stay in their homes and not travel to Manhattan. Fire and smoke are the background for the people of the city as they flee from surrounding buildings. The screen suddenly changes to President George Bush as he delivers a haunting speech that will go down in history. His speech is brief and the lingering line that leaves me speechless is "This was an apparent terrorist attack on our country."

Everything seems to happen in slow motion after that. The news switches back to live footage of the Twin Towers. I stare in shock as fear builds up in my system. In a matter of minutes, students are getting called for dismissal. Mrs. Hammond stands there watching the screen with her hand covering her mouth. The students are in an uproar, some crying, some shooting out of their seats to get closer to the television, and some in shock.

The intercom sounds again, "Mrs. Hammond, Marcy Hillary for dismissal." I jump from my seat gathering my things as I go. I look at Jenny who has tears in her eyes.

"I'll call you later," I say before I rush from the room and down the hall to the main office. Matthew and Samuel are there waiting for me as I approach. Sam takes my books and Matt leans down giving me a hug.

"Mom called and wanted me to come get you. She can't leave her students but she wants to know that we're safe at home." I nod my head not knowing what to say. Just before we walk out of the school, the T.V. over our head shows a plane crashing into the Pentagon. The three of us stand there in shocked silence as we watch the building burning. Shrieks and cries come from the people in the mass pandemonium.

"Come on, let's go!" Matt takes my hand as we rush through the doors. The only thing I remember about the ride home is Sam holding my hand from the front seat and telling me that I was safe and that everything was going to be okay.

Six

Marcy

Well the day is finally here and I'm not any more ready than I was when Sebastian presented me with the idea of throwing this party. I know it's going to be extravagant. There's a part of me that doesn't think there is anything to celebrate since my brother won't be there, but there's also a part of me that wants people to know his sacrifice. I know it's been years and years but I haven't moved on from the fact that he isn't on this Earth with me anymore. I don't know if I ever will. Some days are easier to breathe than others but there is always this shadow following me, reminding me that my favorite person died overseas.

After I shower, I go to my walk-in closet and pull out the dress I bought for the occasion. It's a beautiful green satin long sleeved dress. The neckline cuts into a low v showing off my abundant breasts, the satin then flows from my chest, which has a slimming effect on my curves. I'm definitely not small by any means but I'm finally happy with my shape. I used to be self-conscious when I was younger, but I grew into them and cultivated the confidence I needed to pull off this figure. The dress hits my legs just above my knees making me decide to pair it with brown knee-high boots. As I look in the mirror, the finished ensemble excites me. I decided to wear my long red locks down and painted a beautiful shadowy eye to go with the outfit. I feel good. I feel confident and I can't help but admit that I'm a little excited for this party.

I may or may not have gotten this outfit to impress a growly looking sex god. Surely after tonight he won't see me as his best friend's younger sister anymore. As we grew up, the difference in our ages became less and less extreme. I don't see anything wrong with being with an older man. *Whoa, slow down Marcy. You don't even know if he's with someone or not. He could be married for all you know.* My stomach plummets as I look back to the mirror. I guess I didn't think about the possibility that he could be married. I mean the man is forty-five for Pete's sake. I'm sure he's had many women while here I am, a thirty-six-year-old virgin.

My fingers trail down the smooth satin and for a moment I want to call the whole thing off.

"You know what? I'm not going down that road. If he's married then it wasn't meant to be. I might meet someone else tonight. This party isn't about him anyways. It's about Matthew and me and the fact that I'm so badass at my job my clients want to celebrate me. Put on your big girl panties, Marcy, and go to that damn party. You deserve it." My little pep talk seems to have done the trick. I check my appearance once more as I grab my jacket. Tonight is going to be one for the books. I just know it.

Sebastian texts alerting me that my driver has arrived and is waiting for me downstairs, so I hurry out the door then down the elevator. My boots clink against the ceramic floor in the lobby as I rush to the car. Excitement courses through me when I see the limousine waiting for me. I haven't been in one since my eighth grade dance, the one Sam helped me get ready for. Flutters erupt in my tummy. I haven't thought of that day in so long.

I hear someone clear their throat and I see a gentleman is there waiting for me. As I approach him he opens the door for me.

"Miss Hillary," he gestures toward the open door.

"Yes, thank you." I take his hand as I slide into the car.

"You're very welcome. My name is Charles if you need anything at all." He closes the door behind me then enters the driver's seat. He rolls down the window partition and says, "There is champagne back there if you would like some." I see the fancy bottle but decide to wait until I get to the hotel to have anything to drink. I don't want to overdo it tonight and get sloshed.

I watch out the window as all the lights go twinkling by. Nerves and excitement threaten to overwhelm me but after taking a few deep breaths I'm able to calm myself a bit.

Drawing closer to Hotel Chantelle's entrance, I find myself captivated by its undeniable grace. Despite passing by numerous times, I hadn't truly appreciated its opulent allure until now. Charles stops in front of the doors and parks the car before stepping out to open the door for me. I can't help but to feel like I'm in some sort of fairytale. I take his hand then step out of the limo. Grabbing my clutch tightly, I confidently walk into the lobby of the hotel. Before I arrive at the visitors desk, I am approached by a bellhop.

"Miss Hillary, we have been waiting for you. If you will please follow me to the rooftop, the rest of your party is here. Would you like me to take your jacket?" he asks. I nod and turn, allowing him to pull it from my shoulders. He takes the jacket and heads for the bank of elevators. Following behind, he presses the button to go up. Once inside, we go straight to the top. I'm not prepared for the sight that hits me when the doors open to the rooftop. The whole place looks professionally decorated with black and gold balloons and streamers.

Lizzie and Stormy are the first to greet me by nearly trampling me to the ground. Their excitement is contagious.

"Marcy! You made it!" Lizzie shouts as she squeezes me tightly.

"You look absolutely stunning, Marcy!" Stormy croons over the music playing.

"Thank you both for putting this together. You look beautiful as well," I reply as the two finally pull away from me. Sebastian and Miles are close behind the girls and each pull me into a tight embrace.

"This all looks amazing, you guys. You all didn't have to go through so much trouble for me," I tell them but they aren't having it.

"That's nonsense. You are like part of the family and you have done more for us than we could ever repay." Sebastian smirks and playfully bumps my shoulder. I try to disagree but Miles jumps in and confirms what his brother said.

"He's right. You are an honorary Knight. Now, let's get you a drink." The girls flank my sides with their arms threaded through my own as we walk up to the open bar.

"I love this dress so much," Stormy gushes. "I love satin," Lizzie pipes up and I internally give myself a pat on the back for choosing a dress that I thought was outside of my comfort zone. However I was able to pull it off and I feel comfortable and confident. Exactly what I want to feel on a night that is celebrating me.

"What can I get you?" the bartender asks as he leans over the bar toward me.

"Hmm, I think I want a Cosmopolitan. I haven't had one in a while." He nods his head and slings a towel over his shoulder as he gets to work making my drink.

"I'll be back soon. Sarah just got here," Lizzie says as she trots off toward our mutual friend. As I look around, it's crazy that I know most of these people either from working with them in the past or through mutual encounters with the Knight family.

"Here you go, Miss." The bartender places the drink down on a napkin in front of me. It looks delicious with a bright red hue from the cranberry juice and the lemon peel garnish. Taking a sip, I close my eyes and let the tangy taste flood my senses.

"How is it?" Stormy questions as she takes a sip of her own drink.

"Delicious. Just what I needed," I say. Sebastian comes over to lead Stormy to the dance floor and I use the reprieve to take a look around at all the guests and decorations that I missed when I first came in. I look over to a darkened corner but before I can tell who is there, Amelia Knight appears before me. She is always regal whenever I see her and tonight is no different. I guess being the matriarch of such a prestigious family calls for a certain level of class.

"Happy birthday, my dear. I was thrilled when Miles called to inform me that you finally accepted his offer. You do so much for this family, it's time we celebrate you." She gestures to the bartender who obviously already knows what she is drinking and he gets to work.

"Thank you, Mrs. Knight. I appreciate your boys putting this together for me. It means so much." Amelia nods then picks up her new drink and takes a delicate sip.

"You know you can call me Amelia, dear. We've known each other for years." She grasps my arm and leads me over to a high-top table where we set our drinks. Fortunately, there are tall heaters on this rooftop, or it would be too cold for a party. Guests come up to me one right after another to wish me a happy birthday and I start to get overwhelmed until Sarah cuts in.

She gives me a hug. "You look exquisite, Marcy." I smile at her kind words. She would tell me the truth so the fact that she is raving about the outfit has me feeling more at ease.

"Did you persuade Travis to come with you?" I look around and don't see him.

"Yes, he's here somewhere. I think the guys said something about getting out some really old cigars." She shrugs her shoulders and smiles.

"That sounds about right." I laugh at her rolling eyes. "Are Nora and Ally here yet?" I inquire.

"I haven't seen them but I'm sure they will be here any minute. Nora wouldn't miss this." I nod and take another sip of my drink.

"Excuse me ladies, could I have this dance?" The handsome gentleman bows slightly and holds his hand out waiting for me to accept. I look at Sarah as a huge grin spreads across her face. I feel like he's making an extravagant show of asking me but I can't find it in myself to care. I suddenly like the attention.

I place my drink down along with my clutch as I slide my hand into the stranger's warm hand.

"Sure." He smiles as he straightens then leads me to the dance floor. He graciously spins me around then pulls my body against his, grabbing my waist. The gesture seems almost too intimate for someone that I don't know.

"My name is Alexander Caldwell," he whispers into the shell of my ear as we turn about the dance floor. His warm breath raises the hairs on the back of my neck and for some reason I feel unease with him.

"I'm Marcy," I mention looking out at the crowd for anyone to save me before he twirls me out again. As I swing back into his arms he grabs my waist tighter.

"I know. I'm business partners with Miles and Sebastian and they pointed you out. Forgive me for being forward but you are very attractive." Being a virgin, you would think I'm naïve but I'm quite the opposite. I guess growing up with an overprotective older brother taught me to look for red flags. And this guy only has one thing on his mind and that's getting lucky tonight. He seems nice enough but I came here with one man in mind and I won't be able to rid him from my thoughts until I see his face again.

"Th-thank you, Alexander," I rush out. Now I'm extremely uncomfortable but also hate to be rude to someone that works with Miles and Sebastian. I feel stuck.

"Please call me, Xander." He spins me again and I'm momentarily shocked by his moves then I see *him*. I see Samuel Knight standing in the darkened corner that I was sure someone was standing in earlier. His eyes are on mine as if penetrating my soul. He doesn't look happy to see me. Honestly, he looks pissed off to see me here on the dance floor. I try to look away but my eyes can't help but to wander back to him.

"Marcy?" My focus comes back to Xander as I look up at him to see a questioning look in his eyes.

"Sorry, what did you say?" I ask as I try to keep my attention on him but my eyes yearn to seek out Samuel again. When I look back, he's vanished almost like he was never there to begin with.

"I was asking if you would like to have a drink with me." The song comes to an end but he continues to hold me tightly. I take a step back to think of what I'm going to say to get out of spending more time with him but there aren't any words coming out of my mouth. Just as I'm about to give a response, a large dark figure looms behind me.

"She promised me the next dance," the deep gravelly voice announces. As I turn around, I'm shocked to see Samuel standing before me. The pictures I found on the internet did not do him justice. He's very tall, around 6'4", and pure muscle. He always had some muscles when we were younger but now he looks like he was built like a tank. His boyish defined jaw transformed into strong and masculine. A hint of a tattoo can be seen peeking out of the collar of his shirt. In many ways he looks like the boy I always knew, just grown up. He looks down at me with a ghost of a smile crossing his lips. Taking my hand in his, he pulls me to the center of the dance floor. Neither of us have spoken a word but they don't seem necessary. He brings his other hand to settle on my waist, a little lower than Xander did and a thrill shoots through my body at his touch. My heart is beating out of my chest and all I can think about is when Samuel taught me how to dance when I was in eighth grade.

"Look me in the eyes, Marcy, not down at your feet," Samuel murmurs as the music begins to play on my boombox. I look up into

his eyes and he nods. He takes my hand in his then his other hand grasps my waist pulling our bodies closer.

"I don't know what I'm doing," I confess as I close my eyes, casting my head away from his. Samuel drops my hand and cups my chin forcing me to look up at him.

"That's what I'm here for. I'll teach you everything you need to know, sunshine. There won't be a boy there that will pass up a chance to dance with you." He skims his fingers down my cheek and takes a hold of my hand again. "Now, follow my lead." I nod, keeping my eyes locked on his. As he moves around the garage, I move along with him.

I get caught up in the motions and step on his foot accidently. Instantly I drop his hand and step away, too embarrassed to look at him. I probably broke his toe with how much I weigh.

"Hey, where do you think you're going, princess? We aren't done." He comes over to me and takes up his stance again.

It's not the first time he's called me that, but every time he does I want to melt in a puddle on the floor. I think he started calling me that one night when we were down in the basement playing a video game. I was upset about something and the endearment was born. I never complained because I loved hearing it.

"I can't do this, Sam. I'm not meant to be a dancer. I just stepped on your foot and probably hurt you." Tears spring to the corners of my eyes threatening to fall. I try to look at anything but the beautiful boy in front of me. I knew this wasn't a good idea. I don't even have a date to the dance yet and who's going to ask me? I'm an overweight girl with unmanageable red hair. I don't scream popular by any means.

"Listen to me. You're going to that dance. I know what you're thinking and you didn't hurt me, not by a long shot. Now, let's try again." Another song starts up and we move along to the beat. This time I'm getting more confident and don't feel so self-conscious. Samuel twirls me and pulls me back into his body, his eyes never straying from mine. My breath hitches at his intense gaze he has on me and my cheeks flame.

"See? You're a natural, Marcy. Those middle school boys don't know what they're missing out on." Samuel gives me a wink and my heart flutters in my chest. I have never loved anyone the way I do Samuel. But I know I'm just Matthew's younger sister to him. He won't ever look at me the same way I look at him. My heart rejects the notion and continues to hold on to that fleeting chance that maybe, someday. The song comes to an end just as Matthew steps into the garage. Our bubble bursts and we are back to the real world.

"Hey man, you want to go shoot some hoops? Oh, and mom wants you to come help her cook dinner, Marcy." I reluctantly step away from Samuel and run into the house to help my mother. I didn't know that would be the last time the two of us were alone together. Everything came crashing down after that.

SEVEN

Samuel

I knew the second she entered the rooftop terrace. There was a shift in the air and then there she was, glowing in all her beauty for everyone to see. People flocked to her as soon as she stepped off the elevator. The gorgeous redhead that has held my heart all these years is here, so close yet so far.

I grab my drink from the bartender and walk around the balcony until I'm mostly shrouded from view. I want to be able to stare at her without the distractions of others. Her smile ignites something inside me that I thought was long dead. Her picturesque auburn hair tumbles down her back the way it used to when she was younger. I've always loved her hair. My fingers used to itch to feel the ringlets wrapped around my fingers. It's gotten longer over the years, almost reaching her voluptuous ass. Marcy's luminous fair skin shines bright enough to dim everyone around her. Her curves filled out so beautifully and the confidence surrounding her is like a drug. She walks with a composure she didn't use to possess.

I move along in the shadows in order to keep my eyes on her. I find myself smiling along with her, it's contagious. *When was the last time I truly smiled?* The guilt that has always hung over my head somewhat dissipates when I see how happy she is. She is a sight to behold. Seeing her in pictures and from across the street versus right in front of me is unparalleled. Looking around, I see men drooling over her and anger flares inside me. She doesn't need some skeeze ball hanging around her.

Aunt Amelia approaches her giving her a hug then leading her to a table off to the corner of the patio. Marcy has her back to me but I'm still able to keep an eye on her. That's what Matthew would want. At least that's what I tell myself. As I finish my drink, Xander Caldwell begins moving toward them and I know before he gets there that he's going to try to use his well known charm on her. Xander holds out his hand for her to take and for a moment she hesitates and I find myself holding my breath wanting her to decline the offer. Instead she lets him lead her to the dance floor. When he places his hands on her waist, I see red. No one should be touching her that way. I tell myself that I'm protecting her but I really don't know at this point. I only know that his hands need to leave her body or I will break them. He twirls her around making her green dress rise up and before I know what I'm doing, I'm moving.

I glide out of the shadows letting my presence be known, it doesn't take her long to see me. She stares at me with both intrigue and a fondness that I remember always getting from her. The band finishes the song but her attention remains on me even as Xander leans in to whisper something in her ear. Once he says something again, the spell is broken as she looks up to him. I use this moment to my advantage to make my way by her side.

"I was asking if you would like to have a drink with me," Xander grins down at Marcy, not noticing my arrival.

I use this as the perfect opportunity to get her away from the guy. She wasn't into him anyways, I could tell. I may not know her anymore but I still know her body language and she was looking for a polite way out.

"She promised me the next dance," I announce. Xander looks from me to Marcy with unsaid questions in his eyes but he must see that I won't back down from this. He thanks Marcy for the dance and jets off the other direction.

Marcy is now staring at me with her mouth agape but I take her hand and lead her to the center of the stage. Her small hand fits delicately in my large callused one. Once a new song begins, I turn her around bringing her body flush against mine. The way her body molds into mine makes holding her feel right.

No words have been uttered, a shared silence falls over us as we dance, the crowd falling away around us.

She finally breaks the silence as her brilliant green eyes search mine. "Samuel, it's you." Is all she says but my name on her lips sends chills up my spine. I've never been so viscerally affected by someone in my life. I spin her out keeping our hands locked then catch her when she twists back.

"It's me, sunshine," I murmur as I lean down brushing my lips along the collar of her neck. I can see the goosebumps erupt over her neck and chest when hearing that name. Matthew used to call her sunshine all the time and it became something I started to use as well. In all honesty, she's as bright as the sun. Her personality combined with her beauty makes her shine bright.

"You remembered," she utters as a tear escapes her eye. Keeping my hand on her waist, I wipe away the tear with my other hand. I linger longer feeling the softness of her skin.

"Of course I remembered. How could I forget?" I ask with a smile.

She looks away then back at me with flamed cheeks. She's still so cute when she gets embarrassed. She takes the wrong step and plunges into my chest. Her lavender and honey scent assaults my senses in the best way. I can't help but to grasp her back, tangling my fingers through her hair as I right her.

"Looks like someone doesn't remember their dance lesson." I tsk. "Do I need to show you again?" I smirk. Marcy nibbles on her voluptuous bottom lip making me want to do the same.

"I guess I forgot a few steps," she admits with a smile.

"Then listen very carefully. Don't take those gorgeous eyes off me and follow my lead." She nods as I take her hand back in mine then lead her around the dance floor. I pull her in close, loving the warmth of her body against mine. We dance through several songs with the only words spoken being the ones that our eyes reveal. We are in our own little bubble of musical bliss until Miles comes over.

"I hate to break this up but we are about to give a toast for you and Matthew," Miles says to Marcy. Hearing his name sobers me. I take a step back as though I've been burned by the forbidden fruit. *How did I let things get intimate with her? I'm her brother's best friend. Nothing can happen between us.* My mind is waging a war with my heart. Marcy looks at me but I keep mine on Miles. I can feel frustration radiating off her. I'm doing what's best, keeping her at arm's length. That's the only thing I'm good at. I'll continue to watch her life from the sidelines. She doesn't need someone broken. She needs a whole man, as much as I hate to admit it. But the thought of her with another man makes me clench my fists by my side. Irrationally I don't want anyone to have her unless it's me.

It's good that Miles interrupted when he did or who knows what I would have done. Maybe I would have rented a room here and had my way with her. The thoughts leave me feeling dirty and wrong. Marcy deserves to be with someone that didn't skew her brother's dying request. Having her followed instead of putting in the work myself.

As Miles whisks Marcy away, she turns back to look at me with sadness in her eyes. My gut wrenches with the sight of her unhappiness. She turns back in time to walk up the stairs to the podium where Sebastian joins them. Waiters begin walking around with tall flutes of champagne on serving platters offering one to all the guests.

Miles taps on the microphone making sure it's working before he begins. "Thank you all for joining us in this birthday celebration. We are here to honor a very special day. Marcy Hillary has become an integral part of the Knight family and we are forever grateful to everything she does. And let's be honest, you all know the trouble Sebastian and I can find ourselves in. Marcy is always there to save the day." The audience laughs along as Sebastian comes up behind her and drapes his arm over her shoulders the way a protective brother would. I suppose the Knights have become her adoptive family since her parents' death.

Miles continues, "But in all seriousness, we would be in deep shit without this woman right here. As coincidence would have it, she shares this day with her brother, Matthew, who died fighting for our country. He's a true American hero and we wanted to use this party to celebrate both Marcy and Matthew. Please join me in this toast. Cheers." Miles holds his flute up to the crowd then turns to clink his against Marcy's and Sebastian's. As I look around at the cheering crowd, my heart squeezes with emotions I can't place. Looking back at Marcy, I can see the tears sparkling in her eyes but I know she is holding them in until she can get off stage and out of the spotlight. She excuses herself after she says a quick thank you then moves off to a far corner.

A woman with short blonde hair comes up behind her rubbing her back in calming circles and whispers something in her ear. They begin smiling and laughing a moment later and the relief I feel is palpable. I can't stand to see her sad, especially knowing the reason being that her brother isn't here with her tonight. It makes me question my life and wonder what the hell I'm doing here. If Matthew were here, he would be doing good work and helping those he knew were suffering. Instead, I survived. All I can do is hide behind my computer.

Before I go into a drinking binge, I remember the notes I took earlier and an idea forms in my mind. I could call it the Matthew Hillary Foundation, honoring those that have fallen in battle and aiding those that returned. Maybe that would make me worthy of Marcy.

As I'm looking at her from a distance, Miles and Sebastian come up to me. "Looks like we were right about you two," Sebastian comments as he gestures toward Marcy.

"Yeah, you two seemed mighty comfortable on the dance floor. I think you scared poor Xander off though. I haven't seen him since." Miles chuckles as he takes a drink.

"I was just saving her from the asshole. He wasn't right for her." Before I can take it back, it's out there in the open. Miles and Sebastian both exchange grins then look back to me.

"So, what are you doing over here then? Go get the girl," Sebastian insists. I contemplate his words. It would be easy to say fuck it all and take Marcy as mine. I read the emotions in her eyes. I know she wants this too. The battle of what's right weighs heavily on me because I truly don't know what the right move is. My mind tells me to stay away because I'll only let her down the way I did her brother. *I couldn't keep him alive so why should I be given a chance to protect his sister?* But I want her with every fiber of my being.

"I doubt I'm what Matthew had in mind for his sister," I state as I stare at the red headed siren across the roof. Her laugh is calling out to me with promises while I sail the dangerous seas of my mind.

"He was your best friend. The two of you were inseparable as kids. You don't think out of all men in the world, he would bless you, especially, to be with her. I know you can't get his approval now but don't let that stop you. We saw the way she looked at you. I've never seen her like that, man. Don't blow it because you're worried. I think you are using Matthew as an excuse to not go after what you've always wanted."

It's easy for them to tell me to go after her, they can't see the battle waging in my mind.

Running my hands through my hair, I try to think about what is really stopping me from pursuing Marcy. I can't deny the pull I have toward her. She's secretly been my sole obsession since leaving the military. I've stalked her, telling myself I was only protecting her, doing what her brother asked of me. I knew the lies I told myself would never be able to obstruct the true reason I did it. I want her. No, I *need* her. I need her like my next breath. She is responsible for the only light in my otherwise bleak life.

She must feel my gaze on her because she turns around and looks right at me. I want to go to her. *Would it be so bad if I did?*

EIGHT

Marcy

I see Miles and Sebastian talking to Samuel and I wonder what they're saying. Sam's eyes stay locked on mine while the others are speaking as if he's blocking everything out except for me. I've always dreamed of him looking at me this way but I get the feeling that he's going through some kind of an internal struggle. Sebastian nudges his shoulder causing him to break our contact giving me the opportunity to check out his new muscular build. Before he went into the military, he frequented the gym but now he looks like he lives there. He looks like a beast.

Sarah nudges me when she sees where I'm staring off to. "Ah, so that's *the* Samuel that I used to hear about, huh?" she questions.

"Uh, yeah. I guess it is. I haven't seen him in so long but it's like I still know him and at the same time, I don't. Does that make sense?" I ask as I turn my gaze to her.

"Definitely. People don't change completely but he's been to war so you don't know that side of him. I doubt many do from the looks of it. His body language tells people to back the fuck away." Sarah chuckles at her statement, giving me the opportunity to look back to see what she's talking about. He does stand differently. He doesn't look like the carefree boy I once knew.

Nora and Ally barge into my view of Sam. "Marcy! I haven't been able to get a hold of you all night, love!" Nora beams.

"I'm sorry! I guess I've been stretched out with everyone."

"Don't apologize! This is your day! I just wanted you to know that Ally and I made it to the party."

"Thank you for the invite," Ally gives me a half hug, her usual.

"Of course. I wanted to spend the day with my friends," I reply.

"We are going to go hit the dance floor before this thing dies down." Ally places a kiss on Nora's head then grabs her hand to lead her away. My heart aches at the beauty of their love. I wish I had that.

As dawn draws near, the energy of the party begins to fade. It's been a while since I've indulged in such a high level of alcohol, but my friends' persistent offers for shots were too tempting to resist. Nonetheless, a twinge of regret begins to creep up as I stagger towards a vacant table nestled in the corner. Lifting my gaze towards the spinning patio, my senses swirl out of control causing me to puke in a large potted plant next to me.

Resting my head against the cool table, I close my eyes and wish more than anything that I was already home in my comfy pajamas and in bed. My stomach rolls alerting me that I'm going to be sick again. I lean over just in time to bathe the plant in my vomit. I wipe away the hair stuck to my mouth with the back of my hand.

Groaning I try to stand but I stumble over my own feet and fall face first into a hard body. My arms voluntarily wrap around the person standing before me. A familiar scent of vanilla and sandalwood fills my head and I know it's Samuel that happened to catch me.

"Whoa. Easy there, princess," he croons as he leans over gathering my hair in his large hand. He grabs my arm and pulls me up flush against his body.

Embarrassment washes over me at the state I'm in. I want to go hide in a hole until he leaves so he doesn't have to see me like this. Opening my eyes, I look up at the sexy bearded man holding me up.

"I'm alright. I just slipped," I lie hoping he will let me crawl away in peace.

"Don't lie to me, Marcy," he tuts with irritation. I don't know why he's even helping me when he spent the rest of the party avoiding me like the plague. Every time I would find him, he would look away quickly and suddenly be interested in something else. I guess the closeness I felt during our dance was one sided. *Figures.*

"I don't need your help, Sam. I was just going to call my driver and go home." I push against him so I can remove myself from his grasp. I don't need him or his negativity.

Sam leans down to whisper in my ear. "Stop trying to get away from me, sunshine. You won't be able to." Chills shoot through my body as his warm breath coats my neck. He wraps his arm around my waist and bends, lifting me into his arms bridal style. *What the fuck is happening here?*

"Put me down! I can walk!" I exclaim but he continues walking toward the bank of elevators. I'm confident in my plus-sized body but that doesn't mean I want someone carrying me, especially him of all people.

"More lies," he murmurs. "You know, bad girls get punished. I'd hate to mark that beautiful porcelain skin." He chuckles darkly. Miles comes over and my embarrassment skyrockets because not only is my long-time crush seeing me like this but now my boss. I shut my eyes to avoid their gazes upon me.

"Everything alright?" Miles asks.

"Just making sure she gets home safely," Samuel replies.

"Good, good. We are getting out of here too. Take care, Marcy." As his footsteps recede, I hesitantly open my eyes to find Sam observing me with an inscrutable expression. I absentmindedly run my hands over my face, suddenly recalling the makeup I'm wearing. *Can this night get any worse?* I'm sure I look like a...well, who the hell knows what I look like at this point.

Once Sam steps into the elevator, I try to reason with him again. "You don't need to be doing this. I'm sure I can walk," I mutter with more confidence than I feel. He's probably really doing me a favor because at this point my surroundings are still spinning out of control. Actually, I might have to puke again because my stomach dropped as soon as the elevator did. My saliva starts to thin and I know it's coming. I also know that I will absolutely die if I get sick in Sam's arms or perhaps even worse, on them. I'm talking about faking my own death and moving to another country to live out my days in vomit exile.

As the doors to the elevator open, I risk more humiliation as I jump from his arms barely catching myself on the bellhop standing there. An expression of sheer horror marks his face as the unexpected shower of vomit tarnishes his clean attire. My hurried apology barely registers as I scramble towards the lobby doors, the only thought consuming me is the urge to distance myself from this mortifying scene. The cool fresh air hits me in the face, making me sigh in relief. I'm not sure how it's possible but by a miracle Charles is standing there waiting for me with the door to the limo open. It's almost over, I just have to make it to him. A feat easier said than done. As I begin to stumble my way toward him, I feel a hand wrap around my upper arm pulling me back.

"What the hell are you doing? Are you trying to get yourself hurt?" Anger coats Sam's face as he looks down at me. I open my mouth but no words seem to form. I stand there speechless, for once, not sure if I should be pissed off or thankful. To be honest, I'm questioning several things at the moment.

Sam steps closer to me, reaching up to grab my chin with one hand. "I think you need some manners about respecting your elders," he says with a wicked gleam in his eyes. "Now, get in the car before I bend you over my knee right here." I gasp as the effects of his wicked words course through me. My teeth graze my bottom lip causing him to groan.

Releasing my face, he escorts me to the limo then lifts me into the seat. Before he moves, the buckle comes around me and clicks into place. My body is burning up from all the places he's touched me leaving a lingering effect. Leaning my head against the seat, I close my eyes ready for this night to be over. I hear the door shut then the other side open. I think it's Charles until the seat next to me dips down. My eyes startle open and I see Sam sitting next to me with a smug smile ghosting his lips. My heart pounds in my chest at his proximity but I don't have the energy to figure out what the hell he's doing here. My eyes close on their own accord and don't open until I feel Sam brushing the hair from my face.

"We're here," he whispers.

I pull myself up by the handle on the door and look out the window. This isn't my apartment. Panic starts to course through me but before I get too far down that road, Samuel speaks up. "I brought you to my place so I could watch over you tonight. You had a lot to drink and shouldn't be alone."

"What? I-what? You aren't my caretaker! I've made it thirty-six years on this Earth, I don't need assistance now." His expression turns dark as he clenches his fists by his side.

"You aren't in your right mind and don't know what's best for you, but I do. Now, get your ass out of this car." Sam steps out of the limo and slams his door shut. I cross my arms over my chest because at this point I'm ready to stand my ground. My door opens and he's there unbuckling me pulling me from the car.

"Hey! What the hell do you think you're doing?" I curse at Sam. His irritation with me grows and I feel both proud and nervous that I've tempted the beast. I look to Charles for some assistance but he must know Sam. *Of course he does. He works for the Knights for fuck's sake.*

"Thank you, Charles. I can take it from here," Sam declares as he puts his arm around me, hoisting my body up beside his. My mind is getting so foggy that I don't have the energy to fight back at the moment, but he will be getting an earful tomorrow. He can't treat me like I'm still a child. He hasn't been back in my life but only a few hours and he has the audacity to think he knows what's best for me. *Fuck that.* And I intend to tell him when words are again able to form in my mind.

"Very good, sir," he replies as he closes the door behind me.

Sam is mostly holding me up which makes less work for my legs that seem to be getting heavier by the second. But that's not the only thing getting heavier. I can barely hold my eyes open at this point and I doubt very seriously that I could have made it to my apartment safely. I hate being wrong but even more when it's a man that proves me incorrect.

Suddenly I become more lightheaded and the last thing I remember is leaning against Sam murmuring something about how he always smells so good. Then everything goes black.

Nine

Samuel

I knew she needed me the moment I saw her collapse at the table in the corner. Her friends had since left but she was still there for whatever reason. As I made my way to her across the rooftop, I saw her become ill with none the wiser. I was all she had to truly look after her at this point and I wasn't going to let Matthew down by leaving her there. I didn't expect her to fight me along the way. That's a new development in her personality. She always did what she was told and what was expected of her when she was young but somewhere along the way she grew into Miss Independent. I won't lie and say that it wasn't sexy as fuck for her to speak to me like that.

I got her down to the car with minimal inappropriate comments. I couldn't help myself by taunting her beautiful ass with punishment. The thought of having my handprint on that perfect peach is a sight I might never be able to erase from my mind. I have to adjust myself thinking about it.

Once she passed out in my arms, I lifted her to my chest and brought her to my penthouse. I laid her on the bed and removed her boots one by one, enjoying the feel of her silky calves in my hands. I warred with myself on whether I should put her in something more comfortable or not. I finally decided to dress her in one of my old Army t-shirts. The sheer amount of will it took for me to not gawk at the beauty before me was a true testament to my code of honor. After I got her tucked in, I placed a glass of water on the bedside table for when she wakes.

As I sit on the edge of my bed watching Marcy sleep, in a totally non-creepy way, I take in all her splendor. No one could deny that she is absolutely stunning. Her long red locks lay gently over her pale freckled skin. The sheet falls over her body showcasing the mouthwatering curves she has. I rake my eyes over her body, wanting to explore every inch of her delectable figure. Brushing a piece of hair away from her face, I watch as my beautiful obsession sleeps.

Marcy Hillary is in my bed. I would never have believed it were true if I wasn't seeing it with my own eyes. "You always smell so good" repeats over and over in my mind. *How long has she thought that? Did she believe that when we were kids?*

The sounds coming from the television are sure to upset Matt's parents but they aren't home at the moment. This new game came out today, erasing any plans we had. We haven't left the couch downstairs in hours as we battle it out on the Xbox. The front door opens then slams shut.

"Matt, get up here. I need help in the garage," Matt's dad yells down the stairs. He groans but jumps from the couch to head up the stairs.

"This shouldn't take long," he calls back down.

The door opens and closes again. Thinking it's Matt, I resume the game in single player mode. Soft cries reverberate down the stairs, making me pause the game. The haunting melody pulls me away from the virtual world. I set down my controller, the game forgotten, and follow the sound. The stairs creak under my weight as I ascend, taking two at a time.

Marcy is scrunched at the top with her head buried in her legs. Her red hair spilling in all directions as she whimpers. Anger courses through me at the sight of her like this, making me want to find who is responsible.

I kneel down beside her but I guess I'm not as quiet as I hoped. Her red blotchy face looks up at me but I see the instant embarrassment overcomes her. She wipes her cheeks, murmuring a sorry as she tries to scurry off.

Unfortunately for her, I'm not letting her get away without telling me what happened.

"Oh, no you don't," I declare, pulling her ass right back down to where she was.

"Want to tell me what's going on, princess?" She plays with the hem of her shirt as she shakes her head.

"Hmm... well, if you aren't going to tell me then I guess you need to get to the basement."

Her face shoots up looking at me quizzically. "What? Why?" Her expression makes me chuckle.

"Because we got a new game today that I think you would like." I shrug my shoulders.

"Okay? And you want me to play with you?" She looks at me skeptically.

"Yep." I jump up from the floor, grabbing her hand along the way. "Beat you down there!" I roar in laughter taking two steps at a time.

"Hey! Your legs are longer!" She sprints down then jumps over the back of the couch plopping herself down without me.

Chuckling, I land beside and grab our controllers.

"So, what's this new game called?"

"Mortal Kombat! It will definitely take your mind off things." I wiggle my eyebrows at her which always makes her laugh. This time is no different. Her laughter echoes through the basement, making me pleased that at least she's not crying any longer.

"So, how do I play this?" She looks at the controller like it's an alien.

"First off, there are combo moves which you will have to remember." She rolls her eyes.

"Just start the game, I'll figure it out." With my interest piqued, I start it up. I guess throwing her into the deep end will force her to swim, right?

With just a few games under her belt, she's beating me. The only excuse I can come up with is sorcery. She's spamming all the buttons at the same time. There's no rhyme or reason to her madness but dammit if she isn't kicking my ass.

"Slow down there, princess. These guys aren't fighting you in real life."

"I'm pretending your character is this guy from school. So, I'm having a great time kicking his butt!" she chuckles but I can see the sadness in her eyes. I pause the game to see if she will talk to me this time.

"Hey! I was just about to knock him out!" she whines as she flops back against the couch.

"So, are you going to tell me what got you so upset earlier?"

"Why do you care?"

"Because I need to know who's ass I'll be beating tonight, princess." She laughs, but I'm only partially kidding. People don't make Marcy cry and get away with it.

"It's stupid." She fidgets with her hands then looks back up at me with fresh tears in her eyes. "Do you think someone will like me when I get older?"

"Of course I do! They would be stupid not to. Why do you ask?" She shrugs her shoulders to get away but I won't let her. She always runs when things get hard but she's not running from me. I pull her back, making her collapse on my chest. She scrambles up but stays seated.

"This guy said that I would be alone forever and that no one would want me." She wipes a tear away but continues, "It's not like I like him or anything but his words made me think that maybe he's right." Her emerald eyes shine up at me waiting for an answer.

"Listen to me, when the time is right everything will fall into place. You will find your prince, I promise." I boop her nose making her laugh. I love the melody.

She throws her arms around me tightly, giving me a hug.

"Thank you, Sam. You always know what to say to make me feel better."

"I try, princess." I rub her back in soothing circles until she looks back up at me.

"You always smell so good." Her admission seems to shock her but before I can respond she's standing and rushing up the stairs.

"Thanks for everything, Sam. I've got to do my homework!"

I laugh as I shake my head. That girl is going to be a handful for whoever is lucky enough to have her.

Marcy's moans jolt me back to the present. She's still asleep as she rolls over and snuggles with another pillow. The sound sends an electrical current straight to my cock. I jump from the bed then take a step back. I can't go there with her. She's Matthew's baby sister and here I am getting a hard on from a small moan escaping her lips. Running my hands down my face, I decide to put some space between us.

Walking into the en suite, the lights illuminate as I take a closer look in the mirror.

"I'm too old for her, too damaged. She has no business being with someone like me." If I say it enough maybe it will sink into my thick skull and I can stop obsessing over her.

I glance back at her in the bed, then determine I need to get rid of this tension building in my mind. Shutting the bathroom door, I remove my clothing and step into a steaming hot shower. Maybe this wasn't the best decision because now all I can think about is Marcy wet and naked in my arms.

"Fuck!" I mutter. "Pull yourself together," I say to myself. "She's just another woman, nothing special." But the instant the words are out, I want to reel them back in. She *is* special. Arguably the most special woman I know. And there lies the problem that makes this decision so difficult.

If I'm honest with myself, I've always been intrigued by her. I'm not saying that I liked an underaged girl, but we always got along. There was this coolness between us, therefore I never minded when she would join Matthew and me to hang out. She was always so witty and funny, forever keeping us entertained. I smile thinking back to that little red-headed spit fire. It's true what they say, gingers are impulsive and have fiery tempers, as she proved so eloquently tonight.

The hot water splashes off my face as I submerge myself under the spray trying to rid my mind of images of Marcy but, if anything, it's making the thoughts more pronounced. Sighing in frustration, I quickly wash up then step out from the shower.

I pull on some shorts then brush my teeth before returning to the bedroom. As I turn off the light, I see Marcy shifted in the bed causing her black lace panties to peek out of the covers. I have to bite my lip to keep from groaning at the sight. She is perfection wrapped in satin sheets. I feel like this is a test I need to pass but am bound to fail. Instead of joining her in bed, I get as comfortable as I can in a chair across the room. This way I can be here if she needs something in the middle of the night but far enough away from the temptation.

I rest my head against the chair and drift off with images of her looking up at me while I was carrying her.

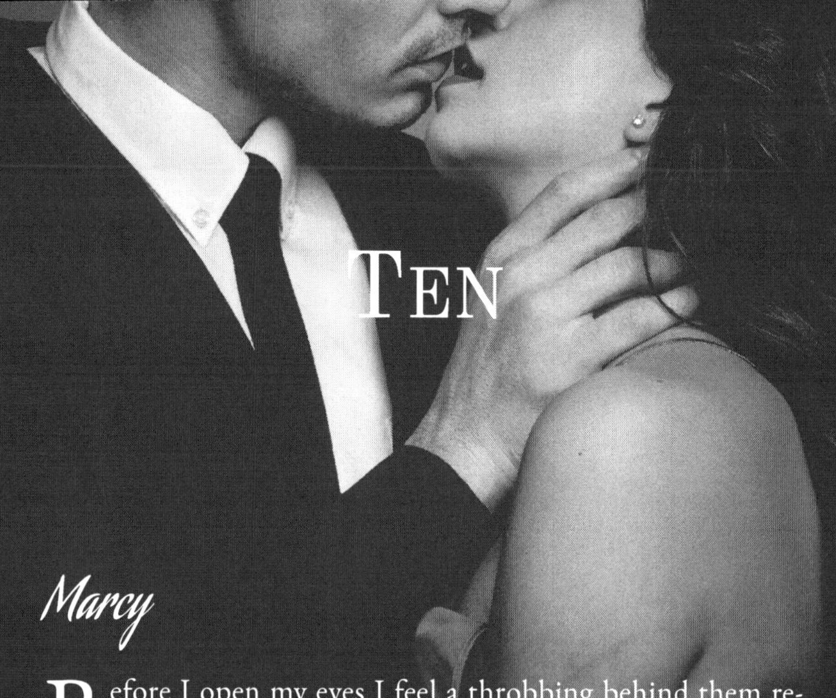

Ten

Marcy

Before I open my eyes I feel a throbbing behind them reminding me that I drank entirely way too much last night. Groaning from the pain, I crack my eyes open, I'm met with an intense light coming from the window. I guess I forgot to draw my curtains last night. A frustrated sigh leaves my lips.

As I pull the sheet away from my body, I feel the silky, satin feeling brushing against my fingers. Even with my mind still riddled with sleep, I know in an instance that this isn't my bed. I shoot up quickly but my legs have other ideas. I wobble around until I get to the nightstand leaning over it, catching my balance. As I brace myself on the table I see the glass of water sitting there, probably for me. *What if it has poison in it? Or a date rape drug? What if I was – Oh fuck*, I push off to a standing position as panic begins to form in my throat. I look all around the room and know for a fact that I have never been here in my life. *Was I kidnapped? Did some villain bring me to their lair to do unspeakable things to me? Fuck*. I look down at my body and realize that my clothes have been replaced by a man's shirt. Pulling it up quickly, I see my panties are still in place. I don't know why but it gives me some sense of calm.

Glancing around the large room, I see my dress draped across a desk in the corner. With no sign of the perpetrator in question, I dash to the desk to put on my dress and boots. I race to the door just as I hear footsteps approaching. *Think fast, Marcy.* I look around the room for a weapon and grab the closest thing I can find, a large book. It's the best shot I have. I knew those crime documentaries would pay off eventually. I remembered how one victim managed to get away and that's exactly what I'm going to do. This man won't know what hit him, literally.

The steps are right at the door and before he sees me I lunge at him with the book over my head, ready to strike him. I don't see his face. I only concentrate on getting in good hits before he tries to take me down.

"Take that you, perv. You won't take me alive!" I scream at him when I jump on his back striking him in all directions. The man is moving around like a wild bronco and I'm doing my best to hang on for dear life.

"What the fuck are you doing?" he shouts as he tries to pull me free from his back but I slap his hands away. This fucker isn't taking me down. I'm going to John Cena his ass.

"You won't get away with this. I'm a secret spy and I know jiu jitsu. You can't take me." I slip from his back and right as I'm about to strike him again he looks at me with blood trailing down his face. Instantly, I drop the book to my feet and step back. Putting my hand over my mouth, the memories from last night begin surfacing in my mind. It was Samuel that brought me back to his place and

I just beat the shit out of him. I don't know whether I should run or try and salvage the situation.

"What the hell, Marcy?" he asks as he brushes his fingers along the cut on his face, wincing from the pain.

"I-uh, I didn't know it was you," I answer quietly as I wring my hands together in front of me. I know the color has drained from my face. Never in a million years did I ever think I would be in Samuel Knight's penthouse, much less waking up in his bed.

"Yeah that part was obvious. Did you seriously think I would let someone else take you home last night?" he asks as his eyes bore into mine. He is not happy at the moment and I don't blame him but I have no idea how to make this situation any better.

"I didn't remember that part, until..." I gulp. "Until I saw your face. I thought you were going to hurt me," I whisper as I put my hands over my eyes. I want this situation to go away. If I hadn't jumped to conclusions none of this would have happened. However, he could have left a note identifying himself for when I woke up alone. So this is partly his fault too. Maybe I do watch too many crime shows. I just manhandled my childhood crush. Although, I have to admit I did a pretty good job for the large beast of a man he is. *Marcy this isn't the time to be giving yourself a pat on the back. Damage control is needed.*

"I'm sorry. Here." I take his hand in mine and lead him to the bathroom I saw earlier. "Let me clean you up." I wince at all the blood dripping onto his white shirt. Man, I've made a mess of things.

He follows along to the bathroom but once we are inside he says, "You don't have to clean this up. I can do it myself," he grunts as he reaches for a wash cloth. I roll my eyes and turn on the lights. Whoa, he looks even worse in the light. Hopefully he can come up with a better story than he got beaten up by a girl. I was wondering why he wasn't fighting back but at the time I thought I had rendered him speechless. *For fuck's sake what am I going to do with myself?*

"Stop being this big macho man and let me take care of you. It's my fault you're like this to begin with. I really am sorry, Sam." I cast my eyes down as I grab the cloth running it under warm water. "Can you sit on the edge of the tub? I can't reach you." He nods and perches on the edge bringing me eye level with him. I can't get over how drastically different our heights are. I mean he was always tall but I don't ever remember him being like a giant to me. I admit the muscles definitely have something to do with it.

With one hand on his shoulder for balance, I take the other with the cloth and begin cleaning all the areas that need attention. He winces when I hit a particularly deep cut and I immediately jump back. I can't stand the thought of hurting him more than I already have.

"I'm fine, Marcy. You can keep going," he murmurs, making the hairs on my neck stand at attention. His voice is so sexy, when it's directed toward me it's damn near irresistible. Letting out a breath, I step forward to continue washing his face.

"Um, where is your medical kit? You need a couple bandages." I rinse the cloth and watch as the red drains into the sink. Guilt rises in my throat as I watch all the red swirl around.

"Marcy?" Sam shakes me from my thoughts.

"Huh? Yeah?" I look up to him as he places a piece of my hair behind my ear. It takes everything in me not to lean into his touch.

"I told you where the kit was. The one you asked for." He holds it up for me to take as I nod my head slowly trying to come back.

"Right. Thanks." Opening the case, I pull out a few bandages and some ointment then spread them across the counter.

"Do you mind having a few bandages? I think you need them until you stop bleeding." I cringe as I look at the cuts on his face.

"Fine." He looks past me to the mirror and he shakes his head. "I sure didn't know you had this in you. I guess I should have, gingers are unpredictable." A small smile ghosts his face and the tightness in my chest eases a bit. Maybe he isn't too angry with me.

"I told you, I thought you were some weirdo trying to get me," I remind him.

"Yes, I got that part." He chuckles and looks back at me. Our eyes lock on each other but I of course have to break the spell because I'm an awkward mess.

"Stay still so I can get these on you." I cup his cheek in my hand and bring it closer so I can apply the bandages. I try not to notice the feel of his skin against mine. We're so close that I want to abandon all thoughts and kiss the man that I've loved for most of my life. *Marcy, get the bandages on and get the hell out of there before you do something stupid.*

I apply the ointment to the bandages then press them to his face in various places. His eyes never stray from mine which makes my job immensely harder. My hands are trembling softly at being this close, but I try to make sure Samuel doesn't notice.

"Okay, all done." I brush my hands together and turn my back to him as I clean up the trash. I wash my hands and move over so he can stand and view the work I've done.

"Thank you. You really didn't have to, but I appreciate it," he mentions as he looks over his face.

"You might want to take some Tylenol to get ahead of the pain." I say as I bite my bottom lip wondering what I should do now. I need to get out of here.

"Nah, I'll be fine." I nod then move to get past him but he catches my elbow. When I look back his eyes have darkened and he's leaning down closer to my face. My breath hitches in my throat wondering what he's going to do.

"I'm sorry I upset you this morning, sunshine. That wasn't my intention. I brought you here last night so I could keep an eye on you. When you passed out in my arms, I knew you needed someone." He rubs his knuckles over my cheek as a chill shoots straight through my body. My ass bumps into the counter as I take a step back to look up into his eyes. His hands drop to my sides as he clutches the edge of the sink, caging me in. He leans in to whisper in my ear, "There's never been someone so fucking sexy in my bed. I barely was able to keep my hands to myself." *Oh gosh, is he really saying what I think he is?* I think my brain is short circuiting. My heart is pounding in my chest as he presses his lips to my neck. My eyes fall closed as his warm breath coats my skin. A moan slips from my lips before I can stop it. Nerves rush to my core making me rub my thighs together.

A growl erupts from his throat as he pulls back, his eyes piercing into mine. "You should be staying away from me. I'm no good for you," he rasps as his hands leave the sink then dig into my hips.

"I-I don't want to," I stutter.

"Is that right?" Sam's lips twitch into a devilish smile as he comes so close that our mouths are nearly touching. I know that he was my brother's best friend and he's older than me but that all flies out the window with how he's looking at me. Like a man starved. It's the same look I saw at the funeral. I'll never forget it.

My words get lost in my throat so I only nod. His finger traces over my shoulder tucking the loose hair behind my back. The sensation ripples through my body. It's almost too much. The way Sam touches me is pleasurable but taunting. I want more. I want everything.

"The things I want to do to you," he pauses, "I shouldn't want them. It's wrong. It's fucked up that you're my best friend's younger sister." He begins to pull back but I stop him by grabbing his shirt in my hands.

"What if I want those things too?" His hazel eyes darken as my words sink in. He cups my face in his hands tightly as he searches my eyes, maybe for uncertainty but it won't find it. I square my shoulders as I lick my lips, readying myself for him.

"I'm a dominant, princess. Do you think you can handle me? I want to tie you so you're at my mercy, squirming but screaming for more." His fingers lightly drift across my skin, making me shiver.

"What if I got you so close but wouldn't let you orgasm, over and over until you were crying and begging?" Sam leans in, his warm breath making my whole body hot and wet.

"How about if you're blindfolded, only able to feel, trusting me to play your body like no one ever has," he whispers into the shell of my ear.

My mind drifts to my collection of dirty books. *Haven't I always wanted this?* Someone to take control and dominate me. I might be a virgin but I've had fantasies about this and I'm not going to let the opportunity pass by.

"If you were trying to scare me, you'll have to try harder, *sir*," I sass as I bite my bottom lip, looking him straight in the eyes.

"I can already tell there will be punishments in your future." He smirks down at me.

"Hmm, sounds intriguing..."

"*Fuck*. This is your last chance to leave, sunshine, before I do something neither of us can take it back," he groans against my mouth.

"I'm not going anywhere, big boy." No sooner are the words out that he smashes his lips on mine. I gasp from the force, allowing him to slip his tongue in. One of his hands slides into my hair grabbing hold and keeping me in place. His forcefulness is something that I never knew would turn me on but my panties are soaked. I rub my legs together, trying to relieve the ache I have, but there's only one thing that can fix it. Samuel.

"Seems like your pussy needs some attention." He chuckles darkly as his hands slide down my body grabbing my ass in his hands. He isn't wrong. It's needed attention for a long time. I don't want to mention that I'm still a virgin. He would probably stop from disappointment, then make me leave. He already seems to be on the fence about whether we should be doing this or not. I'm not giving him a reason to call this off.

He swallows my moans and takes the opportunity to delve deeper into my mouth. Never in my life have I been this lit up by someone. It's like everywhere he touches sends electrical bolts throughout my body. If this is wrong then I never want to be right.

Eleven

Samuel

Marcy tastes like a little bit of heaven mixed with a whole lot of sin. Her luscious pouty lips call to me in a way I've never known before. I need to answer everything they are asking; I can't break away from her. The more I kiss her the more I never want to let her go. I have to stop living in the past with the "what ifs" always floating through my mind. Matthew isn't here and it's damn time I take what's mine. What's always been mine.

She clutches my shirt between her fingers tighter and tighter, pulling me closer. The need to dominate her overwhelms me. I want her to submit to me wholly.

Her forehead bumps a cut but the pain triggers something deeper inside me. "I'm sorry," she murmurs against my mouth but I shake my head.

"Don't." I skim my hands down her soft body then grab her lush ass in my hands. As I pick her up, she wraps legs around my waist letting her arms circle my neck. My hard length presses against her stomach, allowing her to see how much I want her. We move from the bathroom to the bedroom.

I walk us toward the bed and throw her down watching as she bounces in the black satin sheets. Her fair skin glows against the backdrop of the dark sheets, illuminating her exquisite beauty. Her squeals turn to moans as I remove my shirt, avoiding the bandages on my face. Her eyes rake down my chest, roaming over every tattoo marking my skin. The once emerald green eyes have morphed into a darkened mix of sexual desire and longing.

Her boots are the first things to go. I toss them to the floor before I climb on her needing to feel her warmth beneath me. As I crawl up her body, I nip and kiss my way to her chest. Her smooth, creamy skin drives me wild, making me want to devour her.

"I want you so bad," I rasp. I need her out of this dress *now*. Sitting up, I grab fists of the dress looking down at her.

"Tell me no." Marcy bites her bottom lip but doesn't say a word, her eyes glimmering with hunger. The dress rips down the middle of her body and falls away to the sides. It's the only sound beyond our heavy breathing. She pulls her arms free then stretches them over her head arching her back off the bed.

"Fuck, you are exquisite," I groan as I look down at the perfection lying before me. The blush on her cheeks spreads to her chest as she tries to cover herself.

"Don't you *ever* fucking cover yourself in front of me. Do you hear me? I won't take that shit." Marcy audibly swallows as she nods her head and moves her arms from her chest. I grab the ruined dress, ripping a long piece off.

"This will remind you not to cover up." I lift her arms above her head to secure them to my headboard. She pulls to test the restraints but they won't come undone without me doing it. "Fuck,

I've never seen a masterpiece like the one laid out before me." The restraints force her luscious breasts closer to my mouth.

"How's that? Think twice before you hide from me."

"Yes, *sir*," she responds, making my brain misfire hearing those words uttered from her lips. My cock couldn't get any harder if it tried. It's painfully throbbing against my pants, the intensity is like nothing I've ever felt before.

"You better be careful talking like that, sunshine. You've no idea the beast I can become, especially with something I've craved for so long." Her eyes pool with hunger similar to my own. An instant thirst ignites inside me with only one thing to satiate it. *Marcy.*

"Really?" she breathes with a smirk. As I run my hand down her chest feeling the softness, goosebumps erupt over her skin causing her breath to quicken. Hooking a finger in her thong, I rip it from her body in one swift motion. Marcy gasps as the material falls away, finally seeing her completely bare before me.

"Yes, really. I've wanted you when I probably shouldn't have," I whisper into the shell of her ear. I leave it at that and crash my lips down on hers. I don't want to give her time to question it. As my body slides between her thighs, I feel her wet heat rub against me making me lose my damn mind. I need to be inside her. *I need it like the air I breathe.* My cock throbs painfully. It takes everything in me not to fuck her brains out right this minute.

"Me too," she murmurs as she breaks away from me. *Hmm, interesting.*

"Tell me, did you use to lie in bed at night playing with yourself imagining it was me? Have you been a naughty girl?" I question running my lips along the column of her neck.

"I knew it was wrong but I couldn't help it," she admits, breathlessly.

"Fuck, Marcy, what did you imagine when you touched this sweet pussy?" I ask, barely holding on to the last ounce of restraint I have left. My hand skates across her skin until her breast is spilling into my hand. My thumb rubs across her pebbled nipple rewarding me with a small gasp that I swallow down as my mouth ravages hers. My cock pulses in my pants as I imagine fucking her glorious breasts, coming all over her perfect face.

"I always wanted you to touch me. Please," she whines, pushing herself off the bed toward me.

"Please what? What's this needy little pussy need?" I growl my question.

Keeping my eyes glued to hers, I stand from the bed unbuckling my pants then pushing them down my legs. My thick, throbbing dick is harder than it's ever been.

"I just need you to touch me," she whimpers. Her tongue peeks out as she licks her lips but her eyes go wide when she makes her way down to my shaft.

As my hand pumps my cock, I look at Marcy with a grin. "Think you can handle this?" Her startled response is cute.

"I-uh, I don't think that will fit," she stammers as she looks back into my eyes.

"Oh, it *will* fit, sunshine. Scoot up the bed some. I want to taste this sweet pussy first." She hesitates for a brief moment then moves back on the bed. Her breaths quicken as I crawl on the bed kissing her legs until I get to the apex of her thighs. My mouth lowers to her sweet center while my eyes stay locked on hers. I want to see every emotion that crosses her face. Her arousal circles around me invading my senses. I take a long lick from her ass to clit savoring her honey. A growl explodes from my throat.

"Ohh..." she moans as her back arches off the bed. My arm comes around pressing her to the bed. She isn't going anywhere. Not now.

"You *will* take the pleasure I give you," I command, feasting on her, lapping all her juices into my mouth. Her sweet nectar could sustain me for the rest of my life.

"Fuck, you're so sweet," I whisper raggedly. Marcy tries to press her cunt closer to my face, but I have her caged. If I died like this, I would be a happy man.

Her legs begin shaking as I bring her closer to her peak. I press a finger into her wetness and groan from how incredibly tight she is. Her pussy is going to strangle my cock in the best way possible. I continue to lick her clit with my tongue and pound another finger into her tight hole. A shudder wracks her body then she screams my name as her walls contract around my fingers. Her orgasm overtakes her as I continue licking up everything I can. I don't want to waste a single drop. Her head falls to the side as she begins to come down from the high.

"Did I tell you to come, princess?" Shock covers her face as she shakes her head.

"Use your words."

"N-no, sir."

"That's my good girl. I'll give you this one but you better beg for the next."

"Yes. Yes, sir."

A smile crosses my face, which is coated in her slick. She's already learning. I begin nipping then licking my way up her body. I want to leave little love bites behind for when she looks in the mirror, she'll know I ruined this pussy for any other man. I slam my tongue in her mouth forcing her to taste herself.

"Taste your honey. Taste what I did to you," I demand. She swirls her tongue around mine then sucks the juices from it. She hums as she swallows it down. Her vibrations make me want her mouth wrapped around my dick.

I press my fingers back into her juicy cunt wanting to bring her to another orgasm. She needs to be fucking soaked to take me. Her eyes widen as I stretch her little pussy. She writhes under me as I wrap my other hand around her throat.

"You woke up the beast, sunshine. Now take my damn fingers like the dirty slut you are." I can feel her moans vibrating through my hand. Her eyes roll back as her walls begin to pulse again around my hand. I'll be damned, this little vixen likes it rough.

"P-pleasee," she gasps under my hand.

"Come for me, baby."

Just when I didn't think she could be any more perfect, she fucking gets off on me choking her. *Fuck me.*

"You like that, don't you? You like being at my mercy?" She whimpers as I release her throat. Her body continues to tremble as her orgasm wracks through her body.

"Please, Sam," she whines.

"Please what? What do you want?" I want to hear it come from her dirty little mouth.

She closes her eyes but opens her mouth. "Fuck me. Please. I can't take it any longer, *sir.*" Magic to my fucking ears. I swipe my fingers in my mouth, drinking down the honey that I missed out on. Marcy's eyes stay locked on mine watching as I suck them clean.

In one sudden motion I have her on her stomach pulling her ass in the air. She pants as her head is pressed to the bed. Her restraints twist with her. My hands run over her body taking in all its lusciousness. I slide my hand down her spine then grab a hand full of her thick ginger hair.

Leaning over her back, my cock rests between her cheeks. I whisper, "Are you sure you want this?" She tries to nod but I keep my hand in place. "Words. I need your words, sunshine," I breathe into her ear.

"Yes," she sobs into the sheets. "I need this!"

"What's your safeword?"

"Pineapples," she murmurs.

"Good girl. That's what I want to hear," I growl as my hand connects with her round cheek sending a cracking sound through the air.

"Oh, fuck," she rasps. Repeating the motion on the other side, a beautiful red mark appears just like I knew it would. Her pale skin was meant to be marked by me. As I rub the sting away, she brushes her thighs together, needing that friction. Her pussy is dripping down her legs. She's ready.

"Open these gorgeous thighs." Pumping my dick in my hand, precome collects on the tip as I watch her open herself to me. What a fucking sight. A groan leaves me at the thought of her taking my fat cock in her tight little pussy. I have been imagining sinking into this cunt since Matthew's funeral. I knew it was wrong and the timing was bad, but I couldn't help my thoughts. When I left the military, I began following her. The more I watched her, the more I needed her.

I line myself up and collect her juices in my hand, running them down my shaft until I'm completely soaked. "Your pussy is about to be stretched so well around me. You'll be a total slut for my cock after this." I brush the tip around her clit and slide through her folds then back out, teasing her. I want her to want this as bad as I've wanted her.

Marcy groans into the pillow. "Just do it already." *What did she just say to me?*

"Excuse me? I know you didn't just tell me what to do. You take what I give you and that's it. If I don't want you to come then you won't. Better keep that brat in check, sunshine." I slap her cunt with my hard dick eliciting a loud moan.

"I'm sorry, Sam. Please fuck me, *sir.*" She knows what she's doing when she adds that 'sir' at the end. I'd smack her ass a few more times as punishment if I thought I could hold off fucking her any longer.

"That's what I thought." I briefly contemplate taking this slow but the thought leaves my mind as soon as it comes. I need to ravage her and it's not going to be gentle. Without warning, I slam my hips forward sinking my length into her tight channel. Her slick pussy allowed me to seat myself fully inside her in one motion.

Marcy's screams are muffled by the sheets. She's tighter than I imagined and feels fucking perfect wrapped around me. As I lean over her body, waiting for her to adjust to my size, I pull her hair so I can whisper in her ear, "You feel that? You feel me filling this hot, wet pussy with my fat cock?" My warm breath against her skin makes her mewl beneath me. She presses her ass back against me pushing deeper. Pulling my hips back, I slam back into her over and over. Thrusting my hips forward, she begins writhing underneath me. As I lean back up, I drop her hair then take her hips in a fierce hold knowing I'll be leaving marks.

"You feel so good, sunshine," my voice turns gravelly as I continue to pound into her. I look down at where we are joined and that's when I see it. The trace of blood coating my cock. *What the fuck is this? That's not possible. No fucking way. She's not a...virgin, is she? Fuck!*

"Yes, yessss!" she shouts as her tight channel convulses around me but I slow my motions as what I see takes root in my mind.

A growl escapes my lips, "Please tell me you weren't a virgin, Marcy?"

A dampened sob escapes her lips as she looks back at me. My heart drums in my chest at the sight and I know I'm going to hell. I knew I shouldn't have gotten involved with her. Letting go of her hips, I pull out completely as I sit on my heels looking at the sight before me.

"I-I didn't want to tell you. I didn't think you would want me if you knew." She lowers her hips and closes in on herself, trying to hide from me. How could she not think I would want her because of that? I damn near want her even more now knowing that no other man has been there. I want to be the one and only. I want to claim her fucking pussy as my own, never letting her go. A possessive roar bubbles up inside me. She might not know it but she just sealed her fate. She's *mine* and there's not a fucking thing she can do about it.

"I told you to never cover yourself before me." I reach up to untie her wrists and pull her body into my lap. She keeps her face covered by her hands as she cries softly.

"I'm sorry," she whispers.

"Look at me," I demand. My fingers go to her chin, pulling her face up so she can see me. "There's nothing for you to apologize about other than the fact that you should have told me. I never meant to hurt you. I didn't know." My thumbs brush the tears from her flushed cheeks. Her shimmering green eyes look up at me and my heart melts. This woman has me in a chokehold from one look.

"Y-you aren't mad at me?" she asks with concern written all over her face. I take her face into my hands firmly so she knows I mean what I'm about to say.

"Sunshine, I'm not mad at you. I wish I would have known only because I wouldn't have been so rough for your first time. There has to be trust between us or this isn't going to work." I gesture between us.

She chokes back a sob as more tears fall, collecting on my hands. "If it's possible, I want you even more now," I admit. She takes a deep breath.

"What are you saying?" She nibbles her bottom lip and it takes everything in me not to pull it into my mouth, but we need to have this conversation.

"I'm saying that this doesn't change anything. I still want you. Fuck," I run my hand through my hair, "It makes me insane to know that no other man has had you." Marcy doesn't respond, instead she sits there in stunned silence. I'm done running. She's the one I want. All the uncertainty flies out the window.

"I know there's so many bullshit reasons why we shouldn't be together but this is definitely not one of them. Fuck all the excuses floating through our minds, you're mine, sunshine. I just claimed you. You're *mine,*" I growl out the last part wanting to get my point across. She nods as a faint smile ghosts her pouty lips.

"I've always wanted you, Sam. Of course I'm yours." I close my eyes as her words sink in. We're really doing this.

"Then let's do this properly." I lay her back on the bed then crawl up her body, my still hard length pressing between her thighs. My lips find hers in a scorching kiss that has me rocking against her. I need to be inside her more than I need my next breath. I pull away then run my knuckles down her face.

"We can wait," I mention praying she says no. I'd do it for her but it wouldn't be pleasant.

"No, I don't want to wait any longer. I need you." I crash my mouth down on hers as our bodies rock against each other. My hand skims down her belly wanting to make sure she's still ready for me. I press two fingers in easily as her wetness coats me.

"That's my good girl. Spread your legs wider for me baby. This fat cock needs some room." She stretches her legs apart as I line myself up with her entrance.

"Are you ready for me?" I ask.

"Yes, please," she pants. My hips press into hers slowly not wanting to hurt her like last time. With each thrust more of my cock gets sheathed in her. I pull her leg up to rest on my shoulder, allowing me more room. With one final thrust, I'm completely seated inside of her. She's tighter than anything I've ever experienced. I feel her walls squeezing me and I have to fight the urge to blow my load like a teenager.

"Look at you taking my cock so well." She blushes at the praise causing her walls to clamp down. So, my girl likes praise.

With her leg still over my shoulder, I lean down to capture her lips. "Please tell me I can move, baby. You feel so amazing but I need to move." I search her face for any discomfort then she nods and that's all the confirmation I need.

Sliding out, I push back in harder making her eyes roll back. I continue to drive inside her achingly slow until I know she's okay. My hips buck harder and harder forcing myself deeper inside her tight cunt. With every stroke I become closer to my release but I need her to get there first. She will always get there before me. My fingers tweak her swollen clit causing her back to bow off the bed.

"You look so fucking hot taking this big dick," I praise.

"I'm so close. Ahh, so close," she whimpers as her hands dig into my biceps tightly. I pick up my pace as I pound her into the mattress. The pleasure builds far too quickly.

"Come for me, sunshine. Let me hear you scream my name," I grunt as my thrusts grow fevered. I pinch her clit making her shoot off like a firework. Her pussy clenches down on me like a vice sending me to my own abyss. I come roaring inside her.

"Sammmm," she screams as I pump her full of my seed. Jets of come fill her tight hole and for the briefest moments, I wonder if I've bred her. I've never been bare in a woman and I sure as fuck never wanted to fill a cunt until she swells with my child. *What the actual fuck is happening to me?* I'm fucking pussy whipped. No, I'm Marcy whipped.

"Fuck, my little sunshine, you're milking my cock so good," I groan as she continues convulsing around me. My movements slow as we both come down. Setting her leg down, I lean over her to kiss her. I need to feel her lips against mine. My arm holds me above her so I don't crush her with my weight. My cock stays tucked tightly inside her. I'm still hard ready for round two but I know Marcy needs a break. I don't want to over do her first time.

I pull my lips back from hers so I can look down at her gorgeous eyes. They are shimmering and overfilled with passion. As I kiss her forehead, I slowly pull out of her.

"Stay here." Jumping from the bed I head to the bathroom to get a warm cloth to clean her with. My only concern is Marcy and I want to make sure all her needs are taken care of.

As I come back to the bedroom I see Marcy's eyes have fallen closed but an adorable little smile rests on her lips. I spread her thighs to clean up the mess we made taking special care of her red, puffy lips. She might have been a virgin but she took my cock like it was made for her. Maybe it was. As I slide in behind her, I pull her body against mine loving the feel of her soft curves pressed against me. Marcy snuggles in to me letting a soft sigh fall from her lips.

"Rest up, sunshine, I'm far from done with you." A tremble runs through her body stirring my cock back to life.

"Yes, *Mr. Knight.*" She just signed herself over to me. She's mine.

After years of self-denial, the overwhelming desire to consume her, dominate her, and claim her as my own has become irresistible. Marcy will soon discover that she is forever changed, ruined for any other man. The intensity of this longing consumes me, leaving no room for doubt or hesitation.

Twelve

February 17th, 2006
Eighteen years old

Marcy

Rain patters on the windows of the limousine as we drive through the city. The sky is gray and ominous, matching the emotions of the day. I try to hold back the tears threatening to spill down my cheeks, but it's no use trying to contain them. They cascade down my face just like they have since I heard the news. The news that changed my life forever. How will I live without him?

School is finally over and it's time for the weekend. Normally I don't mind my classes but this week something was off with me. I wasn't in the right mind frame to understand what the professors were teaching us. My thoughts often drifted to Matthew wondering what he was doing. I hadn't heard from him in a month which was unlike him. We wrote letters and spoke on the phone whenever we could, but it was never enough. I wanted him home. I wanted him safe. Last night I called his forward operating base but they weren't able to put me through to him. The operator tried several times at my request but the line wouldn't connect so I gave up. I fell into restless sleep, tossing and turning with every boom of thunder.

Dropping my school bag by the door, I head to the kitchen to get a snack. The pantry is full, but nothing interests me. Feeling dejected, I grab a water bottle from the fridge then make my way up to my room. Before I hit the top floor landing, there's a knock at the front door. Unease snakes up my spine as I jog back down the stairs. Mom and dad won't be home for hours so I'm the only one here. Peering through the window, I see a large man dressed in a military uniform. He's standing perfectly still with no emotions playing across his face. Before I close the blinds, a movement catches my eye. Sam is standing behind the other man donning the same uniform.

Without another thought I swing open the door, thrilled to see Sam as I take a step toward him. Heat courses through me at the sight of him in uniform. I expect him to come barreling into the house but he remains outside, a storm of emotions crashing through his eyes. My heart plummets into my stomach as I take a cautious step back looking at the other man. They both remove their hats placing them under their arms.

"Ma'am, I'm Commanding Officer Sanders. Are your parents home?" he speaks evenly as his eyes pierce through my soul. Unable to reply, I shake my head as tears well in my eyes. I look back to Sam but he remains motionless, so close yet so far away. The officer clears his throat, startling me but getting my attention. Panic rises to the surface as my body trembles in fear, chills coating my skin. My heart hammers in my chest as the officer opens his mouth to speak.

"It is with my deep regret and my greatest condolences to inform you that Specialist Hillary was killed in action. He was a true hero to his country that died serving his brothers in arms. He was a good man..." Officer Sanders voice trails off as my world begins spinning out of control. My mind feels like it's been disassociated from my body. Nothing feels real. My legs begin trembling then give out completely. I feel my body falling, falling into a dark abyss. The ground doesn't come for me, instead I feel familiar arms carrying my body as if I'm levitating through the air. There's wetness on my face but I can't move my hands to wipe it away. Sam's beautiful face appears before blackness overcomes me and I'm swept away in a wave of shock.

The limousine pulls into the gated cemetery where most of the guests have already arrived. The driver parks while I stare out of the window at the bleak landscape. Matthew shouldn't be here. He needs to be somewhere sunny and full of life, not in this cemetery that looks like it might be haunted.

Our driver opens the door for my parents then hands them a black umbrella. As I slide out of my seat, Sam appears holding an umbrella out for me. I should be drooling over the fact that he wore his military uniform but all it does is remind me that my brother isn't here. Sam was the last to see him alive and although I don't want to be, I'm jealous. Instead of handing the umbrella off to me, Sam holds it for the both of us as we make our way to the tents that have been set up.

"Marcy," he rasps. He stops walking, then holds me steady so I don't fall from the sudden halt. My eyes slowly trail up to his, not wanting to hear another apology or condolence. I won't be able to take it, especially not from him. No one knows what I'm going through so I don't want to hear how they're all sorry for me. Sam's eyes shine with unshed tears and something breaks inside me.

"Listen, I know you keep hearing this but I want you to know that I'm here for you. *Always*. If you need me, I'll be there." He wipes the tears from my face with the back of his hand. The gesture is something I've always dreamed of, but at this moment my stomach isn't buzzing with butterflies. Instead a lump forms in my throat keeping me from responding. I see the understanding in his eyes and I'm thankful that he doesn't expect a response from me. Sam nods his head, loops his arm back through mine then we continue walking toward the tented area where all my relatives along with all the people that Matthew's death touched are awaiting the service.

I take my seat in the front next to my parents but Samuel goes to stand with the other soldiers that are in attendance for Matthew's funeral. We are asked to stand as the funeral begins.

A team of soldiers carry the casket and secures it in place before us. A beautiful American flag is carefully placed over the casket, then the team salutes Matthew before they step away. An Army Chaplain steps forward and begins his prepared speech. His voice trails off into the wind. I don't hear the generic platitudes. My mind wanders to Matthew. *Was he scared? Did he feel the pain?* I don't know all the details mostly because I didn't think I could handle hearing them. They would haunt me in the darkest of nights.

Once the chaplain is finished, several officers go to the podium to give their speeches of how brave and gallant Matthew was, but we already knew this, didn't we? He wanted to fight for his country after everything that happened on September 11, 2001. He knew the risks and he signed his name on the dotted line anyways. My chest aches when I think I'll never see his goofy smile or feel his heavy arm draped across my shoulders. I stare down at my hands in my lap as the words from the officers' drift away. I don't want to be here. Seeing my brother lowered into the ground isn't something I ever imagined I would witness, and yet here I am. I rise from my seat about to make a run for it through the rain when I lock eyes with Sam. He just approached the podium and his eyes tell me what I need to do. I slowly lower myself back in my chair as he gives me a slight nod that only I would catch. With rapt attention I listen to his eulogy of his best friend.

"Ladies and gentlemen, I stand here today to pay tribute to a true American hero, Specialist Hillary, who dedicated his life to serve our great nation. It is an honor and a privilege to stand before you to share some words that attempt to encapsulate the immense impact Matthew Hillary has had on all of us and the profound legacy he leaves behind.

Matthew Hillary and I met when we were in grade school. He and I grew up together, becoming more than friends, brothers. He may not have been blood but our bond was one to withstand any storm." Sam pauses for a moment as he wipes tears from his eyes.

"Matthew died doing what he loved, caring for others. He was the most selfless person I've ever come to know. He would give you the shirt off his back if it meant that you would be taken care of. That was the kind of man he was. Always giving, he paid the ultimate price as he gave his life for us.

The day before we left for basic training, Matthew, Marcy and I took to the river to celebrate this new chapter in our lives and mourn the one we were leaving behind. We sailed along, cherishing the time we had together. That day will always hold a special place in my heart.

Marcy Hillary was her brother's favorite person. He often called her his 'sunshine' because of the way she brightened his life." I choke on a sob in my throat as Sam continues. "He was thinking of her to the very end." I gasp as I let his words sink in. *Did he say something to Sam?*

"To our fallen hero, you may have departed from this world, but your legacy endures. You will forever remain in our hearts, a symbol of all that is noble and just, and a reminder of the price of freedom. Your wish will be done." The last part is almost a hushed promise to Matthew but I heard it.

We stand as "Taps" begins playing over the loudspeaker, a hushed silence falls over the audience.

"Ready. Aim. Fire." An officer commands as the twenty-one-gun salute commences. I knew it was coming but it's much louder than I expected. As I stand there, the finality of the moment rushes over me, causing me to feel faint. My legs wobble but before I fall, Sam is there holding me up again. I didn't even notice he'd moved but here he is coming to my rescue. I look up at his handsome face as tears trickle down my cheeks. I'm looking for answers. I'm looking for guidance on how I'm supposed to live without my brother, my best friend. He wipes the tears away then pulls me close. He stays by my side as the funeral comes to an end.

The casket team approaches from the side and begins to meticulously fold the American flag. It gets handed off to the Officer in Charge and he comes to present the flag to my grieving mother. She cries as she clutches the flag close to her chest. My father pulls her in close as they weep together at the loss of their son. I haven't taken the time to see how much this affects them. I have been so caught up in my loss in all this.

Once everything is finalized, people begin to disburse as several wait their turns to extend their condolences. I can't be here for this part. I need to get away. Samuel must sense my reticence as he takes my hand leading me from the tents. Before he can open an umbrella, I take off through the rain, loving the chill against my face. He catches up to me but instead of pulling me under an umbrella, he races into the rain with me. We arrive at the cars and I'm breathing heavy not from exertion but with everything going on in my life now.

27 YEARS OLD

Samuel

In the midst of grief, I find solace in the rain, running alongside Marcy. The rain's liberating touch seems to cleanse my shattered spirit. I can't quite explain it, but Marcy had the right idea. I had to get away from there. I sensed her exhaustion from the situation, that's why I pulled her along with me to head to the cars. She's grown up so much from the time we left to now. She's transformed from the little girl once in our shadows to a resplendent woman. She has so much fire in her, just like Matthew. The child I cherished has matured into a woman who evokes newfound emotions within me.

As my pulse races, I draw closer to Marcy, her back against the sleek limousine. Holding her face gently in my hands, I'm captivated by her emerald eyes, which hold a depth I long to explore. My thumbs brush away the raindrops on her cheeks, a futile effort as more droplets gather.

"Marcy," I groan. Her warmth soaks into my body causing me to shiver but not from the temperature. Her eyes hold a fiery passion, locked onto mine. I bend toward her gradually, giving her a chance to stop me, yet she remains silent. Our lips brush as an electric pulse runs through me. It jumpstarts my heart, but in a fleeting moment, I detach myself from her. This was a mistake. I owe this much to Matthew.

"I'm sorry. I can't do this." The moment hangs in the air, suspended between connection and departure. Her lips, warm and fleeting, left an imprint on mine—a promise unspoken, a question unanswered. I back away as I see the realization take over in her mind. She's probably going to hate me but I have to get away. I vowed to take care of her, but not like this. She deserves so much better. Marcy holds her hand to her lips with fresh tears streaming down her face. I fucked everything up. With one last look at the gorgeous redhead before me, I turn and head toward my car. It takes immense willpower to avoid turning back to her, yet I grasp the importance of my decision. I can't start something with her knowing I'll be going back overseas. She's already lost so much and I can't bring myself to add to that.

With my hand on my car, I stand there, heart racing, caught between surprise and longing. *Why did I kiss her? Why did I leave?*

The silence echoes, a void that begs for explanation. I chance a glance back but she is already disappearing, fading into the crowd, leaving me with nothing but the taste of her on my lips.

Thirteen

Marcy

When I turn over in bed to feel for Sam, his spot is cool to the touch. I crack one eye open and see the bathroom door is wide open, he's not in there either. Stretching my arms over my head, I feel the ache between my thighs but can only smile. *Samuel fucking Knight took my virginity*. If you would've told me that's what was in store for me then I wouldn't have believed it. I kick my legs in the air and squeal in excitement. *Is this real life?*

I need to use the restroom but I'm naked with nothing to throw on to cover me, thanks to Sam for ripping my dress to shreds. It was hot as hell at the time, but now I have a problem. Looking around the room, I don't see any alternatives so I wrap the silky sheet tightly around my body then pad to the bathroom. I close the door and lock it behind me letting the sheet pool at my feet. Standing in front of the mirror, I see all the little love bites Sam left behind making my heart drum in my chest. Seeing how he marked me sends chills through my body. My long curls are going in all directions but I can't bring myself to care. As I lean over the counter to look at all the bruises, I feel dried cum between my legs.

It's a foreign sensation but I can't help but welcome the feeling. I'm finally not a virgin. *You need a shower, stat.*

Stepping into the shower, I revel in the hot water running over my body. The heat relaxes my sore muscles making me want to sink to the floor. I'm still tired even after the nap I had. My headache seems to have faded, though, making me wonder if it's true what they say. *Does having sex relieve headaches?* Seems accurate.

I quickly soap up with Sam's body wash loving that I will smell like him for the rest of the day. His shampoo options are severely lacking so I'm forced to use the same body wash and hope for the best. No conditioner for my mane–I imagine my hair will look like something from a horror movie once it dries. The towels are heated and it wraps around my body like a glove. My mind slips into the thought of living like this. It's the little things but it's so luxurious.

Since he shredded my dress like a caveman, I'll have to take some of his clothes. His closet is larger than three of mine combined. A freaking bed could fit in here. Sam has all his clothes perfectly hanging with formal and casual separated by fancy partitions. My fingers graze over the different materials until I come to the end of his closet where I see several formal military uniforms hanging.

Matthew used to wear the same uniform. A lump forms in my throat at the sight. In an instant, the closet feels like it's closing in around me and I can't breathe. I run from there slamming the door behind me. I fall against it with my hand over my chest. It aches, making me think of Matthew and how he's not here. And I just slept with his best friend. My heart sinks at the thought that he would be disappointed in me. I rush to the dresser before me and toss on an oversized t-shirt and joggers. My boots are at the foot of the bed so I grab them quickly making my way out of the bedroom and down the stairs.

I hear Samuel on the phone so hopefully I can sneak out without him noticing. *Shit, where is my purse?* I need my phone to call for a ride or I won't be going anywhere.

My heart pounds in my chest as I look around for the small wristlet that I took to the party. I can't help but check out Sam's penthouse in my search. I love the open concept with huge floor to ceiling windows but it definitely looks like a man's pad. One plus is it's clean and everything seems to have its own spot. I don't remember him being so meticulous before but I guess the military can have that effect on you. Finally I see a sparkle coming from the couch and I know it must be it. As I tiptoe around the side table, I hear a rustling behind me and someone clearing their throat. *Fuck, he caught me.*

"Going somewhere, sunshine?" he taunts as I whirl around. He approaches me with two piping hot coffee mugs in his hands.

"I was, uh, just looking for my purse," I half lie. I mean I *was* looking for it but to get the hell out of here, I happen to leave that part out. Sam has his pajama pants hung low on his hips drawing my attention to his impeccable abs and what they lead down to. I know my face is giving me away because I can feel the heat in my cheeks. It's the curse of a red head. My emotions play across my face like a movie. I have to bite back a moan at the Greek god in front of me. *What was I doing again?*

"Are you sure that's the answer you want to go with? You know what I told you happens to bad girls that lie," he smirks. Dammit, that stupid dimple I've dreamed about for years appears as he stalks over to me. I want to run and jump into his arms and let him tell me that everything is going to be okay, *but is it?* Matthew not being here makes me feel like I don't deserve to be happy because I don't have him to share it with. I feel selfish for thinking, even for a second, that Sam and I could be happy together. It was always too good to be true. Maybe if Matthew was still here things could have been different between Sam and I. Maybe then I wouldn't have this guilt weighing on my chest.

"I, um, I took a shower." I swallow the lump in my throat. "Then I went looking for clothes and your closet..." I try to choke out the rest of the words but they won't come. Tears threaten to spill so I look away, ashamed to feel this way in his presence.

"You saw my old uniforms," he finishes for me. I nod my head as I drop my bag to the couch and wrap my arms around myself. Sam sets the mugs down, taking a few steps closer to me until he's towering over me. I can feel the heat from his body circling around me. He places his fingers under my chin, lifting my face to meet his. His eyes bore into mine with a deep emotion that I can't decipher. Anger? Possession? Whatever it is, I feel like I might slip into its dark depths.

"You think I'm just going to let you run out of here after everything that's happened between us?" he asks, still grasping my chin tightly, not allowing me to run from the situation. He knows me well. He knows I'm a runner when things get tough. I guess I haven't grown up as much as I thought I have.

My shoulders shrug on their own accord, not really knowing how to respond.

"Words, Marcy," he commands.

"It freaked me out, okay? I saw the uniforms and the only thing I could think of was Matthew and how he was your best friend and then I started to panic and..."

Sam pulls me into his chest squeezing me, grounding me to the moment. He rubs soft circles over my back and down my arms making chills run down my spine. I shiver in his arms as I look up at him.

"How about we take this one problem at a time," he suggests. Pulling his arms away but never leaving my body, he leads me to the couch to sit. He plops down then pulls me on top of him. I cringe trying to move over to an empty spot but he isn't having it.

"Why are you trying to get off my lap?" His eyes rove over my body as his nostrils flare. I'm not sure what that reaction is for, but it's oddly satisfying.

"I-I don't want to hurt you. Let me just scoot off really qui–" His finger comes up to my lips and presses them together effectively shutting me up.

"Not another word," he orders. "I know what you're thinking and you need to get that shit out of your head right the fuck now. I thought we went over this." His comment leaves no room for argument but I'm not one hundred percent sure he even knows what he's talking about.

"You don't know what I was going to say and I don't appreciate you talking to me like that. I'm not a fucking child."

Before I know what's going on, I'm hanging over Sam's thick thighs, looking down at the floor. He has me over his fucking lap like he's going to spank me. *The audacity*. I'm so angry that words aren't forming in my mind.

"Now, I've already told you that naughty girls get punished. If you continue to speak down about yourself, you will find your ass on the receiving end of my palm. Now, what's your safeword, sunshine?"

"Safeword?" I repeat.

"Yes, your safeword in case this gets to be too much for you. If it does then say the word and I'll stop."

"I, um, pineapple." *Pineapple? What the hell was I thinking when I picked that earlier?* In my defense, it was the first thing that popped into my mind.

He chuckles huskily, shooting a bolt of electricity straight to my clit. Nibbling on my bottom lip, I can't help but squirm on his lap. *Wait, is he hard?*

"Stay still and count." Sam pulls the joggers that I borrowed down, leaving me bare before him. The cool air hits my fevered skin eliciting a low moan that I definitely didn't mean to voice. I don't want him to have the satisfaction that I will enjoy this little parade of power.

He doesn't warn me before the first slap rings through the air as it connects with my ass cheek. Hot pain shoots through me but morphs into something more pleasurable as it settles into my skin.

"One," I squeak out.

"Good girl," he praises. I don't know why that phrase affects me so, but I find myself growing wetter. If he spread my legs right now, he would see the evidence on my thighs.

Pulling me from my thoughts, another slap connects with the other ass cheek. Am I really going to lay here and take this from him?

"Is that all ya got, big man? I thought this was supposed to be a punishm–"

Sam's hand connects with the back of my things and I can't help but whimper.

"How was that? I was going to go easy for your first time but you had to open that bratty mouth of yours, didn't you?" he huffs."Number?"

"T-three," I breathe out trying to fill my lungs with the oxygen that left them when his hand came down on me.

"Nope. We started over. That was *one*, princess. Ready to use your safeword?" The way he says it makes my blood boil. He's taunting me but he should know I am one to never back down from a challenge.

"One," I repeat, waiting for him to continue. I won't acknowledge that he insinuated that I would be using my safeword. He can kiss my now red ass before that happens.

The next two come in rapid succession, causing me to flinch but I find myself leaning into him still. It's true what they say about gingers, we have a high pain tolerance. Obviously this is being used to my benefit, causing the pain to radiate straight to my pulsing center.

"Two, three," I murmur as I shift on his lap, needing the much needed friction between my legs. I squirm enough that a moan falls from his lips. His hardness is pressing against me. I may be sore from this morning but that doesn't mean I don't want him to slide inside me right now. I'm worked up enough that he could thrust right in.

"I know what you're doing, Marcy. It's not going to work." I lean my head back as far as I can to look into his eyes. Desire radiates from them causing shivers to wrack through my body. I shift more against him causing him to utter, "Fuck!"

Sam runs his hands over my heated backside with slow steady strokes. He smoothes away the pain leaving nothing but need in its place. The joggers get thrown the rest of the way off as Sam pulls me up against his body. My legs straddle him as my wet core rests on his hard cock. It takes everything in me not to rock against him. There is an ache that needs to be quenched or I think I will die right here.

"Don't think every punishment will be that easy," he comments, "I just couldn't focus with you grinding that wet pussy all over my lap." Heat flames my cheeks. *How did I go from a virgin to a wanton woman in twenty four hours?* He pushes a chunk of curls behind my ear then trails his fingers along my cheek then down the column of my throat.

"You're stunning and you don't even know it. How is that possible?" I think the question is more for himself than for me. "If you could see yourself from my eyes," he groans, "you would have a different opinion of yourself."

"Thank you." I'm not really sure how to respond to that.

"You don't need to thank me. I want you to see it yourself, Marcy. I want you to see the beauty I see. And not just on the outside. You are an incredible person." He brushes his hands along my thighs going higher and higher until he almost reaches where I need him the most, but at the last second he pulls back. He smirks at my frustration. *Damn him.*

Against my better judgment, I begin to rock on his lap. If he isn't going to take care of it then I can do it my damn self.

"You aren't too sore?" His voice cracks. I hold in my smile by biting my bottom lip and looking up at him. He curses under his breath, something about not being able to stay away. I don't know. I might have misheard.

"No. Your punishment had the reverse effect and well..." I trail off as I pick up my pace. "Now I have an ache that needs tending to." My hands graze over his sculpted chest then I trail my nails down over his abs. "Fuck, you don't know what you do to me, sunshine." He lifts his shirt from my body, leaning in to capture a nipple between his teeth. He tweaks the other with his fingers giving me double the stimulation. It feels so good that I contemplate if I could orgasm from just this. I'm already so worked up that I don't think it would take much.

"Please," I whimper. Not really sure what I'm asking for but hoping he understands all the same.

"Take me out," he whispers with my nipple still in his mouth. The vibrations are almost too much to bear.

Quickly, I lean up enough so that his pajamas slide right off. Sitting back down, I take his long length into my hands, loving the feel of him within my grasp.

Sam moves his hand down my body until it sinks into my pussy. "Damn, princess, you're soaked. I bet I could slide right in this tight cunt. Think you can take this fat cock again?" His dirty words do something to me, sending a new wave of arousal between my legs. Sam chuckles darkly as he feels the new surge of wetness coat his fingers.

"Does my girl like dirty talk?" he whispers into the shell of my ear. His warm breath sends my body into overdrive, needing him now more than anything.

My hands go to his shoulders as I lean up hovering over his cock. Sam places himself at my entrance then grabs my hips pushing me all the way down on him in one motion. We moan in unison. This new position makes it feel like he's going to split me open in the best way.

Sam lets out a low growl as he cups my face then crashes his mouth down on mine. He licks the seam of my lips until I open up to him fully, allowing him to devour every corner of me. A whimper falls from my lips but is quickly swallowed away by the raging man before me.

"Fuck, you gotta move, baby," he grunts as his hands descend on my hips, helping me to thrust my body up and down on his hard shaft. My body was already on edge and with his movements I'm ready to combust.

"Yes! Oh—" My head falls back as an orgasm begins to flow through my body.

"That's it, sunshine. Come on my cock. Show me how good I make you feel." Sam's hands grip into my hips tighter in a bruising way. Oddly, the thought makes me excited.

"I'm coming, Sam. Ahh—" I chant as I continue to use his shoulders as leverage while I chase my own release.

"That's my good girl. Look how well you take this cock. You didn't know it was made for this pussy but it was." He reaches between us, circling my clit and sending another bolt of pleasure coursing through my body.

"Ohhh—" is the only word I can form as wave after wave of intense rapture crashes into every cell of my body. I'm on fire from the inside out. Burning with need for this man.

"You feel so good wrapped around me. I knew you would. I kept my distance from you but not any longer. You're mine, sunshine. *Mine*," he declares before his mouth is on mine in a punishing, possessive kiss.

Sam flicks my nipples then his mouth is on one, licking and sucking then biting down hard. He grins up at me devilishly as he moves to the other side. He knows what he does to me. He can play my body like a fucking instrument. It's his symphony and I'm in the audience enjoying the experience.

My legs aren't used to this kind of exercise so my movements become choppy. Before I can complain, I'm thrust backwards onto the couch as Sam drives into me from above. His hips piston back and forth like he's competing in a marathon and it doesn't take long for another burst of electricity to invade my body.

"I knew I could get another one out of you. Come for me, sunshine. Milk my cock as I dump everything I have into that sweet pussy of yours." My moans can probably be heard by the whole building but I don't have it in me to care.

"I can't. Not another–"

"You can and you will." Sam pinches down on my slick clit and an explosion erupts, sending shocks to every nerve ending in my body.

"Fuck, you're so damn tight. Your cunt wants everything I have, doesn't it?" he asks before he grips my hips and with one final pump shooting jet after jet of cum in my pussy. The feeling of him filling me triggers something primal in me and it increases the pleasure soaring through me.

Once the high subsides, my body melts into the couch unable to move. Sam collapses over me but holds his weight with his arm above my head. He softly takes my lips kissing me with an emotion that has me questioning everything. *Does he really want me?* He kisses me almost...lovingly? That can't be right. I mean he could have any girl he wanted.

Before I can pass out from exhaustion, Sam picks me up and carries me through the penthouse to his en suite. Placing me on the cool counter, he walks over to his garden tub starting the water and sprinkling in bath salts. He walks back over to me and slides between my thighs pushing my wild hair from my face.

"What are you doing?" I suck in my bottom lip as I look up into his hazel eyes.

"Taking care of you." He kisses my forehead then goes to check on the water temperature. My belly flutters with the feelings I've always had for this man bubbling to the surface. I've always thought the gesture of being kissed on the forehead was sweet and intimate. The man doesn't get anything out of the kiss, it's purely for the sake of the woman. I smile to myself as his back is turned to me.

I take a moment to check out a very naked and very sexy Sam as he's turned away from me. Gah, even his ass is toned. *Is there a part of him that isn't perfect?*

He comes back, lifting me from the counter and placing me into the steaming tub. My ass burns instantly but then it's soothed by the salts.

"You know, you don't have to go through all this trouble, Sam. I've been taking care of myself for twenty years." I sink down in the water loving the feel on my aching body. He cups my chin for me to look up at him.

"And that's exactly why it's my turn to take over." He kisses me then leaves the room with my head reeling. So many thoughts and questions roll through my mind but I can't seem to worry as the relaxation takes over. Resting my head on the side of the porcelain tub, I close my eyes, smiling at the turn of events.

Fourteen

Samuel

Slipping into a new pair of pajama pants, I make my way to the living room, picking up discarded clothing as I go. A smirk crosses my face to see the scattered garments. I definitely wasn't expecting to get her naked again so soon, but the sight of Marcy straight out of the shower without makeup and a mess of red curls surrounding her while wearing my clothes shot an electric bolt straight through my heart.

My stomach growls and I know Marcy will be hungry by now as well. With the events of last night and everything that's happened today, I'd imagine she worked up quite an appetite.

The kitchen stays stocked thanks to Mrs. McCoy. She comes in twice a week with groceries and miscellaneous other things that are needed around the apartment. I hate being anywhere with large crowds, I'm always on guard and waiting for something to happen.

I was just back home after retiring from the Army when an easy trip to the supermarket turned into a nightmare. I'm pretty sure I scared the living shit out of the old lady, but in my defense, she had just dropped a large jar of sauce from the top shelf making a crashing sound behind me. Without hesitation, I dropped my things to the ground and immediately drew my carry weapon. She turned so pale that she vomited right in front of me. I ran out of that store as fast as my legs would carry me, never to return to that particular store. The next day, Mrs. McCoy was hired to do all my personal shopping. I blame the military for the emotional torment I went through that I carried over to civilian life.

Since it's late afternoon, I decide on making pesto pasta with chicken. I remember little Marcy loved pasta. Hopefully, she hasn't changed on me too much.

Switching on the bluetooth speakers, I get to work preparing the meal. Lost in my thoughts and the music, I don't notice when Marcy approaches, leaning against the wall to the kitchen.

"Wow, if mom could see the way you move around the kitchen she would be proud." Marcy smiles with a nostalgic look on her face. She has her hair wrapped up on top of her head and wearing more of my clothes. My breath leaves my lungs when I look down at her, she looks more gorgeous everytime I lay my eyes on her.

"She taught me everything I know. I owe her more than I can express," I reply. She nods her head as she twirls around the kitchen looking at everything. I have to admit that I'm proud of this part of my apartment. When I bought it, the kitchen wasn't nearly what I wanted it to be so I hired a designer and a construction crew to make my visions come to life.

When I was younger, Mrs. Hillary was always feeding me. It didn't take her long to figure out that I watched as she cooked, trying to learn everything she was doing. My parent's both worked long hours leaving me to fend for myself. She ended up pulling me to the kitchen and teaching me the basics before challenging me with more complicated recipes.

"This is a beautiful kitchen, Sam. It beats mine hands down. Not that I use it much," Marcy muses as she turns back looking up at me with those radiant green eyes.

"Is there anything I can do to help?" She wrings her hands in front of her and I find that her nerves don't sit well with me. I want her to feel comfortable here. Fuck, she needs to get used to it.

Kissing the back of her hand, I lead her around the corner to the stools that look into the open kitchen area.

"Sit. You don't need to do anything. Would you like a glass of wine?" I ask as I turn back toward the kitchen.

"Yeah I guess, I didn't realize how late it was. You didn't have to do all this." She gestures to the pots and pans on the stove.

"I was hungry and figured you would be too." I pour a glass of white wine and set it in front of her.

"Oh," she replies. "Thank you." Marcy takes a sip of the wine, closing her eyes as the flavors explode over her tongue. I knew she would like it. A little moan escapes her lips and I have to shift myself to keep from making my throbbing cock noticeable.

"You haven't turned vegan or anything have you?" I smirk.

"Definitely not."

"Good. I knew you couldn't say no to a good bowl of pasta."

"You remembered?" She looks at me puzzled.

"I noticed a lot more than you think."

A cute blush creeps up her neck to her cheeks as she turns away to take another sip of wine. I finish up everything that needs to be done and place the dish into the oven. There's a talk that Marcy and I need to have and this is the perfect time. Wine might be needed for this so I pour myself a glass as well.

"Come with me." My hand links with hers as I lead her back through the living room. I don't think her sitting on my lap will get much accomplished based on our earlier actions, so I take my seat at the couch and gesture for her to do the same.

My leg settles on the couch so I can position myself to look straight at her.

"Is everything okay?" she asks, taking her plump bottom lip into her mouth.

"We need to talk about this morning when you were trying to get out of here as fast as you could." I look at her pointedly. She shrinks under my gaze letting me know that I need to ease her into all this. "I wanted to talk this morning but things...escalated..." I trail off seeing her rosy cheeks appear again. Damn this woman can get me hot and bothered by doing nothing. Marcy leans over and places her glass down then looks back at me

"I, well, this is a lot." She motions between us."I always wanted, but never expected..." Her eyes widen at me like she just let slip a major secret although it's one I've known for many years.

"You were upset about Matthew this morning. What was on your mind?"

She blows out a deep breath. "I guess it made me feel guilty to hook up with his best friend. I always feel guilty when something goes well in my life, like I don't deserve it since he's not here. Like I'm being selfish. Does that make sense?" she asked as she covers her face with her hands.

Pulling her hands away from her flushed face, I take them in mine, squeezing lightly so her attention turns to me.

"This wasn't just some hookup and you know that."

"Do I?" she questions.

"Listen, I've dealt with survivors' guilt. I've asked myself why it had to be him and not me. He had you to come back to. I've had countless nights where I lay awake wondering why it wasn't me." I pause gathering my thoughts. Tears are streaming down her beautiful face and I know I would do anything to take that pain away. Scrubbing my hand down my face, I continue.

"He isn't here for you but I am." She rolls her eyes at my remark, throwing me off. *What did I say wrong?*

"If you were here for me then why did you leave me alone for so long? You could have visited or even written me from the military. Why did you just cast me aside? I thought..." she hiccups now full on crying. She rises from the couch throwing a decorative pillow down.

"At the funeral you-you kissed me for fucks sake. Do you know what that did to me? I was grieving my brother and making out with his best friend..." Marcy wipes her hands across her cheeks gathering the tears. "I felt so guilty but also confused. You just kissed me and ran away as quickly as you could. No words were said. Just vanished." Marcy storms around me grabbing her purse but before she can get anywhere I reach my arm out to stop her.

"You aren't going anywhere, princess. Now get your ass back on this couch."

"I'm not your *'princess'*, Sam! This is so fucked up." She runs her hands through her mess of curls grasping hard out of frustration. "I'm not your anything! Let's just leave it at that, like it was before when you kept your distance. This was a mistake." Marcy side steps my hand and runs toward the door. I'll be damned if I lose her when I just got her. She's mine.

Her hand on the knob, I swiftly pivot her toward me. Our eyes lock, a charged moment suspended in time. The air thickens, anticipation humming between us. What secrets lie hidden behind those eyes? What unspoken desires simmer beneath the surface? The room fades away, leaving only the two of us, caught in this intimate dance of tension and possibility.

"Listen to me," I cup her face between my hands, "I shouldn't have kissed you at the funeral." Marcy scoffs trying to duck away from me but my body has her pinned to the door. "I only say that because it almost killed me when I had to pull away from you." My thumb rubs a tear from her cheek as her attention comes back to me. Her emerald gems gleam up at me.

"Then why did you?" she whispers, her voice cracking. The room pulses with tension, our breaths mingling in the charged air. Her eyes search mine, seeking answers. Demanding truth.

I let out a deep sigh. "I was going back overseas. I didn't know what would happen and I didn't want to cause you any more grief, more heartache. I was trying to protect you, dammit. Don't you get that? I *had* to leave..." I lean my head against hers needing the connection.

"I didn't need you to protect me. All this time I thought you regretted it. It was so unbearable I could hardly breathe." Marcy sobs into her hands letting out all the emotions she had kept hidden away all these years.

"Shh...I never regretted kissing you. *Never*. My only regret was leaving you in the first place. But I'm here now and I'm *not* leaving.

You can't get rid of me, sunshine. I told you that I would always be here for you and it's time I show you how much I mean that."

"Really?" her tone isn't convinced.

"I would never lie to you, baby."

Marcy wraps her arms around my neck, pulling me closer. My lips brush against hers softly before we hear the timer on the oven sound through the penthouse.

I smile against her lips. "C'mon, let me feed you."

I lead her to the dining area beside a large bank of windows. Once I pull out her chair, I kiss her temple then head to the kitchen for our food.

The pesto chicken smells divine as I make two plates for us. Placing the wide bowls on the table, I rush to the living room to grab our forgotten glasses of wine.

"Thought you might want this." I take my seat across from Marcy, my eyes never leaving hers as she leans over to smell the pasta. The euphoric expression that lines her face is all the praise I need.

"Thank you for doing all of this, Sam. It looks amazing." Her eyes glimmer in the reflection of the setting sun behind me making it hard for me to focus on anything else. I'd much rather sit here watching as she enjoys the meal instead of me diving in as well.

"I needed to make sure you were fed." My shoulders shrugging as I take a sip of wine. The delicious notes of fruit and vanilla explode over my tongue.

Marcy takes a bite of the pasta, her eyes falling closed as she sighs.

"I never thought I would taste her pesto chicken again. It was always my favorite Italian dish she cooked. This is incredible, Sam," she gushes as she takes another bite having the same response. The happiness I see on her face makes me want to be the one that always puts it there.

We continue eating and catching up on things that have happened in our lives since the funeral, although we don't mention that event. I already know all about her but it makes me happy that she is opening up to me. We laugh and talk long after our meals are finished. I admit, I've missed having someone to talk to. It's quiet when you work alone from your home office. But what's more, we connect on such an intimate level much more than sex ever could be. Our conversations are as easy as they ever were when we were young. She still holds that fiery temper but has matured into this goddess before me that deserves everything in the world. And I want to make that happen.

We clean up the dishes and Marcy insists on helping with the kitchen. The music turns to "Thinking Out Loud" by *Ed Sheeran*, so I spin her hips away from the sink and into my arms.

"What are you–" Her question pauses as my lips descend upon hers. I pull her around the kitchen taking her hand in mine as my other grips her waist. Her face beams up at me, sending a jolt straight through my heart. We burst out laughing at my goofy moves but we come back together, closer. I decide to leave the rest of the mess for later as I throw her over my shoulder and march to the theater room.

"Will you let me down, you beast?" Marcy wiggles and laughs until I swat her ass hard eliciting a gasp.

"Didn't expect that, did you?" I grin when I hear her humphs. Slowly, I pull her down over my body until the laughter has faded and her eyes are burning. "Let's watch a movie."

In Marcy's attempt to escape, she didn't realize that we stepped into a room that she's never been in. Her eyes widen as she takes in the sight of the plush couches facing a huge screen.

"This is..." she breaks off, still admiring the room. I take a seat on the plush couch and she soon follows. My arms wrap around her, pulling her as close to me as possible. I don't want space between us. It's primal the way I need her touching me always, it simmers a rage within me that I didn't know existed until her.

"Here. Pick whatever you want." I hand her the tablet with every streaming/movie service available.

"Me? I don't want to pick. You pick," she says as she presses the tablet back into my hands.

"You haven't even looked at anything yet. See if there's something you like." She mutters something under her breath but I don't hear. I'm too busy watching her and memorizing every detail that has been too far away for me to notice. My investigator took images of her but they could never compare to the real thing that's in my arms. A pit forms in my stomach thinking of the files I have on her. Before I can go too far down that road, Marcy pipes up.

"How about this?" It's some chick flick but if that's what she wants then that's what goes.

The lights darken and I pull her on my lap as the movie begins. Her head rests perfectly on my chest allowing me to rub circles across her back.

The movie plays on but I can tell she's fast asleep. The small soft snores are a melody I want to fall asleep to every night.

Scooping her into my arms, I carry her through the apartment and into my bedroom.

The blankets are already pulled back from this morning's shenanigans.

I lay her down gently, tucking the sheets over her body. As I come around to my side, a wide grin forms on my face. I love seeing her like this. Wrapped in my blankets in my bed where she belongs. I climb in beside her pulling her body flush against mine, needing the warmth to know this is real. That *she* is real. I've dreamt of this too many times and finally she's right here with me.

The warmth of her head against my chest, the gentle pressure of her arm around my waist—it's a moment of perfect contentment. The world fades away, leaving only the two of us, cocooned in our own little universe. Her breaths are soft, rhythmic, and I can feel the rise and fall of her chest against mine. It's as if we've found our place, our refuge from the chaos outside.

A knot forms in my stomach, a tangle of unspoken words that twist and tighten. The weight of silence presses down, a burden carried within. I need to bury the evidence that I had her followed, that I was always there just out of reach. She doesn't need to know that I watched her from the shadows, that I've memorized the curve of her lips and the way her laughter dances through the air. I danced on the precipice of desire, teetering between the allure of the forbidden and the safety of restraint.

When our lips touched all those years ago, it sealed our fate. The memory of that moment hangs in the air like a fragile thread, connecting past and present. The taste of uncertainty mingled with desire, a bittersweet cocktail that left its mark on both their souls. She was always going to be mine even if I didn't believe for a while.

FIFTEEN

Marcy

I've never woken up in a man's arms before. Snuggled close in a cocoon with the smell of his cologne wrapping around me. In that fragile moment, vulnerability and trust merged. We were two souls, tangled in sheets, navigating the uncharted waters of intimacy. His heartbeat echoed in my ear, a steady rhythm that promised safety. Is it the closeness, the connection I've been starved for? *Longing* for. I've been on my own for so long now it's hard to remember a time when I've had this much care thrust upon me.

My eyes flutter open from the sound of soft snores coming from Sam. A smile crosses my face as I admire this sleeping Adonis lying next to me. One arm rests over his face but his delicious lips are on display. My eyes move further down wanting to discover all of his tattoos. I didn't get the chance to fully explore his body the way he did mine and now I have the perfect opportunity.

His Army insignia is marked on his bicep along with others skating down his arm that I'll have to ask the meanings of. His other arm is resting on his chest with his hand covering his heart.

That's the one I wanted to see closer. I only got a glimpse yesterday and it had me intrigued.

Carefully I lift his hand placing it on his stomach. I hold my breath when he begins to stir, but he doesn't wake. Once I look back down to his chest, I see the tattoo that interested me the most. My heart aches when I see my brother's name written under what looks like his unit patch. 'KIA' stands out to me but only for a moment until I realize what it stands for, killed in action. A knot forms in my stomach seeing Matthew's name and rank inked over Sam's heart. Tears begin spilling down my face but I try to contain the sobs that threaten to spill from my lips. I don't know what I expected but I didn't think it would be this. Seeing "My brother" etched in below is what breaks the dam of emotions I was trying to conceal.

Sam is startled awake and he shoots up from the bed, looking around the room. His eyes land on mine and I see the muscles in his body relax.

"What is it, sunshine?" He crawls back into the bed pulling me into his arms.

"Y-your tattoo–" I hiccup reaching up to place my hand over his heart. He looks at me solemnly as the realization takes over in his mind.

Sam closes his eyes for a moment then says, "I got it when I was overseas. I wanted something that would stay with me always. Something that was ingrained in my skin like Matthew was."

I get it. They were best friends, brothers, even if not by blood. They were close and I imagine that bond strengthened when they went overseas together. They depended on the other. I'm glad that Sam was with Matty in his last moments. It still doesn't mask my shock of seeing his tattoo first thing in the morning. It reminds me that there is an ever present cloud hanging over my head since the day I heard the news of what happened. When I think I've finally stepped out from under it, the cloud sucks me back into the place where his death is hanging over my head. Being with Sam, there will always be something that will remind me of Matty. I don't know if I'm strong enough for that.

Sam cups my cheek, wiping away the fallen tears with his thumb. He continues rubbing soothing circles as he speaks. "Talk to me, Marcy. What is going through that gorgeous head of yours?" I feel his warm breath skate across my skin before my eyes flutter open.

"I don't know. I just didn't expect to see that this morning. I feel like I get comfortable with the thought of us being together then signs of him pop up bringing the guilt back to the surface." I run my hands through my tangled hair reminding me that my much needed conditioner is at home. *Home.* That's where I need to be right now. I need to get away from all this. I need the space to figure everything out because when we are together, hazel eyes lure me right back to where he wants me. I've got to get out of here.

He opens his mouth to speak but I lay my finger across them. I need to get this out. "Sam, I need to go home. I need to figure some things out for myself." His nostrils flare at my admission and I can see the determination in his eyes. That's exactly what I need to get away from right now.

I shuffle off the bed leaving Sam motionless behind me.

"I'm not letting you run out on this. *On us*. This has been a long time coming, princess, and I'll be damned if I let you go now." His voice is still husky from sleep but commanding all the same.

I don't dare turn back knowing what will happen if I do. Picking up my purse and shoes, I head toward his bedroom door pausing for a moment at the entryway. *Am I doing the right thing? Will this screw everything up when I walk out of his door?* I guess that's something I will have to come to terms with if it does, because right now all I can think of is Matty. When I close my eyes, I see him standing there with his goofy smile on his face. I couldn't bear it if that smile faded from my mind, replaced with the look of disapproval.

I hear Sam get to his feet and I nearly sprint to the front doors with tears streaming from my eyes. I feel like I'm suffocating. I can't make these kinds of decisions. I don't think I can pick between the two of them but that's what feels like needs to be done.

"Marcy Wren Hillary, don't you dare turn that handle. Come back so we can talk about this like adults," Sam's thunderous voice booms from the living room. It echoes through my heart like a beacon calling me back to him.

My tears continue to fall with my hand trembling on the handle. "I need time to think," I murmur. As the door opens, I run through the small hallway straight to the elevator. When I turn to press the buttons, my eyes chance a glance up. Seeing a furious and dejected Sam standing there makes my heart break. As the doors close before me, I slide to the floor and weep at the mess my life has become.

I can feel my heart being ripped from my chest. One half going to Sam and the other to Matt, leaving me empty and hollow. *How can I go on without a beating heart?*

The elevator doors open to the main lobby of the building. Embarrassingly, I rise from the floor grabbing my things and dart to the nearest door. I half expected Sam to be there waiting for me, especially with the last look I saw on his face. But he isn't here. I know I should feel relief but I feel even more lost in his absence.

I can't do this. Too many emotions swirl through my mind until I feel like my world is spinning out of control. I need fresh air because the atmosphere surrounding me is stifling. I can't breathe, almost like I've forgotten how to do it on my own. My lungs burn until I'm hit with the cool morning air. The tears on my cheeks turn to cold streams as I make my way toward the edge of the street. I look down at my bare feet wondering if they would make that last step if I told them to. Would they listen? Or would something stop them? The noise in my head is drowning out my sense of reasoning making me believe that stepping into the morning traffic may very well be the best option. Will it hurt or will I just wake up to Matty holding me in his arms? Oh Matty, I need you so desperately. I lift my foot from the freezing concrete as my hair whips in the wind from the passing cars. This is it. This is...

A horn blows before me, sending me flying back on my ass. It takes me a moment to realize where I am but it all comes flooding back as I hear another horn blow.

"Hey lady, you gettin' in or what?" the cab driver bellows from the car parked in front of me. I give a short nod as I rise from the ground to collect my things. My backside stings as I slide into the seat.

"Where are we headin'?" He looks through the rearview mirror waiting for me to answer. *Where am I going?* He makes a disgruntled noise waiting for my response.

"Um, I..." I rattle off my address as the car pulls away from the curb. The glass from the window feels good on my fevered skin.

The buildings go by in a blur, nothing standing out in this city of chaos. People turn into one never-ending smear along the sidewalk as we pass. My eyes close from the emotional exhaustion of the morning, not able to take in any more. I feel weak, small, hopeless, lost.

The cab comes to an abrupt stop causing me to spring forward in my seat. My hands shoot out for anything to grab before I slam into the plastic partition, only missing it by an inch as my hand finds the emergency handle on the roof.

"Fuck, drive much?" I yell at the driver.

"We're here, m'lady," he replies as he rolls his eyes. I swipe my card and slam the door as hard as I can once I'm out on the street. What an asshole.

Now pissed off, I forcibly open my purse trying to retrieve my keys. I slip on my boots over Sam's joggers and make my way up to my apartment. I get weird looks all the way but I have zero fucks left to give. They can stare all they want.

Once in my apartment, I kick off the boots as I head to my bedroom. The previous emotions that brought havoc to my mind have now quieted leaving severe exhaustion in their wake. I don't shower or change, just fall straight into my bed, wrapping myself up in Matty's old blanket. I'm asleep in seconds, my mind finally at rest.

My eyes feel glued shut when I finally wake up. I wipe away the sleep, letting them flutter open. My ceiling comes into view as all the memories of the day come crashing back into my mind like a tidal wave, but I feel numb. Maybe once your heart breaks it takes away all feeling. You're just a living shell of the person you once were. I pull the old, tattered blanket up to my nose but I can't smell him anymore. I haven't been able to for years but it doesn't stop me from trying.

With a heavy sigh, I roll out of the bed. Sam's clothes need to go because wearing them only makes decisions harder. When I turn on the light to the bathroom, my eyes squint from the sudden brightness. The white marble slowly comes back into view as my eyes adjust to the change. The mirror reflects a person who I don't recognize. She looks lost. The once bright green of her eyes seem to have dulled into a jaded color.

With a resigning sigh, I toss the clothes into my bin and climb into the shower. I go through the motions as if on autopilot as I wash. Once I squeeze the excess water from my hair, I reach for two towels. My feet pad back into my bedroom where I pull on some leggings and an old sweatshirt from college. After I wrap my hair in a towel my stomach grumbles. I guess it has been a while since I ate but the thought of food makes me queasy.

I grab a granola bar from the pantry and a water bottle from the fridge. When I close the refrigerator, my eyes catch the calendar pinned to the door. My heart speeds up when I realize I didn't go to Matt's grave on our birthday like I have since he passed. I told myself that I would go Sunday since I was getting ready for the party on Saturday. Yet it's Monday and I never visited him. My stomach twists as I rush through the apartment grabbing my dead phone, I'll have to charge in the car, and my sneakers. Pulling them on, I pluck my keys from the table and race out of my apartment.

I'm so glad I took today off as a forethought from my birthday this past weekend.

Once my phone powers up, I put on my mood music playlist. It's something I made incorporating songs with lyrics that speak to me in an intimate way. Even though it's a cool November day, I ride through the city with my sunroof down and my heater on. It's something Matty and I always did when we were young. It doesn't make any sense but with the air coming in it somehow is freeing.

The trip to the cemetery is rooted in my mind, making driving it feel like second nature. I park in my usual spot then grab the bag I got from the grocery store on the way. As I walk through the memorial park, my eyes focus on the dark clouds above. They seem to follow along the path to Matthew's grave. I lay out the towel and sit beside him pulling my knees up to my chest.

"I'm sorry I'm late, Matty. I didn't forget, I just–life threw me a curveball and I didn't handle it well." Wind blows, making the leaves rustle around me. I sit quietly for a moment stewing in indecision of what to say next. I pull out the candy from the bag I brought and hold it up.

"I brought our favorite candy. I figured eating it would be like old times when you would take me to the store and we would sneak it past mom and dad so we could have a movie marathon with good snacks." I tear open the package and the fruity smell hits me like a brick. I haven't had Sour Patch Kids since Matty passed away.

"You know, you didn't always have to let me pick the movie. We could have watched one of your crazy action movies instead." I pour some of the gummies in my hand and divide them by colors. I always ate the red and orange and he wanted the green and yellow. We would split the blue ones between us.

"Sam came to our birthday celebration on Friday. Miles and Sebastian put it on for us. I hadn't seen him since your funeral. I didn't even know he still lived in the city." Emotion clogs my throat and I'm not sure where to begin with this conversation.

"So, Matty, I—um, well I ended up drinking way too much and Sam actually came to my rescue and took care of me." I look around the bleak cemetery trying to find the right words. Guilt threatens to overwhelm me but I have to get this out before it eats me alive. I take a deep breath, letting the cold air into my lungs, causing them to burn.

"I'm just going to say it. I slept with him, Matty. I'm so sorry. I know he was your best friend and I shouldn't have betrayed you. I got so caught up in my feelings for him that never seemed to have faded over time. Instead they were stronger than ever before." Tears stream down my face as I take a bite of the sour candy. The flavor explodes in my mouth bringing me right back to all those years ago when I would cuddle up with Matt on his bed.

"Did you ever realize my feelings for him? I know you never mentioned it but could you tell? From the first time you brought him home, I was smitten. I can't describe it. It was like all was right in the world when he was around. I didn't mean to fall for him the older I became. It just...happened." I wipe the tears from my face with the sleeve of my sweatshirt.

"I wish you were here. I need you now more than ever because I don't know what to do. I can't choose between you two. I wouldn't survive it, especially now." The wind picks up causing my hair to swirl around me sticking to the wet patches on my face. The sky darkens with the looming threat of rain.

"Since you've been gone, I feel guilty if something good happens in my life. Like I don't deserve to be happy because you aren't here for me to share it with. But I also know in my heart that you would want me to be happy. It's so hard to know which one is right. Please tell me what to do. Please, Matty, please tell me." I cry silently into my hands as drops of rain begin to fall. I don't want to leave. I'm not ready. I haven't figured out what to do yet.

"Do you remember that time that we danced in the rain after one of your football games?" Smiling, I stand up then scroll through my playlists until I come to the song I'm thinking of. I hit play and set the phone down on his headstone.

"Do you remember, Matty? Everyone was scrambling to leave but you picked me up and twirled me around singing "Everlong" by the *Foo Fighters.* We laughed so hard as we screamed the lyrics together getting questioning looks in the process but we didn't care. We were in our own little world. Our bubble." I dance around him. I can feel him with me. I'm laughing and shouting the words to the song getting some wrong but I don't care. It's just us. As I'm spinning, jumping and acting a fool the rain starts pouring down on me. I twirl with my arms out embracing the cold rain, my face looking up at the sky letting the water cleanse me of my transgressions.

My knees hit the ground as my hands grip my hair and I scream. I scream for having to be here without Matt. I scream for his short life. I scream and scream because I'm mad as hell that he was taken from me.

"Why did you have to leave me, Matt?" WHY? Why did you have to be such a fucking saint and go fight for our country? I'm selfish, Matty! I wanted you with me. I needed you with me. I hate you so much but I love you the most." I scream as loud as I can until my voice begins to crack; I feel the strain on my throat. My fists punch the ground with all the strength I have left, over and over and over until I collapse to the ground in a heap of fucked up mess. That's what I am. My chest is heaving and my eyes are overflowing with pain and loneliness, mixing with the rain and cascading down my face away from me. My emotions sink into Matt's grave as I lay there sprawled out.

"I don't really hate you, Matty. I never could..." I whisper.

"Can I date your best friend? Being with him sparks my soul back to life, Matty. It's been dead since you've been gone. I know you were so protective of me but I think you would approve of him. You already know he's a good man. Tell me, Matty. I'll listen. I always listen..." I trail off as my phone sparks to life playing a new song. "Santeria" by *Sublime* blares around me. Matt was always singing this song. He even sang it one night at this karaoke party we were at. My eyes close as a fresh set of tears stream down my face. I know it may seem crazy but I know he just answered me.

"Thank you," I breathe.

Smiling, I look at his name engraved above me.

"Thank you. I'm proud of you in case I never told you. You will always be my hero, my best friend."

My hand runs back and forth over the cold, wet marble until I hear footsteps approaching. My emotions tore through me so ferociously that I don't have the energy to look. I close my eyes as I curl into myself, exhaustion taking over.

Warm hands wrap about me but before I can scream, I hear him. "Shh, it's me. It's just me, princess." Sam's words calm my racing heart as he picks up my drenched body. He slings the wet towel over his shoulder and grabs my phone, silencing the loud music.

"How–" I mutter, my voice barely above a whisper.

He doesn't answer me right away, he just walks us to the parking lot in silence.

"Put me down, Sam! If you aren't going to talk then put me the fuck down. I don't need a savior if that's what you think you're doing," I shout as loud as my voice allows which isn't much. I wiggle in his arms until he drops me to my feet. His gorgeous hazel eyes have turned stormy.

"I followed you. Okay? You ran out on me. I was fucking worried about you." He slams the towel on the ground in front of us. *He followed me?* "I could see the darkness and desperation seeping into your eyes," he pants, running his hand down his face as the rain continues to pour down on us. The only sound around is our labored breathing as the rainstorm pounds the ground. His eyes lock back on mine and a chill runs through my body not from the cold but from his intensity.

"Do you know how I saw that?" I shake my head.

"I saw it because it's what I see when I look in the mirror. It's what haunts me." He takes a step toward me and cups my face.

"But I didn't see it this morning." He pulls me flush against his body.

"What are you–" His finger covers my lips then tilts my chin up forcing me to look at him.

"I didn't see it this morning because of you." I gasp as more tears flood down my cheeks but my focus remains on Sam's unwavering gaze. His thumbs stroke the tears from my cheeks. Leaning down he rests his forehead against mine.

"I'm broken, sunshine, but your fire got in through the cracks of my soul. You showed me what it felt like to live again. Life threw us a curveball and we found ourselves shattered but you brought light into my life, even during our darkest moments. It ignited my spirit. When we're broken, it's easy to forget what it feels like to truly live. But then someone came along—you—and suddenly, the world became vivid again. Life isn't just about existing; it's about feeling, experiencing, and embracing every sunrise. That's you, Marcy. You're my sunrise, my sunshine."

"Say something, Marcy." His lips brush against mine so lightly it would be easy to miss. My brain is already exhausted from all of the events from today culminating with talking to Matt. My thoughts are sporadic and I can't form the words I need to say. I don't even know what the words are.

"I—" He pulls back from me searching my gaze for answers that he won't find. It's all too much.

Sam drops his hands from my face as he steps away, turning around in the rain. His head falls back as the rain continues its assault upon us. My heart is drumming against my chest threatening to break free.

Sixteen

Samuel

The raindrops fall, a symphony of liquid notes, but my gaze remains fixed upon her. She stands there, a vision carved from moonlight and stardust. Her eyes, deep pools of mystery, hold secrets that beg to be unraveled. The delicate curve of her lips, a half-smile, hints at stories untold. And her hair, a cascade of red silk, dances with the wind, defying the storm.

In this tempest, she is my lighthouse, guiding me through the chaos. Her presence ignites a fire within me, a warmth that defies the cold rain. I wonder if she knows the power she wields—the way her laughter can chase away the thunder, the way her touch can heal wounds unseen.

As the rain continues its relentless assault, I find solace in her existence. She is my refuge, my muse. I am a moth drawn to her flame. Nothing can diminish her radiance; it only grows stronger with each passing moment. I stand here, drenched and mesmerized, lost in the storm but found in her beauty.

The rain intensifies, its rhythm echoing the rapid beat of my heart. She glances at me, her eyes holding so much emotion. Without hesitation, I step closer, needing the warmth only her soul can give. The raindrops cling to her lashes, glistening like diamonds. I reach out, brushing a droplet from her cheek and she smiles.

The world fades away, leaving only her and me—a flame burning against the darkness. And as the rain washes away our pasts, I know that this moment is a beginning, an unwritten chapter waiting to unfold.

"I'll say it then. For years I sat on the sidelines of your life never giving us a chance because–" *because I was a fucking coward, but no longer.* I run my hands over my face trying to find the perfect words. I grasp her cheeks in my hands eliciting a magnetic pulse that races through me.

"Fuck all the excuses, mine and yours. You're mine, sunshine. Do you understand me? *You* are the one for me. You always have been, but circumstances were never right but now...now there is nothing in our way. It's our time now. When you walked onto that rooftop, I felt your presence before I even turned around. This is where our story begins. Life is too short to hold back any longer. Tell me you don't feel the same. Tell me this isn't what you've always wanted."

Her emerald eyes, like shards of jade, pierce through the veil of my composure. Each blink, a razor's edge, flaying my defenses. I stand there, vulnerable, caught in the crossfire of longing and fear.

She reaches up to brush the hair from my eyes. Her gentle touch, like a whisper of silk against my skin, sends shivers down my spine. The way her fingers trace the curve of my brow, brushing away stray strands of hair, feels like an intimate secret shared between the two of us. It's as if she holds the power to unravel me completely, leaving me breathless and yearning for more.

"Sam, of course it's what I want. It has always been you for as far back as I can remember." Her words send jolts straight through my heart. I lift her up against me tightly and her legs wrap around me as our lips crash together in a fevered kiss. Our moans tangle together as we rock back and forth.

"Home?" I whisper against her lips. When her head tilts slightly, lips pressing against mine, her eyes lock onto mine with a nod. It's a silent agreement, a shared desire. Shifting her in my arms, I pull the door open to my car, setting her inside.

"Wait! What about my car?" she questions.

"I'll take care of it." I reach in to buckle her then kiss her temple. I race around to the other side seeing the discarded towel on the ground. I throw it into a nearby dumpster. I'll buy her ten more.

Jumping into the car, the engine purrs to life. Marcy slipped off her shoes and has her legs pulled up against her body shivering. I can't have that. I have this deep rooted need to protect her from everything, even sickness. I crank up the heat and reach in the backseat for a hoodie I threw back there the other day.

"Here, put this on until I can get you into some dry clothes."

"T-thank you." Her teeth are chattering as she reaches out with trembling fingers to grab the sweatshirt. I turn up the heat as we head back toward the city. The gentle notes of the music envelop us, creating a cocoon of tranquility. It's as if the melody knows our unspoken words, weaving them into the fabric of the car. The silence feels like a shared secret—a comfortable pause in our conversation.

Darkness falls over the roads with the exception of the street lamps as the storm continues to blast from above. The normal chaos of New York City is eerily quiet, allowing our journey to be a quick and easy one. As I park in my usual spot at home, I look over to find Marcy fast asleep bundled up in my sweatshirt. My eyes trace the outline of her soft face against the dark features of the car. She glows bright without trying, beautifully mesmerizing. I truly don't know how I kept my distance from her for so long but once I felt the electricity in her touch at Matt's funeral and again at her party, our fates were sealed.

Looking out of the window at 40,000 feet above ground, my mind wandered back to the expression on Marcy's face after I kissed her. When I came home for Matt's funeral, I didn't anticipate finding my best friend's younger sister to have grown into such a gorgeous woman since we had been gone. I know the years drifted by but I didn't expect them to have affected her so much.

When Matt and I left, Marcy was a silly fourteen year old with braces, but when she opened that door I felt like my brain misfired. Gone were the slouched shoulders, braces and frumpy clothing, replaced with the brightest smile I've ever seen, perfect posture and clothing that hugged her curves in all the best ways. She was a vision, a goddess. Fucking stunning.

What was she doing right now? Was she crying? Did she need me? Did she hate me? The questions cycled through my mind so much that I debated reaching out to her but as soon as I picked up the phone or began an email, I would decide against it, telling myself that she wasn't thinking of me.

I'll never forget the way her black lace dress made every man at the funeral turn their heads. I wanted to snap them all off for daring a glance at what wasn't theirs. Not that I believed Marcy to be mine. But fuck did I want to fall to my knees and beg. I knew her. I grew up with her always tagging along. I'd always loved her but somewhere along the line it blurred into something more. More time thinking about her witty comebacks, more dreaming about how her red hair fell in waves down her back and more fantasizing about her pouty lips on mine. She was everything I wanted but never thought I would deserve.

When Marcy and I ran through the rain after the funeral something came alive inside me. It was like I had been a zombie over the past week just going through the motions until she lit me up, mending the part of me that had died with Matthew. I never intended to kiss her but when I pressed her up against the limousine there was a fire in her eyes that I knew mirrored mine. My hands cupped her cheeks as the rain around us seemed to slow like we were in the eye of a storm. It was just us. Me and her. Together. Suddenly everything made sense but nothing was as it seemed and so I fled.

The hurt I saw in her eyes gutted me more than anything had in my life. I knew I couldn't be what she needed while I was in the service. She had already lost so much and I couldn't stand the thought of being the reason more tears ever touched her cheeks again.

Once I got back to base, I threw myself into work and missions. I worked harder and longer to keep the memories at bay. It was going for the most part until a package arrived for me. For a moment, I thought it was from Marcy until I opened the letter.

Dearest Samuel,

I hope this letter finds you well and that you're healthy and happy. I know the toll of losing a best friend can take on a person. The heart breaks in a unique pattern each time, taking a special person to glue the pieces back together in their own way. The heart may never be the same but in many ways it's better and more beautiful than before.

Do you remember the lovely antique Japanese vase that you asked me about once? Well, I bought it because of its intricate design. Once you asked me about it, I began researching the item. I came across the word 'kintsugi'. It's an old technique for repairing broken ceramic. Instead of trying to piece it back perfectly, the Japanese believed there was beauty in flaws. So, they made the glue gold before adhering it together again. Everyone would know that it had been broken at one time but would see the piece as more exquisite and meaningful than it was to begin with.

All of this to say, it will mend and work better than you ever dreamed. Marcy is familiar with this technique and has taken to collecting similar pieces.

Speaking of, Marcy is in survival mode, not truly living. I believe losing Matt and then yourself has done a number on her. I haven't seen her bright smile in many, many months. I actually haven't seen it since the funeral. When she ran from the tent with you, she looked more carefree than she had in years. It was heartwarming for a mother to witness, even on one of the hardest days of our lives. She's always had a connection with you. I attributed it to puppy love for far too long. Having met my husband at a young age, I knew the look on her face well and should have recognized it for what it was.

Soulmates.

It always takes the stubborn man longer to realize what he has in front of him and with the age gap, I knew you wouldn't see it for some time.

But if I'm not mistaken, you finally saw what I've known for years. You did the right thing even if it seems like the biggest mistake of your life. It wasn't your time yet.

Your times will align at the exact moment that has always been drawn in the stars for the two of you. I truly believe that. Don't beat yourself up, kid. Get your job done and find your way home. It isn't the same without you here. My kitchen has never been lonelier and Marcy doesn't have a cooking bone in her body.

I've sent something that you'll know what to do with when the time comes. I love you like a son, Samuel. Thank you for serving our country.

With love,
Mrs. Hillary

With tears streaming down my face, I folded the letter and placed it in a small pocket of my bag ensuring its safety. I unwrapped the small package that came with the letter. Instantly my mind went to Marcy when I saw what was enclosed. I smiled at Mrs. Hillary's way of giving me a push that she knew I would need. Shaking my head, I laughed out and held the gift to my chest. I just needed to get through this chapter of my life.

Life often unfolds in unexpected ways, and sometimes it takes a serendipitous encounter to reveal what has been there all along. Our reunion has only cemented the feelings I had for her at the funeral. Matt brought us together in ways I didn't understand, until he was gone. That has been his greatest gift. His actions toward me in our youth, bringing me into his family like one of their own, had a lasting tether that tied me to his sister. Through deployments and stupidity, the tether never diminished but only grew stronger the closer I was to her.

Seventeen

Marcy

My vivid dreams from the car mix with reality, leaving my mind foggy with everything that happened at the cemetery. It takes me a moment to realize where I am and why I feel like I'm levitating through the air. My eyes spring open to the bright lights of Samuel's penthouse lobby causing me to shield my face from the intrusion.

"Hey sleepyhead. I didn't want to disturb your sleep plus there was no way you would have been able to get your soaked shoes back on," he whispers, which I appreciate while the drowsiness takes its time to dissipate from my system.

"You know, I could have walked. You don't need to carry me everywhere." His hazel eyes dart from mine as his handsome face morphs into one of irritation. Sam's jaw clenches, making me wonder what I said wrong. I didn't mean anything maliciously. I truly don't need to be babied and carried everywhere as if an invalid. Not to mention that I feel very uncomfortable when he babies me. It just reminds me that I'm nowhere near a supermodel's body frame, which he's probably used to being with. I'm comfortable in my skin most days but that's totally different when someone is carrying me. All of my old insecurities come rushing back to the surface making me feel like a burden, especially a heavy one. I can do this on my own. My mind wanders trying to think of something to say to fix this uncomfortable wedge between us that sprouted from my comment.

The elevator doors close behind us and the sudden pressure from climbing floors quickly makes me queasy. It's a silent ride to the top as I stew over what to say, but no words form. Sam doesn't respond to my comment like I expect him. He carries me into his apartment, placing me on the ground and keeps me steady until my legs are stable beneath me. He tosses our soaked shoes by the door then takes my hand in his, leading me somewhere in this giant palace.

"Sam, I'm sorry–" His grip on my hand tightens, making my comment die on my lips. We pass through his bedroom doors and into the bathroom. Sam releases my hand without turning. I stand there wringing my sore hands together in front of me waiting for some sort of response. The shower head springs to life then he stalks back to me. His eyes are burning with...anger? Desire?

"On the counter," he commands. A beat passes without either of us moving both testing the other. He steps closer bending so his warm breath coats my neck as he whispers, "I said get your ass on that counter, Marcy." His words paint an evocative picture of longing and desire. My body awakens by the mere presence of him. The need for him to touch me heightens but I know he won't until I submit to him. I can see my independent, girl boss visage happily fly out of the window as I do what he asks.

My wet clothing squishes as I jump on the counter but I don't dare move until more instructions come. A wicked smile crosses his face as he separates my thighs, coming between them.

His fingers trail over my cheek and down my throat, leaving goosebumps in his wake. "Such a good girl for me," he murmurs as my body begins to tremble from his praise.

"Let's get these wet clothes off." Sam's hands skate down my body until he reaches the hem on the hoodie he offered me in the car. Slowly he peels the damp garment from my body, tossing it to the floor. He continues until the only thing remaining is a purple lace bra that barely contains my heaving breasts.

"Did you put this on hoping I would see it? Hmm? Did you want me to rip this from your skin?" He chuckles darkly, his eyes never leaving mine as his warm hands cup my chilled skin. The heat from his body coupled with his hands on me has me squirming on the counter, needing more. More heat, more touching, just more.

I nod but he tsks. "Words, sunshine," he growls. Something about the sound of his voice sends jolts of pleasure between my thighs.

"Y-yes, I hoped you would see." I pull my bottom lip between my teeth biting down as I wait to see what he does next.

"Mmm, you can't do that baby." Sam pulls my lip from my teeth then soothes it with his thumb as he rubs it back and forth. Without thinking, my tongue peeks out to stroke his finger. His eyes close as a groan vibrates from him. I love seeing I have the same effect on him that he has on me. It makes me feel like we are on equal ground even if he's the one in control.

His eyes open with more urgency than before. My bra pops open before I know what happened. It's added to the pile on the floor.

Not wanting to be the only one on display, I lean closer to slide his shirt off.

"Is there something you're wanting to see, princess?"

"It's not fair to only have me out of my clothes." I look up at him with a pout, making him give in instantly. He pulls the shirt over his head the next moment laying over the pile of wet discarded clothing.

Sam slides me from the counter then falls to his knees before me. His hands grasp the waistband of my leggings, sliding them slowly down my legs torturing us both. My panties go next which I'm surprised aren't ripped. His hands slowly slide up my body as he nips and kisses a path from my legs, up my tummy, over my breasts and along my neck until he's standing, leaning over me. Electric shocks from every point of contact spread through my body as if hitting every nerve until I'm a panting mess.

"Fuck you're exquisite. I want to devour every inch of you," he breathes into the shell of my ear eliciting a moan to fall from my lips.

In a haze of desire, my nails scratch down his chest until I reach his pants, pulling his belt free and dropping it to the floor with a loud clank that seems to vibrate around the marble. The intensity of his molten pools of hazel is almost too much to bear. Before I can finish, he sheds his pants then pulls me flush against his body. I can feel his hard length pressing against my stomach, making my pussy throb with need. Sam squeezes my ass in his hands forcing me to stand on tip toes as he crashes his mouth over mine.

He's overwhelming.

All consuming.

Obsessive.

His heat burns my cool skin but ignites something deep inside me.

The steam from the shower begins to billow out, surrounding us in a cocoon of warmth.

"C'mon, sunshine, let's get you warmed up." The twinkle in his eyes causes a blush to creep into my cheeks because I know exactly how he intends to warm me up. His fingers gently stroke down my arm until his hand encompasses mine, leading me into the shower. I'd follow this man anywhere.

The warm water is almost painful against my chilled skin making me flinch away. I didn't realize how cold I was even though I was standing in the rain in November.

"Here, is it too hot?" Sam questions, reaching over my shoulder to adjust the temperature.

"It's okay. My skin being cold makes it feel hotter than it is." He nods, pulling me in to wrap his arms around me.

"I want to kiss every freckle," Sam pauses, kissing my forehead, "along," kissing my cheek, "your," kissing my nose, "body," then finally kissing my waiting lips. He spins me around to face the glass wall forcing me to put my hands up to steady myself. That's when I see the damage I did to my hands when I was screaming in the cemetery. I try to slide them down, not wanting Sam's attention to focus on the cuts and bruises.

"Marcy, what the hell happened?" I hesitate, pressing my hands against my stomach. He smacks my ass hard getting his desired effect. I turn around to rub the sensitive skin before he does it again.

"Why the hell did you do that?" I seethe.

"I asked you a question and you didn't answer me," he replies matter of factly like he can get away with shit like that. I roll my eyes, which is a huge mistake that I realize after the fact. Sam takes a step closer, caging me into the cool glass shower wall. My teeth pull my lip in to nibble on, only because I know it drives him wild. Two can play at this game.

Sam groans as his darkened eyes rove over my mouth. He bends to grab my wrists from behind me, pulling my hands out for him to observe. My eyes glance away not wanting to see the emotion written across his face.

He brings my hands under the stream to clean away the caked on blood.

"Ow!" I whimper, snatching my hands away quickly.

"Marcy, I need to see the damage." Hearing my name fall from his lips instead of an endearment makes me feel like I'm in trouble. It's stupid because it's my name but I can't help the disappointment. I lift my hands back up to his so he can continue his perusal.

"I'll have to wrap these up when we get out of here," he explains, letting my hands dangle by my sides.

"I don't think–"

"Don't," he commands, effectively shutting me up. There is something about his tone he must have gotten from the military that makes me *need* to do what he tells me. "Turn around so I can wash your hair."

As he grabs his bottle of 3-in-1 soap and shampoo concoction, I can't help but giggle.

"Something funny?" he asks as he takes my hair in his hands, lathering it then massaging my scalp. It feels so good I could fall asleep.

"I was just noticing your variety of shower products," I murmur with an unmistakable sass that has me smiling.

"I don't usually have guests." That intrigues me. We never had a talk about if we were single or not. I suppose I just assumed, which makes me wince. I don't respond because I'm trying to think of what exactly to say. Why the hell didn't we already have this talk? He never even asked me if I was with someone. Did he not care? Or was it obvious that I didn't? Maybe my imaginary boyfriend couldn't make it to the party. He doesn't know. The more I think, the pissier I get.

Sam takes the shower head from its stand and begins rinsing my hair.

"You might as well say what you're thinking before you explode," he chuckles, continuing to rid my hair of all the soap.

"How did you–"

"Your shoulders are so tense, they look frozen in place. Just spill it."

"Ugh, I was wondering why we never talked about if we were seeing other people. I mean you could have had a–"

"I didn't," he answers before I finish, which makes me angrier. He puts the shower head back in place making it the perfect time to turn and confront him.

"You didn't let me finish!" I fume.

"I didn't need you to. I didn't have a girlfriend or wife or anything else your mind was trying to cook up." He shrugs like it's not a big deal. I guess he just *assumed* a girl like me would be single.

"Why do you still look mad? Wasn't that the right answer?" he smirks, making me want to smack that look right off his face.

"It was! But, what? You just assumed that I wasn't with anyone? You never asked!" I try to shout but my voice just squeaks it out. That definitely wasn't as forceful as I wanted it to sound. I can't win.

"I knew you were single," he states, squeezing more soap into his hands before he lathers his own hair.

"What? How could you have known that? Because I didn't show up with someone?" Sam's lips come down on mine and I don't know whether to lean into the feelings or push him away. *Men are so frustrating.* He pulls back, kissing my forehead then finishing his hair.

"Do you know how fucking sexy you are when you're all riled up?" He grins, rinsing.

Sam makes me so crazy! He sees my frustration and cups my face, his thumb running circles over my cheeks.

"I knew because I asked Miles and Sebastian before the party."

"Oh." Well, that makes sense, I guess.

"Do you feel better now?" I nod absentmindedly.

"Use your words."

"Yes," I sigh. There's still this nagging feeling that he's not telling me everything but I can't put my finger on it. However it doesn't take long for all of my negative thoughts to drift away. Sam grabs my ass, pulling me up so we're face to face. I circle my legs around his waist loving the feel of him pressed right at my entrance. He leans in sucking that special spot behind my ear that he's found, knowing it makes me desperate. My nails dig into his shoulders as my hips press into him more.

"Tell me what you want, sunshine," he purrs into my ear, nipping and licking down my throat. Pressed up against the cool glass,

Sam finds my needy clit and begins to rub in slow even strokes. He's teasing me until I answer him.

"You. I need *you*," I pant.

"I asked what you wanted, sunshine. What do you want me to do to this gushing cunt?" he asked again but with more edge than before. He wanted me just the same.

"Fuck, Sam. Stop being so difficult. Fuck me dammit," I demand. His devilish chuckle wraps around me before thrusting inside completely. My breath whooshes out of me, like when I was a kid and fell off of a slide. A muffled cry escapes my lips as my head bangs against the glass behind me.

"Take it! This is what you wanted, isn't it, *princess*?" he grits.

"Take it like the cock hungry slut you are." My moans catch in my throat as he stretches me, thrusting hard and fast. My release builds quickly with a ferocity that makes my eyes roll back.

"Yes! Right there," I hum as the tingles of an orgasm begin in my tummy.

Before the pleasure rolls through me, Sam pulls out, setting me on my feet.

"Hey! I—" He presses his hand around my throat tightly. The look of his eyes is fierce but confident. My tongue dips out to lick my lips. I can't help but taunt him.

"I don't think you remember how this works. You don't command me. I'm the one in charge," he whispers in my ear, twisting my nipple with the other. The pain shoots jolts straight to my pussy, keeping me right on the edge.

Sam bites my shoulder then smoothes it over with his tongue. I can't help but to wiggle under his firm grasp.

"I give you pleasure but I can also take it away. Now, on your knees, brat," he smirks but his command isn't up for question. I'm realizing when to pick my battles with him.

Without my eyes leaving his, I slink to my knees before him. His large body blocks the water spray enabling me to keep my eyes open. I've never sucked a cock before but I want to please him. I don't want my inexperience to shine through.

Not waiting for instructions, I run my hands up his slick thighs. With my tongue sticking out, I lick from the base to tip in one motion. His accompanying groan rings out in the shower spurring me on. My lips wrap around his head as I suck the precome into my mouth. The mixture of our desire dances on my tongue.

"You look so pretty on your knees," he croons. His praise has me diving back in for more. I take him down my throat until tears are streaming down my face and my lungs are burning. He fists my hair, pulling me to look up at him. "Remember to tap my leg if it's too much."

"Yes, sir," I accentuate with a smile.

"Fuck! Open up." It's the only warning I get before he thrusts himself into my mouth, further and further with every stroke. My hands tighten on his ass pulling him closer to me. I want everything he has even if I can't handle it.

"Breathe through your nose, sunshine. Let me in."

I relax as much as possible while his thick shaft pounds my throat. My hand massages his balls making Sam call out my name. A sense of pride falls over me for giving him pleasure. I can sense he's close but he pulls me off before he comes.

"There's only one place my cum goes." He lifts me then presses my front to the wall, keeping my hands locked behind my back.

Sam kicks open my legs and pounds inside me. His other hand wraps around to circle my clit bringing me back to the edge within minutes.

"Please let me come, sir!" I whine as the explosion bubbles within me waiting for permission to combust.

"That's my good girl." He bites down on my lobe causing a strangled moan to escape.

"Do you think you learned your lesson?"

I nod furiously

"I need those words, baby."

"Yes sir. I'm sorry. Please!" I beg as more tears rush down my cheeks.

He pinches my clit hard, lighting the fuse. "Come with me," he urges. "Tell me who owns this pussy. Shout it for the whole building to hear."

"It's yours. It's always been yours, sir! Fuckkk—" A garbled mess erupts from my mouth as Sam stills inside me. I feel each pulse of his hot come spurt into my channel, causing my release to continue on and on.

Once my hands are free, I wipe the hair from my face but continue to lean against the wall for support. Sam slides out and I instantly miss the connection. His arms circle my waist, pulling me against his body.

"My beautiful chaos," he purrs into my ear, his voice a velvet melody that dances through the air.

"Hmm, beautiful chaos. I like the sound of that," I muse.

He turns me to face him, his eyes full of emotion. Sam presses a kiss to the top of my head as he whispers, "You're bold, unapologetic and beautifully messy, princess. The tempest that stirs my heart." My heart drums in my chest at his words. This is what I've always wished for. We stand there together until the water begins to cool.

"Better finish washing up." He adjusts the knob on the shower to allow us a bit more warmth as we scrub quickly. Sam gently washes between my legs with more care than I've ever seen from him. He takes care of me. He actually likes taking care of me. He may be a Dominant in every way but he also enjoys the aftercare aspect. Maybe even more, making him even more irresistible.

Eighteen

Marcy

"Hop on the counter so I can bandage your hands," he instructs. Without hesitation, I climb on trying to hold the towel in place. Sam rummages through drawers until he finds what he's looking for. It hasn't been long since I used this first aid kit on him. It seems like so long ago but it's only been a few days. My emotional limit has been pushed and pulled in all directions, making me exhausted.

"Let me see." Sam grabs my hand and places it on my thigh. The bruising is really starting to show. He tsks but pulls out some ointment and bandages. The cuts aren't too bad but considering they were packed with mud, I'm sure he wants to take precaution against infection.

Before he gets started, he hesitates for a moment then looks up at me. I can see the irritation before the words come. "How am I supposed to take care of you, if you can't take care of yourself?" he questions. I'm lost for an answer. I can take care of myself. I've been doing it for almost twenty years now.

"How dare you say that? I've been the *only* one who cares for me for more than half my life. I've made it this far!" I seethe as my breathing picks up.

"Your hands tell a different story." I pull back from him as if his words burn me. Tears prick at the corners of my eyes from the anger boiling inside me.

"I got emotional at the cemetery. It doesn't mean I can't take care of myself, Sam!" I scoff and turn away, crossing my arms over my chest.

"Hey, it's me, sunshine. Why are you getting so defensive?" He brushes a wet chunk of hair from my face, then firmly tilts my chin to look at him. "I don't like seeing you hurt. It makes me feel like I'm not doing my job."

"You don't have to take care of me. I've said it over and over. I can do it all on my own, dammit." The floodgates break and tears flow down my cheeks like intertwining rivers.

"I'm not going to say this again so you best listen. It is my responsibility and pleasure to care for you. It's something I don't take lightly. Not only am I your Dom but your mentor, teacher, and protector. I want what's best for you no matter what." Sam cups my face, swirling his thumb over my cheek. I don't know why I have the urge to fight him on this. I'm just...scared.

"I finally got you, princess. I'm not letting anything take you away. So deliberately hurting yourself or putting yourself in danger, that shit stops now." My eyes glisten with unshed tears as they stare into his.

"So," I hesitate.

"I meant everything I said at the cemetery tonight. You are it for me. But I need you to understand what that means." He takes a few moments before he says anything further. The thick silence stretches out between us making me uncomfortable.

"After Matthew died in my arms, my commanding officer insisted that I go through therapy. My mind was in a constant state of battle with itself. I was miserable but I didn't think I needed help. I fought it until I broke down one night. Nothing even initiated it, but I'd hit rock bottom and I knew I needed to talk to someone about everything I kept bottled up inside." Sam runs his hand down his face then places his hands on the counter on either side of me.

"I see it in your eyes. I see the pain you try to hide. I see how broken you are when you hold yourself together. I see all that because I've been there. You haven't moved on from your parents' deaths or Matt's. That depression and loneliness follow you like a cloud. Of course no one else sees because you're good at faking it. You're good at putting on the face that everyone expects from you. But I truly see you. I see the hurt that never healed. I see that little girl that was forced to grow up before her time. I see the fear in your eyes, the fear that everyone you love will leave you in the end. I see you, sunshine. And I don't want that pain for you." Sobs wrack through my body as I try to reel in the emotions, but the more I try the more everything comes pouring out. Sam takes my injured hand in his, kissing my knuckles lightly then holding it up for me to see.

"This is from anger that has accumulated over time and finally was set free. You're hurting yourself." He pulls me into his warm embrace as my cries continue. I can't deny what he's said even though I want to. But I'd be lying. He's right about everything.

"How do I make it better?" I murmur against his chest. "How do I make the pain go away? I'm so tired of hurting, Sam. So tired." He holds me tighter, rubbing my back in comforting circles.

"You need to talk to someone. You've got to get it all out or you're never going to be okay. You'll always have that darkness hanging over you. I don't want that for you. I want you to be happy. Full of life. I need you, sunshine."

I nod my head in agreement. "But what will people think of me?"

"Who cares what anyone thinks? If they aren't a positive force in your life then they don't deserve a spot to be there. Fuck them. It's time to take care of you." Sam kisses the top of my head then pulls my chin up.

"Let's get your hands cleaned up so we can get in bed. I think some cuddles are needed. It's been a long day. Why don't you take tomorrow off? I'll make some calls and move around my schedule, you try to do the same." The thought is intriguing. I hardly ever just take a day off, but I'm starting to think I need to begin listening to my heart and not be consumed by the need to progress in my career. I think I've worked so hard to keep the pain away but it never disappears does it? It hits you when you least expect it.

Once Marcy's hands are bandaged, we slide into bed.

"Oh, let me message Sarah and Nora about tomorrow." She grabs her phone to send out a couple texts then puts it away. I already called Philip, my second in command, to set up some time off. He'll only call me if there is a breach in someone's security. He does well stepping into leadership if ever the need arises.

The heavy conversation still lingers in the air like echoes in an empty room, refusing to fade away. I know it's still not the right time to tell her about my private investigator following her or the fact that I've been funneling business to her to ensure her continued success. Using the 'trust card' earlier but not using it myself is going to bite me in the ass. I know it. I've got to find a way to tell Marcy everything without her freaking the fuck out.

Marcy snuggles in close as I wrap my arm around her, pulling her in tighter. The warmth of her arm around my waist, and the gentle weight of her head on my chest, ease the fears I have when she finds out the truth. I close my eyes, wishing there was an easier way to approach this subject with her. She's going to see it as a betrayal and I'm not sure I disagree with her. I let out a deep sigh trying to live here in the moment with Marcy.

"Hey, is everything okay?" Marcy runs her hand through my hair, pulling softly.

"Of course, it's just been a long day." I lean over kissing her forehead then return to my pillow. She hesitates for a moment then follows suit.

"Thank you for tonight. All of it. Even caring enough to follow me to the cemetery," she whispers after a beat.

"I told you I would always be there for you and I meant it, even all those years ago."

"I'm starting to realize that." Her foot drags across my leg before she drapes it over.

I love that she's getting more and more comfortable with me. She's the perfect fit beside me. Our bodies mold together like clay on a potter's wheel—soft, yielding, and shaped by the hands of intimacy. In this delicate dance, we become one, our contours fitting seamlessly, as if the universe conspired to create this perfect fusion. And so, we both become art—a sculpture of passion, a masterpiece of connection. In this moment, I find home.

Nineteen

Marcy

Weeks pass, weaving threads of connection into a tapestry of shared moments. Sam's laughter becomes a familiar melody. It dances through the rooms of his penthouse, echoing off walls. I often find myself laughing as well from the silly and completely lame dad jokes that Sam seems to have saved up just for me. Words spill forth—dreams, fears, childhood memories. Sam tells me stories about the military and shows the accompanying scars written across his skin. Mentions of Matt and the military become easier and easier to bear, even though I haven't gone to therapy yet. Maybe the night in the cemetery was enough to get everything off my chest. I've felt lighter since that night, even if I have slipped back into the habit of putting on the brave face everyone has come to expect. Sam sees the truth but he hasn't pressed the issue again.

We spend our nights either at Sam's or mine, although it's mostly his. He plans dates that blow any others I've had out of the water. I think that's his goal, he wants to wipe away any thoughts I have of other men. He doesn't realize they were just placeholders until my real prince came along. Nevertheless, he's making up for lost time, planning starry rooftop picnics, midnight rides with his top down and the heater on to keep from freezing. We've even taken to finding small second hand bookstores throughout the city.

But lately he's gone overboard with the flowers sent to my office, surprise lunch dates and even romantic dinners at fancy restaurants. Not that I'm ungrateful but he knows money doesn't impress me.

"You really hit the jackpot with this one, Marce," Sarah gushes as the newest bouquet arrives at the office. I try to smile at her as she plucks the card from the vase. The flowers seem to be getting more and more extravagant, bordering on insanity. Something doesn't seem right. This isn't the Sam I knew when I was younger. It's like he's forgotten the things that made him unique, instead turning into someone that tries too hard. I guess people change, sometimes imperceptibly, until one day, we look at them and wonder where the familiar contours went. Sam, once a constellation of quirks and idiosyncrasies, now seems to wear a different skin—a borrowed one, perhaps. The essence that made him unique—the way he laughed at obscure jokes, the freckles on his hands, the way he hummed while cooking—has faded like an old photograph left in sunlight.

Sarah hands me the card and I hesitate to even open it. I have this overwhelming feeling in my mind that he is doing all of this to hide a part of himself that he doesn't want to be seen. Or more specifically doesn't want me to see.

"Well, what are you waiting for? Open it! Let's see what Mr. Knight has to say today," Nora chimes in. I nod meanwhile wishing I didn't have to do this with an audience.

Sunshine,
Give your all to me, I'll give my all to you
You're my end and my beginning
Even when I lose, I'm winning
-John Legend
Yours,
Sam

"I think Travis needs some pointers from Mister Smoothe over here," Sarah swoons at the message in my hands. I murmur something unintelligible as I think about what the hell is going with Sam. I don't have the heart to tell her this is a copout. Nervously I shove the note in my pocket as I turn back to gathering my things. Staying here isn't going to solve anything. I don't know what's going on with him but I intend to find out.

"I'm taking the rest of the day, Nora. Call me if you need me!" I grunt as I try to pick up this new monstrosity of flowers.

"No problem, boss ma'am. Have fun," she chuckles as she wiggles her fingers goodbye like she knows something sweet is coming, but fear tugs at my heart as a bitter taste of uncertainty creeps in. I couldn't take it if Sam let me down again. My mind takes me back to my parent's funeral.

It's sunny out, which is the total opposite of how I feel inside. My mind is a storm threatening to spill out at any moment. Here I am again, in the same cemetery where my brother was buried. I was forced to come back here because some drunk driver had to cross lanes one rainy night and slam into my parents' car, killing them instantly. Never in my life have I felt more alone. No family. Barely any friends. I've isolated myself since Matthew's death and my friends gave up on me. So now it's just me.

I sit alone in the front row but I save the seat next to me by placing a card in the seat. I know it's silly to think he would come. Who knows if he even knows about their deaths? I haven't heard from him since he kissed me then ran. I thought he would have called or sent a message but of course he didn't. I held out hope that by some miracle he would be here for me. But he isn't.

Once the ceremony is over, I am forced to stand up front for people to come by to give their condolences. This is the worst kind of torture. These people don't know a thing about me or what I am going through.

I close my eyes, wishing I could slip off my heels and run as far and as fast as I could from this place. The weight of everything suddenly overwhelms me and I can't take it any longer. The only person I yearned to see was Sam but he let me down. I am utterly alone in the world now.

I feel like pieces of my soul are drifting through the wind like the universe blew my dandelion, leaving me with only fragments of myself.

The wind brings dark clouds over our heads. A sense of peace rises in my chest as the rain begins to fall. I take the sign from the universe and take off through the cemetery. People call my name but their voices drift off into the storm. I am on the run, my heels digging into the mud as I go. I slip out of them, leaving them behind. The rain pelts against my face, freeing me from the confines of my mind. I don't slow until I'm standing in front of Sam's family home. No one seems to be home so I go around back to the tire swing he used to push me in. The rain makes it easy to slip inside then I dig my feet in pushing myself higher and higher.

"Sam, where are you? Why aren't you here for me?" I yell through the rain, weeping as I swing along.

"You p-promised you would always be here for me. YOU PROMISED!" I scream. The swing comes to a stop after I give up pushing. I lay my head on the tire swing as I cry. Cry for Matthew. Cry for my parents. And cry for me. Rain always washes away some of the pain, even if it returns later. I can always count on rain to cleanse my soul for a time.

The drive to Sam's penthouse is filled with anxiety. He had a meeting across town this afternoon and expects me to be at work which will give me time to see if I can find out what he's been hiding from me. I wish with all my heart that there is nothing to find but I trust my gut and know something is amiss.

My keys clank into the bowl beside the door as I step in. The door closes behind, making me jump. Okay, I definitely don't like the idea of snooping but I've asked several times if everything was okay and he always responds that it is without looking me in the eyes. Enough is enough. He is supposed to be my partner in all things and that doesn't mean keeping secrets from me. He has to know that I could see through his fake façade.

I don't even know where to start until I pass his office on the way to the bedroom. A room that I have never been in before. He never gave me a tour of his office when he showed me the rest of the apartment, making this room a beacon for me to follow.

Before I enter, I look down the hall even though I know I'm here alone. My hand trembles as I open the door, as if expecting something to jump out at me. To my relief, this room looks like any typical home office. I pad over to the bookcase that spans an entire wall. The shelves are filled with countless books and sporadic framed photographs. One sticks out to me and I immediately pick it up, swiping away the dust that's gathered. My finger skims over Matthew and my mind instantly goes back to when this was taken. They had just graduated high school and I squeezed between them to make sure I was in the picture, even when my mom insisted she wanted just the graduates. Sam was the one to tell her it was alright then leaned down to let me hold his diploma as we smiled for the picture. It makes me smile that he kept this and makes me wonder why there are no pictures in the rest of the apartment. A question for another time, I suppose. Turning from the bookshelf puts me directly in front of the computer. He does most of his business here but there is a nagging feeling inside me to click the mouse.

Just as I assumed it's password protected. Lifting my foot to leave, I turn back to the screen. *What would Sam's password be?* I make several attempts until my birthdate pops into my head. *That's not it, right?* I type out 1-1-0-1-8-7 then press enter expecting to be declined access again but the screen changes to his home page. My heart accelerates as I take a seat in his chair to get a closer look.

The background is a picture of me in black and white that I can't recall where it was taken. Strange. I look at all the titles of his folders and am about to give up when I find one called 'sunshine'. My stomach plummets as I click open the folder, seeing thousands of black and white pictures of me from a distance just like the one on his background. They couldn't have been from Sam because he was still in the military until a few months ago. Someone was following me and Sam has the proof on his computer. Did he orchestrate this or did he find someone stalking me? Neither thought offers reprieve from the pit in my stomach. As I scroll though the pictures, I come across a folder entitled 'Big Apple PR'.

"What the hell, Sam," I mutter to myself.

Clicking on the folder opens documents and receipts. I'm not sure what I'm looking at until I pull them up one by one. The first is a proposal from years ago sent to Miles and Sebastian Knight asking them a favor. Sam recommended my "new and up and coming PR firm" to them requesting to give me a try as a favor to him. He prefaced it by saying their 'playboy lifestyles' needed to be handled and he had the perfect person to represent them.

It wasn't my hard work that landed them as clients, it was Sam. All the clients that followed suit after them had nothing to do with me but everything to do with Sam. Tears fall from my cheeks as I go through every single document as my heart breaks into a million tiny fragments on the floor around me. He was an anonymous donor that helped move my in-home business into a full blown empire with multiple employees.

My hand comes to my mouth as the things I thought I built were molded by someone else's hands. Samuel's hands. I never achieved anything. I've been a puppet in some sick twisted game he was playing.

I hear the front door open but I have no energy to move or respond when I hear him call out for me. The sound of his feet echo through the hall until he's standing at the open doorway. I don't look up right away. I can't.

"Fuck, Marcy, I can explain," he utters, taking large steps until he's quickly by my side. I pull away from his embrace as he leans over me. "Please don't do this," he pleads.

"I-um, I don't understand. What the hell are you doing with all this?" I gesture to the computer frantically.

"Did you have me followed? No, actually, *why* did you have me followed, Samuel?" I yell.

"Sunshine, calm down. I-" I cut him off before he can even finish whatever bullshit explanation he has.

"No. Don't you dare call me that! You don't have that right!" I scream as I jump from the chair, rounding the other side of the desk to put distance between us. My tears continue to fall from anger and sadness, mixing together until they drop to the floor.

"Marcy, I'm sorry. I fucked up. I was going to tell you everything." Sam runs his hands through his hair as he rocks back and forth in place, probably trying to decide what to say next.

"When exactly? When were you going to tell me, Sam? I've told you everything," I sob. "I've told you things I've never told anyone and all this time you've been hiding this! When did you think was the best time to tell me that you basically built my firm and had me followed for how long exactly?" I grip my hair in desperate frustration, needing the pain but already feeling it deep inside.

"Listen, I needed to tell you something and I never knew how." Sam looks at me with pain in his eyes. He runs his hands down his face then tries to step toward me, making me back away.

"There's something I didn't tell you about when Matthew died." My breath hitches in my chest at the mention of my brother. He hesitates but looks over to me with every emotion playing across his face.

"He, um, was lying there in my arms and I couldn't stop the bleeding," he laments as tears form in his eyes.

"I tried! Fuck, I tried to save him but I couldn't, Marcy! I couldn't save your brother but before he passed he made me promise that I would take care of you," he sobs, squeezing his eyes closed with his fingers.

A huge lump forms in my throat at the image.

"So, is that what you are doing now? 'Taking care' of me?" I scream. I can't hear anything over the pounding in my ears from my own heartbeat.

Samuel steps over to me trying to grasp my hands in his but I slap them away. I just can't. Before it was just the shit on his computer and now with everything he's said about Matthew, I can't touch him. I don't *want* to.

"Is that why you had me followed? Is that why you pushed clients into my lap? Has that been what all this has been about?" I gesture between the two of us, barely able to hang on to my emotions any longer. "You decided once you got back into town a couple months ago that you would, what? Insert yourself into my life?" I wail, wrapping my arms around myself.

"I've been in the states for two years," he confesses but I don't believe the words I'm hearing. He couldn't have been here that long. *Could he? Has he just been watching me this whole fucking time?*

"I don't think I heard you correctly. Did you just say that you have been in the states for *two* years?" I whimper feeling a surge of desperate emotions needing to wreak havoc on anything in their path.

"I didn't know what to say to you. I wasn't sure Matthew would want me with you no matter how desperately I needed you. A battle waged a war in my mind over what to do."

"You didn't know what to say," I repeat with an ominous chuckle. Sam doesn't say anything, just waits for my response. I leap toward his desk dragging my arms along until everything falls to the floor. Papers fly then land on the mess at my feet.

"So you were here when I needed you most. You were hiding behind your fucking computer when I was alone in the world. You were just sitting here building this security empire and never came for me."

He tries to speak but I hold up my hand immediately. I'm not done yet.

"You sent out a minion to follow me while you were in here safe from the real world," I huff incredulously. "You made a promise to my brother but did the bare minimum."

"I did this for you. Everything has always been for you, Marcy," he pleads. "You have to see that. I couldn't be there but I made sure you were taken care of."

"No, you could have been there, but you weren't. Why didn't you come for me?" I whisper. "I've been waiting on my prince just like you said, but you didn't come."

"I fucked up. I'm sorr–" I scoff.

"No! You can't undo what's been done. You got what you wanted from me, right? You wanted to fuck me, manipulate me, then bury me along with my brother." I tried to shove him but he doesn't budge.

"I can't undo it but forgiveness is a choice, Marcy!" I scoff as I continue to fight my way past.

"Stop!" he commands but it doesn't do anything to me anymore.

"You're wrong about us and you fucking know it. You're just running like you always do, dammit." The slap rings through the room before I realize what I've done. The pain radiates up my wrist, making my arm tremble.

"Get out of my way, Samuel!" I hit him repeatedly in the chest until he finally relents, allowing me to pass. Regret paints his face, but the only thing I can think of is getting as far from Samuel Knight as I can.

I run from the office grabbing my things. As I leave, it feels like a death. The words circle back in my mind, haunting me. Then all of the good memories flood in—the laughter, the tears, the late-night conversations. All of it now wrapped in a shroud of finality.

The words hang heavy in the air, a weight that presses against my chest. The penthouse, once familiar and comforting, now holds a different kind of silence—a void where laughter and shared moments used to reside.

I slam the front door, leaving a part of me behind. My once beating heart becomes sharp shards ground into the carpet. My blood probably accompanied the shredded organ.

Why did I leave? The question echoes louder now. Regret gnaws at the edges of my thoughts. Maybe it was necessary, maybe it was inevitable, but that doesn't make it any easier. The ache settles in, a dull throb that feels like mourning.

Outside, the world continues its usual dance. People hurry past, lost in their own lives. The sun dips lower, casting long shadows. I wonder if anyone else feels this way—like leaving was a little death, a part of themselves severed. A part of me was severed.

Maybe it was for the best, I tell myself. Maybe I needed this closure. But the ache persists, a phantom limb that reminds me of what is lost. I glance up at the sky, seeking solace in the vastness above. The stars blink, indifferent witnesses to my departure.

The adrenaline courses through my veins as I grip the steering wheel, the engine roaring in response to my desperate plea for escape. The world outside blurs into a chaotic mix of colors and shapes. Sam's face, etched with surprise and fear, lingers in my mind—a fleeting connection before darkness envelops me.

Twenty

Samuel

When I returned to my apartment after the meeting, I instantly knew something was amiss. Marcy's car was parked here, meaning she left work early. Opting not to tell me could only mean one thing. My mind wandered back to anything that I could have said to make her suspicious of me. I knew I wouldn't be able to pull off the secrecy forever but with each passing day, the truth seemed harder and harder to reveal.

A deep pit formed in my stomach as the elevator climbed the floors. My anxiety and fear rose along with the elevator, leaving me a bundle of exposed emotions once I reached my apartment. As I opened the door, Marcy's lavender and honey scent filled my mind like a drug, releasing some of the tension in my body. Here, the walls held memories—the laughter, the whispered promises, and the quiet moments when words failed us. All of it faded away when I realized my office door was open.

"Marcy," I call out as I slowly walk down the hallway. My controlled breathing techniques failed me the closer I got to her. It was as though I could already feel the turmoil and anguish running through her, down the tether that connected us.

I turned the corner into the office. Seeing Marcy there on my computer is the worst kind of fear. *How could I not have told her?* I wonder how I could have kept this secret— a deliberate omission. The unspoken words hang heavy, like unsent letters waiting for a reply. Regret, that relentless companion, whispers: *How could I not have told her?* The missed chances, the unspoken truths—they accumulate like dust, cluttering my mind.

Her tear drenched eyes shoot to mine as questions dance through them.

"Fuck, Marcy, I can explain," I confess as I take large steps to be within her reach. She moves as if frightened of me, shooting pain straight through my heart. "Please don't do this," I plead.

The relentless back-and-forth of the argument feels like a storm—winds whipping, lightning striking, and thunder echoing through my thoughts. Each word exchanged becomes a raindrop, soaking deeper into my conscience. And yet, absolution remains elusive—a distant shore beyond the tempest. Marcy has every right to be angry, demanding answers. This could have all been avoided if I would have told her everything up front.

The waves crash, each one a memory: the lies I told, the trust I shattered, the fragile bridge I burned. I watch the wreckage—the fragments of trust, the shards of connection—sink into the abyss.

Marcy throws everything from my desk in her rage but I don't care. Everything can be replaced. Everything except her. Papers flutter like wounded birds, pens roll off the edge, and my chair tips backward. She's a storm incarnate, and I'm caught in her path.

"You're wrong about us and you fucking know it. You're just running like you always do, dammit."

The fury and pain in her eyes is something I never want to see again. Without warning, a powerful slap sounds through the office. Her hand absorbed her pain and sought out vengeance. The taste of copper floods my mouth as my mind races trying to piece together the events that led to this moment. My decision to hide the truth hurt us both in the end.

The office quiets. Marcy's storm rages down the hall and out of the apartment, leaving behind a silence—an aftermath of the hurricane we were both caught in. My knees hit the floor clutching a picture in my hands that miraculously didn't crack. It was a moment caught in time. Marcy's flaming hair twists and turns from the wind making only her vivid green eyes shine through the chaos around.

I stand at the precipice, looking down into the ravine wondering how far the drop would be. *Will it hurt? Will my screams be heard or swallowed by the raging waters below?*

No! I take a step back knowing where I need to be. I can't give up. She is my forever. My whole life has been orchestrated for us to be together. I won't let that effort be in vain.

floor, I speed through my apartment and down the stairs, jumping over the handrails to lower levels to get to her faster. I have to get to her before she's gone forever.

I reach the ground floor, bursting through the doors in time to see Marcy's pained emerald eyes glance to me. In that suspended moment, the world blurs—the cacophony of the street, the rush of footsteps—all fading into insignificance. Until she blinks. One flutter of her eyes and the spell is broken. The dam of pandemonium breaks, flooding the street with witnesses—a chorus of gasps and exclamations.

"Marcy! Marcy!" I thunder over the commotion as I race to her car. My heart is in my throat as I approach the terrifying scene before me. Smoke hits my senses first then the unmistakable scent of blood. The same scent that has haunted me all these years from the battlefield.

"Someone call 9-1-1! Now!" My voice booms over the crowd causing several people to pull out their phones.

Her car was hit head on making it roll over in the street. My shoes skid across the debris as I drop to the ground by Marcy's side. She's suspended upside down from her seatbelt. The world narrows—a tunnel of debris, a spotlight on Marcy. Her car, crumpled metal, hangs like a pendulum. The scent of gasoline mingles with the metallic taste of fear.

Blood streaks her face forming a crimson river. "Marcy," I say, my voice raw but coated in panic. But she's beyond words—lost in the upside-down world. Her hair, once sun-kissed, now clings to shattered glass. I reach for her trembling hand—the skin cold, her pulse erratic.

The rain drums—a requiem. The street is a theater of chaos. Witnesses gather, their umbrellas like black flowers. They'll remember this, the moment when gravity betrayed us, when my life tilted.

I unclip her seatbelt, each second an eternity that stretches on. She slumps, her head lolling. Her eyes meet mine, maybe a plea, a question. But answers elude me. I'm just a witness.

"Stay with me," I whisper. But the world blurs—raindrops, tears. Marcy, the girl who laughed at sunsets, who whispered secrets in the dark, hangs between existence and oblivion.

I try to cradle her head as though it's a fragile moth's wing. The rain baptizes us—cleansing, but drowning. Her breath becomes a delicate thread. I want to tell her: "I've loved you since the first raindrop." But words are inadequate, like trying to catch smoke.

The sirens wail—a chorus of urgency. Rescuers descend from every direction. Their hands strong, their faces masked. They'll cut her legs free, mend her brokenness. *But will they mend mine?*

As they lift her, I watch, realizing for the second time in my life that there is nothing I can do. Matthew died in my arms, blood coating us both. It almost seems tragically poetic that I held his sister in the same position. But I won't give up hope. *I can't.* She is my lifeline to this universe and without her, I'll jump from the precipice.

Losing her would be the final nail in my coffin, two graves needing to be prepared. The lovers who couldn't be separated even in death, they will say. The lovers, bound by fate and circumstance, stand at the edge of eternity. They'll say we were twin souls—two halves of a fractured whole.

Twenty One

Samuel

The fluorescent lights flicker, projecting a Morse code of uncertainty. I pace like a caged animal—my shoes squeaking on the linoleum. The waiting room is like purgatory, holding my breath.

The door swings open. My heart leaps. *Is it her? Is it the doctor?* But it's just a nurse, clipboard in hand. She glances at me with sympathy in her eyes. How does she do this job? How can she stay so strong when she's surrounded by chaos, never knowing how it will end?

I want to scream: "Tell me!" But I swallow the words.

Back and forth, back and forth.

The chairs are hard and unforgiving, witnesses to my restlessness. Other families sit—each with their own story, their own prayers. It's as if we're bound by fear like a silent fraternity.

The door opens again. My pulse races. This time, it's a stretcher—a patient wheeled in. Not her. Not Marcy. But someone else's loved one. I close my eyes and send them a silent prayer.

The clock mocks me. The never ending ticking has synced with my heartbeats. Minutes stretch into hours. The walls—sterile and indifferent—absorb our collective anxiety. The scent of disinfectant mingles with the unmistakable tang of fear.

Once I arrived, it was too late to see her. I cursed and tried to throw my money around, anything for me to see her. I'd spend my entire fortune to see those emerald eyes shine up at me again.

She'd been rushed back into emergency surgery. Thankfully I had the forethought years ago to put my name as her next of kin contact or they wouldn't speak with me at all. The tiny silver lining from my stalking days, not that we would need that had I not been a coward.

That's how we got here in the first place. I grip my hair pulling the strands needing the pain to be refocused from my heart.

I want to trade places, to be the one suspended upside down. Me, it always should have been me. The thought takes hold of my mind and doesn't release once its claws have been dug in.

Marcy, the girl who danced in the rain, who traced the tattoos on my skin—now lies on an operating table, her life hanging in the balance. I grapple with the fragility of existence, the intricate dance of fate, and the profound impact people have on our lives. Marcy now rests in the hands of skilled surgeons, their actions guided by science and compassion. Hopeless and alone, all I can do is wait. Wait for the doors to open with news.

If Marcy returns, a promise echoes across time—a vow etched in the fabric of my soul. If Marcy's eyes flutter open, if her heartbeat steadies, I'll be there forevermore, a steadfast partner, a man shaped by love's crucible.

My promises are whispered under the fluorescent lighting, rippling across all existence. I vow to be more in every way. More of anything she needs. I'll be the shelter in her storms, the laughter in her quiet hours, the hand that steadies her steps. I'll learn the art of patience, the grace of forgiveness for myself and others, and the alchemy of shared dreams. I'll make this right, even if I die trying.

Twenty Two

Marcy

"Marcy, wake up sleepyhead. Oh, come on, sunshine," he chuckles. That voice. It's so familiar but I can't place it. My eyes flutter open even though I feel like I could sleep for a lifetime and it wouldn't be enough.

"There she is," he croons, tucking a strand of hair behind my ear. It's so bright, white coats everything as if the scene hasn't been painted yet. I turn my gaze to the voice and that's when I see him.

Matty.

My Matty.

My arms fly around him, a desperate embrace—a collision of longing and vulnerability. His warmth seeps into my soul, a slow infusion of hope. It's as if he carries sunlight in his veins, stitching together the fractures left by life's relentless hammer. He pulls me into his arms, smelling my hair like he always used to.

"I've missed you so much, sunshine," he whispers as my tears coat us both. I can't make words, I can only hold onto him like my life depends on it.

He pulls back enough to wipe the tears from my cheeks. His beautiful green eyes shine down on me, a sight I'd thought was lost forever. His bright red hair shines above me like a halo. My fingers trace the familiar ridges like a delicate dance across time. Each contour, each line etched into his skin, becomes a memory I'll carry like a secret talisman. The warmth beneath my touch, the way his jaw curves, the flutter of his eyelashes—they're all part of this fragile tapestry I'm scared will evaporate before me.

"H-how is this possible?" I whisper.

"I just needed to see my sister. You've grown up so much, sunshine. Where has all the time gone?"

"It was lost. The clocks moved but I didn't. I've been waiting on you. I've been waiting on you for so long, Matty!" I sob into his shoulder as he rocks me in his arms like he did when I would have night terrors as a child.

"I promise, I wanted to come back to you. I'm sorry I let you down. You have always been the light of my life and even in death I held on to that light. You saved me, sunshine. But now it's time for me to save you. The universe still needs you, Sam needs you. It was my time to go, but it's not yours." He cups my face. His soft hands almost melt away the pain of losing him all that time ago.

"I can't lose you again, Matty. It hurt too bad the first time." My hands tremble as mine cover his.

"You never lost me, sunshine. I've been with you every step of the way. Always."

"Can I stay here with you?"

"You have a new chapter to live. The pages are fresh, waiting to be splashed with new ink. Your's and Sam's story isn't over, sunshine. He's waiting for you. Your love has been written across the stars for a long time. He's the one, Marcy. He is your beginning and end." He chuckles softly, a melody I wish to save forever.

"You know, I always knew there was something special about the two of you. I guess it was destiny for him to come into my life so that he could be in yours."

"But he hurt me, Matty."

"But did he? He was there on the sidelines waiting, watching, helping. He did what I asked, more than you can understand."

"Forgive him," Matt insists.

"But–"

Matty looks at me with a stern expression I remember. "Forgive him, sunshine. He was going down a path of self destruction until you forged the pieces of his heart back together."

"Thank you," I sob. "Thank you for being my brother, my best friend, my everything."

"You will always be my sunshine, my only sunshine." Matt leans in, gently kissing my forehead.

"It's time for you to go now."

"No! I'm not ready! Please, I can't leave you–"

"Marcy, you are the strongest person I know. You can do anything. Now lay down like old times."

Matt snuggles behind me, forever the big spoon. "Everything will be okay, sunshine. Do you trust me?" I nod against the cool pillow beneath me.

"With my whole heart," I murmur, grasping his arm draped over me with all the strength I can muster.

"Embrace your fire. Let it guide you through the shadows." I let the words sink in as he hums a song he made up for me long ago.

My eyes close, feeling at peace as his song washes over me one last time.

"Close your little eyes and dream of good things, dream of good things, like I once did.

Close your little eyes and dream of good things, dream of good things, like I once did.

You can dream of dragons, witches or fairies so, just close your little eyes and dream of good things, dream of good things..."

"Marcy! Can you hear me?" someone shouts above me.

"Paddles ready?" he shouts.

"Clear!" Suddenly I feel this powerful warmth travel through my body straight to my heart.

"There she is! She's back!" I hear cheering surround me. The pain in my body radiates back to life and relief floods me knowing I made it back. I have a new chapter to write. Our chapter.

Samuel

Exhaustion, that silent companion, settles into my bones. It's more than weariness; it's the weight of waiting—the hours stretched thin, the minutes echoing with unanswered questions. My mind, a labyrinth of thoughts, navigates the twists and turns. Each tick of the clock, each heartbeat, becomes a move on the board. I strategize, analyze, and wonder if the next call will bring solace or upheaval.

I've forgone phone calls until I have information to share. Right now is a game of waiting. The anticipation hangs in the air, a taut string waiting to be plucked. My fingers, like restless birds, tap their silent rhythm on the chair. Each beat echoes the seconds of the damn clock above my head.

And then, the doors spring open again. The hinges groan, releasing me from the confines of waiting. Someone approaches—a figure blurred by distance, yet unmistakably real. Their steps, deliberate and purposeful, carry them straight toward me. This is it. My weary eyes try to read the emotions on his face but they remain locked away in a stony gaze.

Jumping from my chair causes a sudden burst of movement—a ripple in the otherwise static waiting room. The chair now lies sprawled on the floor, the commotion forces all eyes to turn toward me.

"How is she? How is Marcy Hillary?" I question rapidly as the doctor comes to a stop. The doctor stands before me, answers hang in the air between us. Finally, after what seems like a millennium, he responds.

"She made it through surgery, Mr. Knight. If you will come with me, I will explain everything further." Nodding seems like the only thing I can do at the moment as the news sinks in that she's at least alive. Tears of relief skim down my face from the emotional turmoil that I've been living with for several hours. I know I won't feel peace until I can see her, until I can wrap my hand around hers. I follow the doctor through the emergency room to a bank of elevators.

"She was given a room in the ICU so we will be able to monitor her overnight. Once she wakes from anesthesia she will be placed there." As we enter the elevator, he begins going over the details of her injuries.

"When she was brought in, her condition wasn't stable. The paramedics suspected she had a traumatic brain injury, which was confirmed with a CT scan upon arrival. However, Ms. Hillary had internal bleeding causing severe pressure on her occipital lobe. We were successful in relieving the pressure. Are you with me so far?" he asks with a genuine look of concern on his face. I know I must be pale with the news he's giving me. I can feel myself growing faint with every uttered word. I press myself against the wall to stabilize my trembling body that threatens to plummet to the floor.

"I am." I pause trying to collect myself. I've been through fucking war but hearing about my love's injuries makes me want to crumble to the floor. "This is a lot to take in." My hands scrub through my already disheveled hair trying to absorb everything he's telling me.

"As I was saying, we relieved the pressure but as we were stitching her back up, her body went into shock. This caused her body's blood pressure to drop significantly resulting in cardiac arrest. Fortunately, we were able to stabilize her after several attempts with the defibrillator. We won't know if there are any lingering effects to her brain until she wakes. Her brain was without oxygen for six minutes but Ms. Hillary is lucky to be alive."

As his words circulate in my mind, the air feels like it bursts from my lungs leaving me bereft and reeling. The elevator doors open making me rush from the confines of the small metal box.

"Mr. Knight, are you alright? Is there someone we can call for you to be with during this time?" His touch, firm and reassuring, anchors me to the present. Now that I know she survived surgery, it's time for me to do everything I can to help her, starting with her accommodations.

"No, thank you. I will make some calls once I have seen her. I would also like to have my doctor come in to go over her records just as a second opinion. I want Marcy to be placed in the best ICU room available with the leading team of doctors and nurses tending to her, no expenses spared. Do you understand? There will be a significant donation made to the hospital for your cooperation. I'm sure you understand how beneficial that would be for this facility."

"Yes, of course, Mr. Knight. I will get in touch with the hospital administrators to have those arrangements underway immediately. I will have a nurse come inform you when Ms. Hillary is in her room"

"Thank you. Now, would you please direct me to a quiet room where I can make some phone calls."

I settle into a comfortable leather chair, closing my eyes as the events of the day wash over me. Never would I have imagined I would be here where I woke this morning. It shows how life can change in an instant, as if I didn't already know that.

Pulling my phone from my pocket, I pull up Miles' contact. I need to let him know what's happening so he can share the news with Big Apple PR.

"Sammy! How've you been," Miles' voice booms from the speaker making me wince. My head is already pounding from the events of the day, I don't need yelling in my ear.

"Listen, I called because Marcy was in a car accident early this afternoon. She had to have emergency surgery but she's in recovery," I manage.

"What the fuck, man. Why didn't you call me sooner?"

"I didn't have any news to give you. I only just received the news myself that she was out of surgery."

"Sam, we're family. Seb and I would have come and waited with you. Hell, she's basically family too, especially now..." he trails off.

"I know. I just needed some time to process everything. I still haven't seen her yet."

"What happened to her? Have you spoken with her doctors?" Miles questions.

"Yes, just now. She had internal bleeding in her brain causing a pressure build up. They had to operate immediately." I don't want to add the part where she died on the table for a few moments. I can't speak that out loud. I don't want it sent out into the universe.

"Fuck man. Tell me what we can do."

"Can you get in touch with Marcy's office to let them know. Nora is her assistant so she can handle Marcy's schedule. Sarah also needs to know but I don't have her contact information." Honestly I don't want to make any more phone calls. The more Miles can take care of the better. I want all my attention to be on Marcy. I need it to be on Marcy.

"Consider it done. Anything else?"

"Can you call Dr. Petterson? I want him down here to look over her records to make sure they are doing everything they can. I trust him."

"I agree. I'll call him first. Text me if there is anything else that you need from me or Seb. I will fill him in on everything. I love you, Sam. We are here for you, don't forget that." Tears prick my eyes. The weight of emotions well up, threatening to spill over. Family has always been so important to Marcy, a lifeline that she cherished even when circumstances were harsh. Yet, I've been avoiding mine—a realization that hits me like a sudden gust of wind. Family fortifies you, like roots anchoring a tree, providing stability and nourishment. It's time to reconnect, to mend the frayed bonds and find strength in each other.

"Thank you, Miles. I appreciate it. I truly do. You're like my brother and I've been a shitty one to you and Sebastian. I promise to rectify that. This whole ordeal has given me time to think and there are things I need to change, beginning with my family. I love you, man."

"Sam, we knew you would come around eventually. You had shit to work through but I'm glad that you finally got your head out of your ass. Now, let me go so I can make these calls."

"Heh, thanks again. I'll call with updates."

Relief floods through me knowing Miles will ensure the news spreads to the appropriate people allowing me a small reprieve from the chaos of the day. However my anxiety spikes when I think of Marcy.

The news that Marcy died on that table today, even if only for a few moments, will forever haunt me.

Marcy. Died.

Died.

Almost gone forever.

Now the chair doesn't comfort me, its once supporting embrace is replaced by restless energy. I'm back on my feet, pacing like a caged animal. Helplessness wraps around me, a suffocating shroud. Desperation claws at my chest, and fear bubbles up, threatening to overflow. Sweat covers my forehead, from the intensity of my emotions. My heart races like a wild stallion. Erratic breaths mirror the chaos within. At this moment, I'm both the storm and the ship caught in its fury.

Fuck, it's happening again. Fear of the unknown overtakes my mind. The downward spiral is coming. I can feel it taking over my body, starting with my heart and shooting through the rest of me. I fall to my knees, gripping my hair until the pain erupts from the roots. Darkness envelops me in its sinewy grasp. I can't breathe. My heart is going to burst. Heat courses through me making my skin slick with sweat. I can't breathe. Flashes of Matt bleeding out in my lap plague my mind, playing over and over like a broken record. My hands fall from my hair.

Blood.

Blood is on my hands. Matthew's or Marcy's? I couldn't save them. I couldn't. I feel the bile coming. Abdominal cramps as I clutch my chest. Dry heaving.

Bile.

Or blood.

Death is coming. It's coming for me as punishment. I feel it. It's ripping my heart from my chest. I can feel each snap, each rip of my veins and arteries. My body falls to the floor. What is this chill? Is that it then? Am I dead? Gone? My whole body shudders without abandon. I've lost control of everything. Darkness is everywhere. I can't breathe.

Blood.

I smell it.

Take care of my sister.

Take care of Marcy.

Marcy.

Dead.

Failure.

With trembling hands, I pull my phone from my pocket. I can barely see the screen through the tears and my shaking hands. I can't see. I'm dying. Can she help?

"S-siri c-c-call doctorrr Willl–iamssss"

Ring.

Ring.

I can't breathe.

Too late.

Ring.

Blood.

"Hello, Samuel. How are–"

"H-h-help..."

"Take a deep breath. In through your nose then out through your mouth. Listen to the sound of my voice. Deep breaths. In through your nose out through your mouth. Hang on to the sound of my voice, Samuel. Are you still with me?"

"I c-can't–"

"Samuel, listen to me. Listen to me. Breathe. Deep breaths in through your nose then out through your mouth. Listen to my breaths. Do it with me. Samuel."

In.

Out.

In.

Out.

"Yes, I can hear you. Listen to my voice. It's not going to take you. You are safe. Breathe. Breathe, Samuel. In through your nose out through your mouth. Listen to me breathing deeply. You can do it. In and out. In and out."

In.

Air.

Out.

Fuck, I need air.

In.

Out.

"Keep going. I can hear you. Feel your chest. Your heart isn't gone. It's there. Beating. Keeping you alive. This is your mind, Samuel. Deep breaths."

My chest, my heart. There isn't a hole. My mind. Just my mind.

In.

Out.

In.

Out.

"Good, now tell me something you smell. Close your eyes and tell me three things that you smell, Samuel. Keep breathing."

"Ummm, fuck, I-I smell sterile, c-clean, some sort of c-cleaning de-detergent."

In.

Out.

"Good, Keep breathing. In through your nose and out through your mouth. Okay, now tell me what you see. What is around you?"

Brightness. It's too bright.

"I can't–"

"Samuel, listen to my voice. Breathe. Yes, breathe just like that. Open your eyes. Focus. Tell me what you see."

"Sofas, chairs, magazines, television–"

In,

Out.

"Are you still with me, Samuel?"

"Yes, here. I'm here. It's coming down. It's-I can breathe. I can breathe."

"Good, just focus on your breathing."

I nod. My eyes fall closed as I continue the breathing pattern.

In.

Out.

"You're doing good, Samuel. I can hear you breathing."

In.

Out.

In.

Out.

"My breathing is better. My heart rate, fuck," my watch is vibrating telling me it's too high. "It's still elevated but it's better than it was."

In.

Out.

In.

Out.

"Check in, Samuel. What's your color?"

In.

Out.

"It's yellow-green. I'm-I'm okay. I'm coming down. Fuck, I haven't had one in so long." I wipe my forehead with my sleeve.

"You did the right thing. Even if it wasn't me that answered, you would have been taken care of. I'm glad I was on call tonight."

"Thank you, Dr. Williams. I need to schedule more sessions. I know I've missed several. I thought I was better because my girlfriend took the nightmares away and I haven't had the urge to drink until I passed out, but it's not fair for me to lean on her. I need to take care of myself for her sake."

"I'm glad you came to that realization before things spiraled more out of control. Would you like to come in next week?"

Exhaustion. That's all I feel. My body is weak. That attack pulled every ounce of energy I had left. But I have to see her. I have to see Marcy.

I check my watch, seconds ticking by like slow heartbeats. Waiting for someone to come tell me that Marcy is in a room and that I can see her. The sterile hospital corridors echo with anticipation, the scent of disinfectant clinging to the air. If someone doesn't come soon...my patience is already fraying at the edges, unraveling like a worn thread. I'll go out there and demand some answers. Determination fuels my resolve, a fire burning beneath my skin. The need to see her is overwhelming, a tidal wave threatening to engulf me. I cling to the surface, trying to stay calm. Breathing deeply. Each inhale a lifeline, each exhale a prayer.

"Mr. Knight, if you want to come with me. Marcy is awake and in her room," the nurse announced, gesturing for me to follow her.

"Thank you! I was about to come ask for information on her. How is she?" I ask as we walk through the bleak halls, passing random pictures hanging on the walls.

"She's still very groggy, going in and out of sleep. She's on pain medication that is keeping her sedated. She broke several ribs along with the injury to her head so she will need some time to recover." I just nod. My stomach rolls when I think of her hanging upside down in her car, blood streaming down her face. The image will be forever etched into my mind.

"Right in here, Mr. Knight. Press the call button if you need anything. My name is Alicia, by the way."

"Thank you, Alicia. I'll call if we need anything." She closes the door behind her and my hands tremble as I grasp the curtain, pulling it open.

My heart sinks when I see her lying there covered in various bandages. Her frail form, once vibrant and full of life, now lies hooked up to so many machines.

Slowly I walk to her side, brushing a lock of hair from her beautiful face. Her emerald eyes flutter open and lock on mine. She takes a deep breath as she tries to raise her hand for me.

"Sam..." she whispers.

"Shh, princess. I'm here now and I'm never leaving. Now rest my love." My hand intertwines with hers. The world tilts back on its axis, as if acknowledging this pivotal moment. She's going to get through this. We will get through this.

Together.

Always together.

The world could be collapsing around us but the only thing of importance is Marcy being alive.

Twenty Three

Marcy

After a few weeks, I'm starting to feel like myself again. The pain from my ribs has begun to fade. Sam took time off from work and has been by my side through it all, just like he promised in the hospital. His unwavering support and promise to be there during this challenging time demonstrates his compassion and loyalty. Whether it's through comforting words, acts of kindness, or simply being present, Sam has undoubtedly made a positive impact on my healing journey. When I was released he insisted, or rather declared, that I would be living with him and not just as I healed. He made sure I knew this was permanent. That we were permanent. I tried to give him a hard time but I knew in my heart that being with him was where I was meant to be. I was surprised when we got home and all my things were already there and put away. I just rolled my eyes, knowing damn well he probably did all this while I was still sedated.

While I was in the hospital Sam and I talked about the disastrous argument from his office the day of the accident. I can still see the fear in his eyes when he thought I wouldn't forgive him.

"Sunshine, please forgive me. I was wrong and scared." He squeezes my hand, rubbing his thumbs in soothing circles.

"At first I convinced myself that I was looking after you for him. That I was doing what a big brother would do and the more it went on the less it became about watching for him, because you fucking consumed me, Marcy. You became my focus, to get out of bed and pretend to be a human inside a hollowed shell. I thought if I waited and watched long enough that some part of me that's long been broken and missing would finally fix itself and I would be worthy of you because that's all I have ever wanted. Heaven and hell be damned." Tears pour from my eyes as his words echo through my mind.

"I only helped with your business because I wanted to see you flourish without pressure. I knew you would succeed on your own, but you've had to work so hard your entire life that I wanted to do something to ease the weight on your shoulders. Never did I have the intent that you couldn't do it on your own. Believe me, sunshine. I know your drive. I only wanted to build you up even if you didn't know it was me helping." Before I could respond, he continued.

"Punishing ferocity. That is the only way I know how to love. My heart, scarred and battle-worn, has learned to fight for what it wants. And it wants you—the girl with the haunted eyes, the one who carries the weight of the world on her shoulders. I am completely and utterly in love with you. You are my obsession. My drug. My fire. I need you more than the air in my lungs." Sam gets up to cup my face.

"Please forgive me. I'm begging you, sunshine," he whispers softly against my lips. He presses a gentle kiss to my temple then gets on his knees beside the hospital bed. My hand is still grasped tightly in his hand.

"I know you love Japanese pottery with the gold glue that mends the broken pieces." I nod not sure where this is going.

"I will repair your heart and trust in me by restoring your broken pieces, one by one. I'll be the gold glue that fills the gaps in your heart making you stronger, unique, resilient. Please give me the chance to show you how devoted I am to you. Your broken heart will be more beautiful than ever, shining with the gold of my love."

I take a deep breath, remembering the conversation with Matty. I know what I have to do even if it scares me. I'm scared to be hurt again but even more scared of losing Samuel from my life. I have to take a leap of faith and trust that he will be there to catch me.

"Okay," I murmur above the beeping of machines surrounding us. Sam jumps to his feet, relief written on his face.

"I will take care of you for the rest of your life. I promise. I'll always be here for you." Sam brushes some hair from my face, peppering kisses along my forehead then down my cheeks. Finally his lips press against my lips, electricity jolts through my body causing chills to cover my skin.

"You know I love you too, right?" I whisper as his lips brush softly against mine before trailing along my jaw. Then he whispers in the shell of my ear, his warm breath sending chills over my entire body.

"Those are the most beautiful words I have ever heard." He crashes his lips down on mine tenderly, not to disturb the bandages on my head. His lips whisper promises to me–silent vows.

"Say it again, princess," he pleads.

"I'm in love with you, Samuel Knight. I have been since I was young and didn't even know what love was, but I knew. You have always been the only one for me. That's why I waited for you. I hoped you would come, like you promised."

"I'm sorry it took me so long, but I'm here now. I'm here, sunshine. You're mine."

"Yours," I agree.

I never told him about the dream or experience I had with Matty. It's a precious memory that I will cherish the rest of my life. It was a beautiful gift I was given. It finally made me feel like it was okay for me to experience happiness without him.

My therapist tells me to keep a journal, it's like giving my mind a safe outlet to express what's going on inside. It helps keep the anxiety at bay.

"Hey princess, where do you think you're going?" Sam comes up behind me, embracing me in his strong arms. I sink into his warmth, loving the safety only he can give me.

"I was going to get some fresh air on the balcony, why?" He leans down, nipping and kissing my neck.

"Because I had something to tell you," he whispers. I turn in his arms to look up at his glistening hazel eyes staring down at me.

"And what would that be?" I ask.

"The Matthew Hillary Foundation is a go! We got all the backers we needed. Miles and Sebastian spread the word and it all came together. This is really happening. We are going to help so many soldiers, sunshine!" Without hesitation, I jump into his arms knowing he will always catch me. He spins me around the room as we laugh together. This foundation has been our sole focus since I was released from the hospital. Big Apple PR will be representing it and I can't wait to launch it to the public.

"I'm so proud of you, Sam. You are a true hero. Don't ever forget that."

Twenty Four

Samuel

Dr. Petterson finishes up his exam of Marcy, clearing her for normal activities. Thank fuck because I've been craving her body and lying next to her every night was the worst kind of torture knowing I couldn't take her.

"Thank you again for coming, Doc," I repeat as we walk to the front door.

"Not a problem. You Knights sure keep me busy," he chuckles.

"Never a dull moment around here that's for sure," I reply.

"You've got my number if anything else comes up." He heads out of the door toward the elevator. I wait until he's inside to close the door and lock it.

Turning around, I see Marcy leaning against the bedroom door in nothing but a black babydoll. Her beautiful long red hair cascades down the front of her body, sweeping along the sides of her voluptuous breasts.

"Seems like someone is ready for their punishment." Her cheeks flush but she looks at me questioningly as I walk closer. "If I remember correctly, someone disobeyed me," I tsk, running the back of my hand down her soft cheek.

"I didn't do–"

"Nu uh. You continued your little temper tantrum that day and stormed out of here." Fire flares in her eyes as the memories of that day come flooding back in.

"I was mad. You can't be ser–" I press my lips to hers, silencing the argument before it begins.

"You may have been mad but then you put yourself in danger by storming out of here. I won't tolerate you hurting yourself, Marcy." The air hangs heavy with anticipation. The room, dimly lit, seems to hold its breath, waiting for the inevitable. She stands there, her eyes wide, pupils dilated, waiting for her instructions. She isn't getting out of this one. Not with all the pain and suffering we both endured because of her rash decision. Tonight she'll be learning about consequences. She pulls her bottom lip into her mouth, knowing exactly what she's doing to me. *Naughty, naughty girl.*

"Now, be a good girl and go get on the bed, ass up for me," I whisper along her neck, sending shivers through her creamy, delicate skin.

"Yes, *sir,*" she murmurs as she turns to walk toward the bed, swaying her ass purposefully along the way. She won't be such a brat after I get my hands on her.

I follow her into our room, throwing my shirt in the hamper. Marcy does as she's told, crawling on the bed positioning herself on all fours with her beautiful round ass pushed out for me, the babydoll slides from her ass and pools around her waist.

Leaving her to wait with anticipation, I head toward the closet to retrieve a few items I purchased for the occasion. I smile as I reach up top to pull the boxes down knowing this will be a night for the books.

"What a good girl you're being, still holding that position like I said," I praise as I set down the toys on the bed behind her so she can't see. My fingers run lightly over her skin, along her calves, up her thighs, over her ass, across her back then tangling in her hair pulling her head up to face me. Her body arches beautifully under my hands.

"You're fucking stunning, princess." I drop her hair as I band my hand around her throat. Her whimpers vibrate through, shooting an electric spark straight to my cock.

"I've got some surprises in store for you tonight. Remember your safeword?"

"Yes, Mr. Knight," she purrs. My lips crash down on hers with a punishing ferocity. She gasps against my mouth. Her lips are soft, yielding, but there is a fire within her—a hunger that matches my own. I only release her when I know she's about to pass out. Her eyes darken with desire as she nibbles on her swollen lip. She's ready.

Spreading the items out on the bed, I know exactly what we will be starting with. She tries to look over her shoulder but she won't be able to see. She's only going to feel.

"Remember to relax, sunshine. If you don't it'll only make your torment longer for my pleasure." I pick up the tube of lube and slick two fingers. I grab a handful of her ass until she squeals, knowing it won't be the last one heard from her sweet lips.

"We're only getting started."

Pulling her cheek to expose her ass. She shuffles on her knees, parting her thighs. My fingers dig into her flesh, my eyes catch sight of her dripping slit, it would be so easy to divert and give into my tongue's and cock's demand.

Stiffening in my resolve I swipe the cool gel on her ass. My hand cracks down when she tries to shift away.

"Marcy," I tsk. Her reply is muffled in the blanket.

I move closer to her on the bed, invading her space, making her *feel.* I part her thighs again, widening her position. I press my knee against her calf, anchoring her exactly where I want her.

"Breathe." I push my middle finger against her resistance. I feel her thigh shake but I don't ease up the pressure.

"Fuck."

"Yes, princess. That's exactly what's happening," I chuckle darkly. My middle finger presses clear past the first knuckle and further than the second until my palm is pressed flush against her skin.

I smirk at Marcy's muted muffle into the sheets. My cock throbs while she tries to move away from my unyielding invasion.

The more she bucks the deeper she pushes my finger. I crook my finger upwards and she stills. Like the beautiful puppet she is beneath me, her back bows and her breathy moans echo through the room.

"That's it, fuck back against my hand."

Her hips roll and I slip a second finger against the first. Her muscles grip tightly, pulsing in time with her moans and rocking.

"You're going to strangle my cock, sunshine. Are you going to rock back this eager when I fuck your freshly spanked ass?" She whimpers at my words. Releasing her hip, I reach out and grab a fist full of her hair and wind it around my hand.

The grip forces her to arch to me and rest her full weight on my fingers.

I lean in and kiss her temple softly. "You're taking it so well. That's my good girl, I know you can. One more, baby." Marcy's pitiful whine goes straight to my cock.

Fumbling with one hand, I reach and add another dribble of lube over my slick fingers. Sawing them back and forth, slipping my ring finger in with the first two until it forces her wider.

My thumb slips between her thighs and presses inside her wet warmth.

Marcy's movements stop, her back bows and her fingers dig tightly in the fabric beneath them. "S-sir..."

"More? Yes, I agree." I let go of her hair and spank her cheek.

She cries out and any movements of retreat are snuffed by my weight and the way my fingers sink deep into her core.

"Sit up," I command.

Marcy grabs my arm for support and I kiss her soundly, swallowing her moans while she rides toward what she hopes will be her release.

"Do. Not. Come," I warn.

Her bright green eyes meet mine in desperation and I can't wait to taste every frustrated tear she sheds.

"You won't sit for a week if you do." Even though that's already in the cards for her.

I hold up a medium sized plug to her gaze. "Open," I instruct, marking to memory the way she shudders and clenches against my slowly thrusting fingers at my harsh tone. Pushing the plug past her lips, I study her every reaction.

"Suck. Run your tongue over it and know that'll soon replace my fingers. Leaving that tight, needy hole open when you take the first part of your punishment."

Her eyes flutter closed on a moan. Her chest moves rapidly, her pulse erratic.

I can't resist leaning in and running my tongue over the slope of her shoulder to her neck. She tastes of honey and sin. I press my teeth against her skin, wanting to mark her creamy skin. Marcy stills beneath the pressure and the tension in her thighs eases; opening herself further to me.

"I'll never get enough of you. Fuck!"

I hold the T-base of the plug between my fingers. She runs her tongue over the intrusion, her eyes fill with a mixture of hesitation and desire.

"Let go."

Marcy pulls away and swipes a drop of spit from her lip with her tongue.

"There's no way that'll fit," she argues, her eyes pleading.

"Stubbornness and physics are against your argument. Relax, princess. Lean forward, palms flat on the bed."

"Sam..."

"That's not how you address me right now. Is it, sunshine? Do you think it's wise when I can simply do this–" I spread my fingers inside her tight ass and brush the pad of my thumb against the opening of her pussy. "–and remind you that you're not coming until I split you open with my cock."

"Sir," she corrects, rocking her hips toward the intrusion. "We can have spanking and butt fun later," Marcy pleads, her head tipped back, her eyes meeting mine. "You can punish my pussy with your cock, sir. Please! I need to cum."

"That's not how this works, sunshine," I tsk. "But I promise you'll regret those words someday."

Marcy's cheeks flame as she looks away.

"You're supposed to remember punishments, princess. It seems my hand wasn't enough last time and as your dominant, I won't make that mistake again. I plan to correct you the way I should have."

"Sir?"

"Look at me," I urge.

She does quickly.

"I'm not mad at you. None of this is from anger. You need to understand that, Marcy." I brush her hair from her eyes. "I would never harm you, but I will hurt you within your limits."

She can live with a blistered ass but I *can't* live without her.

"Your safeword is always an option, don't forget that."

"I know. Okay. I do. What are you going to use?" She glances nervously at where I placed the implements earlier. Some are part of my original plan for the evening. The rest is to gauge her reaction and assure her that no matter how or where I push her limits, I'll never knowingly break them. Or her.

"No belts, crops, or other implements tonight. You'll take six strokes from the paddle and you're going to say thank you after every one. You will be given three seconds for your reply or the count starts over and I will add another to the tally. Do you understand?"

"Yes, sir."

"Good, now be an obedient little slut and present your ass before you lose the kindness of this plug and get my cock as punishment. Spoiler, sunshine, it's not as nice or teasing as my fingers."

One of these days that beautiful sassy mouth of hers is going to get the punishment fuck she'd regret.

She was mine to mold and forever to cherish. There'd never be another soul that would see her this way. Her curvy body was on display for every dirty and depraved thought either of us would have.

Marcy's body relaxes as she rests on her forearms, her forehead presses against the mattress as though it will hide her moans of need. The sheer black fabric skates down her body with her movement, releasing her breasts for my viewing.

"Such a beautiful sight," I croon. "Might as well let the rest of it fall off. I need to see all of your creamy skin on display for me."

I pull my fingers from inside her and pick up the plug, taking my time and slicking it from tip to base. I hold it between my fingers, satisfied with the long gentle curve of the base. Ensuring that it won't slip or be uncomfortable at any point during her paddling, I place my hand on her back and position the plug at her lubed hole.

"I'll go slow like I did my fingers and I promise, good girls like their ass split open and filled too."

Marcy gasps and I use the distraction to slip the first third past her tight muscle. Her back bows but she holds her hips still, her breathing is rapid but she doesn't dare move away from the intrusion.

"That's it, it's more than halfway. Are you ready for the next knot?"

She shakes her head but quickly changes to a frantic nod from the renewed pressure of the toy as I push it deeper.

I drag my nails over the curve of her ass and dip between her thighs to cup her pussy.

It squelches and gushes against my hand and just as I expected, she arches her back toward my touch and pushes the next bulb stretch into her.

"What a fucking goddess. Wet, needy, soaking my hand while I fill this virgin ass."

Her mouth opens wordlessly and she rises from her arms as I wrap my forearm around her middle. Twisting her body, I grab her breast and press her back against my chest to hold her steady.

"You've got two more tapers to go, baby." I hungrily lick my lips, watching her expression for any signs of distress. My cock throbs and I still, taking the moment to reign myself in at the sight of her moaning and begging. "Use your words."

"It burns when it–*oh fuck!*"

I push the next notch in and press the last and largest one against the ring of her asshole.

Marcy grabs my forearm to steady herself at the sudden invasion. "I'm so full! I can't."

"You can," I punctuate my words with a steady pinch to her nipple. Flicking with the tip of my finger, then pinching and rolling the stiffened bud. I repeat the soft soothing motions and she begins to relax.

Her head rests against my shoulder, her soft mewls whispering against my skin, finally accepting she has no control and can't sway my pursuit.

I kiss the top of her head and increase the pressure of the toy. "Look at me."

Marcy licks her lips, swallowing a gasp but meets my eyes.

"I know you feel it. When the widest part gets pushed against your hole, it will spread you open."

She nods.

"When it feels like too much as the thickest part stretches making you want to resist, push it away until it doesn't burn and pulse."

Another nod, and I notice the flush on her face.

"Enjoy it while you can. Once I slip my cock inside you there'll be no relief."

Her moans are half awe and half fear.

"That's right. You'll be filled with every fucking inch, princess. Bouncing and crying, begging me to let you come."

"Come, yes, please. I want to come!"

"What is your pussy weeping more for? The thought of my hips brushing against your freshly reddened ass..." I bring my face closer to hers, drinking in every facial expression. "Or knowing that I'll be the only one to fill, fuck, and make you cum from filling your asshole like the needy little whore you are?"

I punctuate my words and slide the plug fully into her ass.

"Good girl. Know that next time you get punished, my cock and cum before the plug. And no orgasms."

Marcy's shuddering cry echoes through the room as she falls forward and lays with her cheek against the mattress. She stays on her knees, her plugged ass high in the air.

"You're a fucking vision." I run my hands over the curve of her ass and up to her shoulders. Shifting on the bed, I reach for the paddle and set it in her line of sight.

"There's more?"

"Yes there is. Now be a good girl and tell me you want it."

"I'm a good girl and I'd like an orgasm or four please."

"Duly noted. Now ask."

"Please sir, fuck me."

"Seven spanks with the paddle you say?"

"What?!" she screeches.

"I can make it eight..."

"Please paddle me, sir. I'd like my punishment please."

"I love when you beg, princess."

I pick up the paddle and trail the soft leather over her hip, the curve of her breasts and belly. I round up onto her ass then tap the area several times to bring the blood to the surface. Prepping the skin will prevent bruising and keep the integrity of the sting without creating a biting pain.

I want her to secretly crave it, not fear it.

Marcy wiggles her ass against the paddle, inching her thighs closer together to gain friction.

Swinging the paddle down sharply against her thigh she quickly stills and lets out a frustrated and needy sigh. "Please! May I have my spanking now!?"

"Quite the eager girl. Are you in a hurry, sunshine?"

"Yes. The faster you can put that down the faster you will fuck me."

"I do love how fiery and demanding you are." Seeing her this way, needy and begging, makes me want to abandon my plans to sink into her tight cunt now. Her desperate whimpers send electric bolts straight to my cock.

Dropping the paddle between us, I thread my fingers in her hair and pull her in for a deep kiss. My tongue invades her mouth as she willingly submits beneath me.

Her body automatically turns toward me but I grab her hip and still her movements. My hand reaches back, grabbing her ass tightly.

I move my carefully placed fingers and brush along the plug, stoking the fires that are turning her into a beautiful mess beneath me.

Hooking my finger under the curved base, I tug gently to increase the tension.

Marcy moans against my mouth, shifting on the bed to release the pressure of the plug.

I bite her bottom lip making her whine softly with need. My hand cracks across her sit-spot and the force ricochets against the plug stilling her movements.

"I need," she pleads.

Her needy moan does me in.

"Okay, sunshine." I cup her jaw and kiss her softly. "I can't help myself, you're so beautiful when you're wet and needy for me." I brush my lips over hers again. "I'm so fucking addicted to you."

"Yours."

"Yes, you are."

I pull away and help her shift to her previous position on her forearms and she presses her forehead against the bed.

"Don't forget to breathe and your requirements."

My fingers wrap around the handle of the paddle, flexing as I study her luscious curved ass.

I land the first strike on her right cheek and I'm automatically counting the seconds in my mind.

"Thank you, Mr. Knight!"

The second lands harder on the left cheek.

"Thank you, sir!"

I land the third across both.

"Fu-thank you, sir!"

"Good girl. Halfway."

Marcy's back arches and she nods with a soft whine.

Four and five are met in quick succession to the backs of her thighs, giving Marcy no reprieve.

She stumbles over her double thank you's, her breath caught on a sob.

The final stroke lands against the plug effectively mixing pleasure into her pain.

"Thank you, Mr. Knight!!" she cries. Her body sags against the mattress.

Setting the paddle down, I prop myself on my elbow next to her panting form. My fingers run across her sweat-slick skin. Her breathing picks up when my nails score across the lines of fire.

"Are you still with me, princess?"

"Yes, sir," she whispers, her eyes wide and glassy. A lone tear runs down her cheek as I trace the trail with my thumb. I caress her cheek soothingly until her eyes focus on mine. They are the brightest green when filled with my tears.

"What was the lesson?"

"No danger for me or you light my ass on fire."

"I'll take that as an acceptable answer, this time." I brush her hair from her shoulder, pressing my lips against her warm skin.

"How do you feel, sunshine?"

"I need you. My skin is on fire. Mr. Knight, please. I can't take it anymore."

"That's my needy little slut. I've got to have you."

"Does that mean my ass, sir?" she whimpers her question.

"You don't know how bad I want to sink my cock into that snug little hole."

I move my body over hers, pinning her wrists with one hand and straddling her thighs.

Wrapping my fist around my hard cock, I brush the tip between the cheeks of her ass then lower until she coats me in her wetness.

"Hearing you beg, sunshine. I can't wait anymore. I need you."

She writhes beneath me as I notch the head of my cock against her opening.

"Wait, you're n-not, *oh fuck*!" Marcy's realization flits across her beautiful blissed-out face. "It's too much! Sir, oh!"

With one hand on the mattress and the other in Marcy's hair, I thrust my hips against her plugged ass, my cock sinking into her clenching pussy. Her cries hitch in her throat as she chokes back a sob, her arm blindly grasping for me, sinking her fingers into my skin. The bite spurs my thrusts to a faster pace. Hard punishing thrusts, my cock sinks into her gushing cunt. Every time I bump against the plug she cries into the pillows. My hips roll and my locked hips trap her beneath me.

"Where's that bratty mouth now?"

Marcy's breath is heavy against the mattress as I continue to thrust into her. I can feel her tight cunt already clenching around me. I love that my girl likes the pain only I can give her. Her gushing pussy is proof of that.

"I think we need a change of scenery." I smirk as Marcy looks back at me, questions swirling in her mind. I slide out of her tight channel, instantly missing her warmth. My hand goes out to her to help her off the bed. Pulling her along, I press her against the cold floor to ceiling windows in our room.

"Fuck! It's c-cold!" she whines.

"We'll heat it right up." I kiss behind her ear as I slide her palms on the glass. I grasp her hair, pulling her head back to me.

"Are you ready to get fucked where anyone can see us? Anybody walking on the street can look up and see your pussy taking this fat cock." She nods with a new blush coating her cheeks. Well, I'll be damned. My little vixen likes to be watched. I can't wait to find out everything she desires.

I press her front to the glass, eliciting a deep moan.

"I've got a naughty girl. You like this don't you? You want them to see your man fucking you like the dirty slut you are?"

"Yes!"

I roughly kick her thighs open, holding her arms in place then slam inside. This angle shifts the plug, making her pussy even tighter.

"You're going to take what I give you because you trust that I know what you need."

"Yes, sir," she gushes. My thrusts increase until her body is helpless but to bounce back against me to accept more of my cock. I wrap my other arm around her tummy, keeping her in place as I pound deeper.

"That's my beautiful good girl," I praise.

I hum against her throat, "It's not the plug in your ass that you have to worry about now." I trail hot kisses across her neck and shoulder, giving her enough time to stew in my words.

"You should be worried how full I'm going to fuck this pretty cunt of yours with my cum." She moans, chalking my words to bedroom talk and I feel her muscles tighten around my shaft.

"Fuck, you're the perfect little toy, princess. You're just so responsive." I bite the back of her neck and kiss my way to press my lips against the shell of her ear.

"I'm your good girl! I'll need your cock, sir!"

"Say it again."

"I'm–" her breath hitches, as I rest my full weight against her back.

"Hmm? What was that?" I whisper.

"I'm your good girl, sir," she pants. I know she's close and all I would have to do is tweak her swollen nub to make her see stars. She was good for me after all so I decide to give her this one.

"How bad does my girl need to come?" My hand slowly travels down her belly until I'm almost where she needs me to be. I begin rubbing circles above her clit, almost where she wants me, but not quite.

"Please, Mr. Knight," she gasps as my fingers connect with her sensitive area. It only takes a few strokes and her pussy begins squeezing me so hard I feel like I could pass out just from the pressure.

"Ouuuu...FUCK!" she screams as she explodes around me. Her body trembles as I continue to work her through her orgasm. Wave after wave of pleasure rolls through her as she presses her ass back against me harder, needing me deeper. Her release gushes out as I continue my thrusts.

It doesn't take long for the tingle in my spine to begin, my impending orgasm right on the horizon.

"I'm going to fill this pussy up so much that you are dripping for days." Marcy only nods, too strung out to reply.

"I'm so glad you agree since they took your birth control out at the hospital." I chuckle darkly wishing I could see the expression that crosses her face.

"Wha–" I grab her face and crash my lips to hers. She takes everything I give and even fights for control. *Heh, oh sweet Marcy. That will never be the case.*

"It had to be removed because they were worried about blood clots after your surgery," I groan at the thought of filling her womb with my seed.

"But they never–" No, they didn't mention it at my request. I nip the base of her neck then suck to ensure I leave my mark.

"I can't wait to breed this cunt. When your belly begins to swell with my child, mmm, fuck! I won't be able to control myself around you. Not like I can anyways, right?" My balls tighten and after two more thrusts, I'm emptying myself inside her. Jet after jet of cum dumps into my girl. Chills run through me at the thought that I could get her pregnant tonight. The thought shoots more cum from my cock.

Coated in sweat, I pepper kisses along her shoulders and up her neck. "You did such a good job, sunshine. I'm so proud of you." I slowly pull out then turn her around so I can see her beautiful face. My cock is still hard, ready for the next round but I don't think she can handle more.

Pushing her hair from her face, I lift her chin so she looks up at me.

"You didn't use your safeword," I acknowledge.

"I didn't," she smirks, "don't you know gingers have a high pain tolerance?" she giggles as she wraps her arms around my neck, pulling me down to her.

"You're such a brat, you know that?" I chuckle as I lift her ass in my hands, pressing her back against the window.

"So I've been told." She squeals when I thrust back inside her hot, wet cunt. I press my face into her neck as I fuck her hard and slow. I want to take my time because I never want it to end.

"Princess, I see so many punishments in your future. That mouth of yours is going to get you into some deep shit one of these days." I smile against her skin, knowing I can't wait for that day to come. I might be a sadist but my little sunshine wants as much as I'll give. She will match me every step of the way.

Twenty Five

Marcy

I feel like I've been put through a fucking triathlon with the severe exhaustion but extreme satisfaction. Never in my life have I experienced anything like Samuel Knight. I know I was a virgin before him but I'm pretty sure his brand of fucking could be compared to an ultimate sporting event.

"How is that bath feeling, my love?" Sam whispers, leaning over to kiss my forehead. After our scene, Sam carried me to the bathroom gently. It's amazing how quickly he can go from the punishing dom to the loving/aftercare dom. I'm not complaining because I love both and all the others in between.

"It's amazing but it's missing something." His eyebrows cinch in question.

"And what would that be?"

"You," I murmur, as I move some of the bubbles for him to see my chest on display.

"Is that so?" He smirks down at me. His gaze sends heat straight to my core. I nod and crook a finger, inviting him in. He doesn't hesitate and slides in the other side, pulling me to straddle his legs.

"Is that better?" he whispers into the shell of my ear, making goosebumps break out over my skin. He knows what he does to me.

"Much," I answer. I lay my head on his chest, loving the gentle thrum of his heart. Sam cups some water in his hand and pours it over my back and shoulder. I know he's making sure I keep warm. He begins rubbing soft circles on my back, nearly lulling me to sleep.

"How's my sunshine feeling?" he asks as he kisses the top of my head.

"Very cozy," I murmur against his chest, wrapping my arms around him tighter.

"I meant your tender ass that got some extra attention tonight."

"Oh, well, I'm okay," I reply. Obviously not happy with my answer. He presses me up and pulls my chin over to look at him.

"It's okay, princess," he presses a sweet kiss to my lips then looks back at me, "you don't need to be strong all the time. That's why I'm here. Now you can rest." Tears spring to my eyes as I look at the beautiful man before me.

"I am a little sore, I guess."

"Show me where so I can make it better." I pull my bottom lip into my mouth to nibble. "Is someone being shy all of a sudden?" I nod as he smirks at me.

"I guess I'll have to find these spots myself then," he whispers against my lips. He holds himself there just barely grazing my lips, taunting me until I can't take it anymore and pull him closer. He chuckles against my lips.

He slides his hand down my back slowly making his way to my sore ass. He gently rubs soothing circles around my puckered hole.

Never in my life did I think I would like having something in my ass but oh how wrong I was. Sam knows my body better than I do it seems.

"How's that feel?" he asks softly. My eyes fall closed from the wonderful sensation. I find myself slowly rocking back against his hand.

"That good, huh? I think I know what will make it even better." He smiles and I melt into him. He skims his other hand down my tummy then further until he reaches my bundle of sensitive nerves. Simultaneously he rubs both spots making my body come alive once again under his touch.

"Yes, that feels so good," I moan against his chest. My hips thrust against his hard cock, standing between us.

"If you keep that up, I'll end up back inside that sweet cunt of yours," he teases.

"Maybe that's what I want." I tilt my head up for him to see I'm serious.

"Fuck, princess. You're as insatiable as I am."

"I guess that makes us a good team." I smile. He shakes his head in disbelief but grips my hips, raising me in the water.

"Put me in," he urges.

"Yes, sir." He pulls my chin for me to look at him.

"Right now it's just me and you, baby." I nod as I take his hard length into my hand, loving how it pulses from my touch. I center him at my entrance as Sam slowly pushes me down onto him. We both groan from the immense pleasure.

"Fuck, I'll never tire of you. You were made for me." He cups my face as I continue to bounce slowly up and down on his cock.

His kiss is slow, sensual, consuming. I don't know where I end and Sam begins.

"I was supposed to be soothing your aches away, not making love to you in the tub."

"You are soothing me. My pussy ached and needed you," I giggle against his neck.

"Well in that case I guess I better tend to it." He grabs handfuls of my hips as he thrusts up inside me. The slow strokes make me frenzied.

"Sam, I need to come." He kisses up my neck, around my jaw then finally presses his lips to mine. As I keep the same pace, Sam's hand slides between us to rub my clit. It doesn't take long before I'm a writhing mess on the brink of another orgasm.

"Come with me, sunshine." His words send sparks through my body jolting the pleasure to hit every nerve I have.

"That's it, fuck! Marcy!" He presses me down on his lap as his cock goes off inside me. I can feel each spurt egging my orgasm to continue until I'm too weak to hold myself up. My whole body feels like a limp noodle. I don't think I could walk right now even if the building was on fire.

"Maybe l put a baby in your belly tonight," Sam purrs in my ear. I'd forgotten what he'd said earlier. I shoot my eyes up to his and see he isn't joking.

"Are you serious?"

"More than ever," he replies. I don't even know what to say. Before any words form in my mind, he continues. "I want to start a family with you, princess. That shouldn't come as a shock to you. I want everything with you." He entwines our hands together then kisses my knuckles. "Please tell me you want the same." He looks so vulnerable right now that it tugs at my heart.

"Of course I want the same. I want it all. I just can't believe you didn't tell me about my birth control."

"Oh, I was keeping that as a surprise. I've been dying to get inside you but I had to wait until you were cleared by a doctor. Don't think for one second that I didn't dream of fucking you every night," he groans in my ear.

"I want to fuck you so hard then keep my cock in place until my seed takes root. I'm not letting you get away."

His lips smother mine is a ravenous kiss, only stopping when we both need air.

"I fucking love you. Today. Tomorrow. Forever. Through this life and the next."

He lifts us from the tub and wraps a towel around me then uses one to dry my hair as much as possible, taking his time to pamper me. Then Sam leads me to the bed, instructing me to lean over it. He opens a container sitting on the bedside table then begins massaging a cooling lotion over my ass and thighs. The effects are instant and the burn no longer stings. He continues to rub and massage, making sure it all rubs into the skin.

"Now, crawl in the bed, love."

He scoops me into his arms and pulls me against his warm body, cradling my head against his chest. I wrap my leg around his wanting to be as close as possible. He pulls the covers over us as we snuggle in closer.

Sam rubs his hand over my belly and I can see a faint smile ghost his lips from the moonlight flickering through a crack in the curtains. He reaches down between my legs, feeling his cum leaking out but he presses it back inside me.

"Just in case..." he smiles.

"I love you even if you are a bit crazy," I murmur.

"I love you most."

Twenty Six

Marcy

Rolling over in the bed, I feel Sam's heat pressed against me. It envelops me like a safe haven. His contours fit seamlessly with my own, as if we were two pieces of a puzzle finally finding their match. His arm is draped over my waist, pulling me closer. Even in sleep he makes sure there is nothing separating us. My eyes fall closed as I listen to his soft breathing, his chest rising and falling like a steady metronome.

Sam's lips brush my forehead, making me gasp. "I thought you were asleep!" I squeal as he rolls me over to face him.

"I was but I felt your sweet ass wiggle against me and it woke me." He's leaning above me, resting himself on one arm.

"I'll try to contain my wiggles next time, *sir*," I tease, knowing I just lit a fire inside him.

"Did my princess not get enough last night?" He brushes the hair from my face then pulls me in for a sweet good morning kiss. Sweet. That's the flavor of this kiss—a blend of vulnerability and desire. I lose myself in him—the thought of coffee forgotten, the day's agenda erased. I could stay like this forever.

"Let's go shower then I'll whip us up some breakfast. How does that sound?"

"Absolutely amazing," I sigh. "You're too sweet to me."

"That's impossible." He kisses my nose. "But I'll spend forever trying." He winks as he jumps from the bed, dragging me along with him. This man, in all his craziness, holds my heart.

"I planned a special date for us tonight, princess," Sam breathes into my ear. Turning in his arms, I place my hands on his shoulders, pulling his face closer wanting to feel his soft lips against mine.

"Is that so? And where will we be going?"

"You can't seduce the answer out of me, little vixen. You'll have to wait and see. But there is something special for you in our closet." He winks then slaps my ass as he begins to walk away.

"Hey! That's mine!" I giggle as I run away from him but he's right on my tail. We get to the bedroom and he jumps on the bed after me, pinning me down.

"Oh I don't think so, sunshine. This ass is mine." He squeezes it hard.

"So is this perfect cunt that you saved just for me. It's all mine." Sam cups it in his hand showing me exactly who's in charge. Shivers run through my body at the intensity of his gaze on me.

"And these," he runs his hands up my body until my breasts fill his hands. "Mmm, these are mine to lick, suck, bite and anything else I want to do to them." His eyes darken.

"Wouldn't they look beautiful with clamps hanging from them? Dangling and tugging as I fucked you from behind." A whimper escapes my lips. I want any and everything he wants to do to me because I trust him explicitly.

"Fuck, you're exquisite," he croons in my ear, "too bad we have to start getting dressed." He smirks, pressing a chaste kiss to my lips then gets off the bed. Dammit, he got me all needy and then takes it away, like dangling sweets in front of a child. I breathe out a huff.

"Aww, something wrong, sunshine?" He holds his hand out for me, helping me from the bed.

"Yes, you know what you did. I don't appreciate being teased." I cross my arms over my chest.

"I see someone's brat is showing." He brushes the hair from my face then leans down so his face is right in front of mine.

"You haven't seen teasing yet, baby." He pulls me in for a deep kiss, sweeping his tongue into my mouth. I can feel his hard length pressed against me. I need him now, I don't want to wait. I trail my hand down his chest to grab his cock as it strains in his pants. A growl erupts from him as he pulls away.

"You're playing with fire, little girl. You wouldn't want to get burned. Now go get ready. We'll be leaving soon."

He heads toward the door as I mutter under my breath, "maybe I like fire." He stops at the door, not turning around.

"Oh, I can't wait to get you back here tonight. You have no idea what's in store for you now."

"Yes, sir," I murmur loud enough for him to hear. He turns his head back and tsks. With that he's out of the door and heading down the hall.

A giggle bubbles up as I skip to the closet to see what he got me. I really can't wait to see where he's taking me. He's been very secretive for a couple days so I knew he was planning something. Nerves ricochet through my body thinking about all the possibilities.

The lights dim and the curtains begin to draw back. Sam's hand slides to my thigh with a light squeeze. My eyes are peeled, anxiously waiting for the first scene to unfold so I can understand why he was so secretive bringing me here.

And then I hear it. The first note of the Overture. He brought me to see the Phantom of the Opera. He knew. He must have heard Matt and I on the boat that day. He squeezes my thigh again as his thumb gently strokes my skin but I can't look at him. I can't look away from the images before me.

Tears fall from my eyes as the beautiful stage comes to life. This is what I've always been waiting for. This is what we were waiting for. Matthew was a sucker for this play and we always said we would see it together. He promised he would come back to me and that we would see it one day. It's been eighteen years and I'm finally seeing it. Not with Matthew, but with Sam.

I don't know if he understands the magnitude of what he's done. As the play progresses I feel lighter. This was the last string of Matthew I had tethered to me and now that I'm here it snaps, setting us free. It sets me free. Matthew can finally rest in peace because his last request has been fulfilled by his best friend.

I know he truly meant for Sam to take care of me. In all ways. In his last moments, he knew Sam was what I needed to get through this life without him.

I close my eyes because the tears begin blurring my vision but I continue to listen. I hear the melodies weaving through the air and I know Mathew can hear them too. A wave of peace washes over me, leaving me breathless.

"Thank you," I whisper, knowing he'll hear even though I'm not looking at him.

"I promised to take care of you, sunshine. That includes helping you to let go."

He knew. He knew I was still holding on to that last string. I have been for years. I haven't been living, not really. Until Sam.

Sam stormed into my life filling it with emotions I never knew I could feel. He sparked me back to life and resuscitated my heart. I can hear the beating in my ears. I'm alive. It's time to start living.

Opening my eyes, I look at Sam.

"Come here." He opens his arms allowing me to sit in his lap. I snuggle in close as I lay my head on his chest. I hear his heartbeat intertwining with my own.

"You have given me more than I can even describe. You brought me back, Sam. You gave me what no one else could. Peace. I've finally found peace and it's because of you," I pause trying to continue without fucking up the most important part. With a deep breath, I vow, "I love you, Samuel. You have forever been my always. I knew it from day one. It wasn't a silly little crush. Your soul called to mine in the most desperate of ways. I—" with the back of my hand I wipe my eyes, smearing the black mess painted across my face but I don't have it in me to care. Sam sees me. He sees my heart and soul. His called out to mine as the actors dance together in the theater.

"Marcy, when I met you I was enchanted with your stories. At just nine your mind fascinated me. I couldn't explain it. I knew you were special. When I saw you again at the funeral, the fast, all encompassing, obsession consumed me to where I could barely breathe. I knew in an instant that you were it for me. You, whom I had known for half my life. You had been irrevocably weaving yourself into my heart until I was nothing without you." Sam swipes his fingers under my eyes then tangles his fingers into my hair, positioning my head where he could fully see me.

"I didn't give a shit about the age difference. I knew you were placed in my life for a reason. You became a permanent fixture that all my thoughts turned to. I knew I couldn't have you until I was out of the military because I would die over and over again forcing punishment on myself from beyond if I didn't make it back to you. So, I waited, biding my time. But then I faltered, wondering if I would ever be as good as what you deserved. So I watched from afar believing you were living your best life, until your birthday party. That's when everything changed inside me. My body craved yours with a ferocity that I've never known. Being that close to you felt like I was burning alive but I knew my only salvation was having you in my arms."

Sam took my lips in his, losing ourselves in each other. Once he pulled back I could see there was still more he wanted to say.

"I didn't understand your brother that day. But his words were clear. He knew. Somehow, he always knew." He chuckled thinking back.

"He entrusted you with me. His final wish had been what I had longed for but denied myself. But when I took your hand in mine that night, I knew I could never be apart from you again." He presses a longing kiss to my knuckles, his eyes never leaving mine. Chills run through my body from his words, his touch, his everything.

He places my hand on my lap then digs through his tux, revealing to me a small velvet box. My heart, already on the edge of bursting, somehow manages to accelerate.

I don't know where to look but my eyes land on his. His hazel pools of unending passion shine down on me. I faintly hear the box opening but I'm more focused on his words.

"I would have asked permission but it was already granted to me long ago." A pang of sadness hits my heart but it's quickly washed away as a tear slides down his beautiful sculpted cheek. I've only seen Sam cry three times. First at Matthew's funeral then when I woke up in the hospital and now. Emotions bubble inside me threatening to rupture.

"Sunshine, please allow me to take care of you. Allow me to be your rock when your mind threatens to drift you away. Your shield when the world is too much. Your support when you need it. Allow me to be your equal in all ways, sharing my family with you so you're never alone again in this crazy huge world. Marcy, please allow me to be your husband, lover, partner, your forever for the rest of our days."

Nodding, I look down at my hand already donning the most perfect diamond I've ever seen. He didn't give me a chance because he already knew the answer. My finger wiggles, the diamond twinkling from the stage lights. It's then that I recognize the ring.

I gasp, bringing my hand to my mouth. He smirks like he was waiting for me to notice.

"How did you–? How–" I stutter, more tears begin streaming down my cheeks.

"A few months after Matthew's funeral, I received a letter from your mother while I was overseas. She'd seen our connection at the funeral and knew we would find our way to one another, eventually. She knew you'd always dreamed of having this wedding ring as your own." I nod in disbelief.

My Nanny's wedding ring was the most precious possession in the world. I always wondered what had happened to it after my parents' funeral. I figured it got misplaced and was lost forever. My sweet mother would let me play dress up with it when I was younger.

I'm twirling in my beautiful green dress my mom bought me for the dance coming up. I look in my mirror seeing Sam leaning up against the wall with a smirk on his face. I turn around, embarrassment flooding my cheeks that he saw me.

"You're mom sent me. It's time for dinner, sunshine." He gestures behind him toward the kitchen. "But now I'm intrigued. What do you have here?" He asks moving closer, turning my hand over so the ring sparkles around the room.

"It's, um, my Nanny's wedding ring. It will be mine one day." I gulp at the nerves tickling my belly. Sam's cologne floats through the air making me hazy.

"I see, but what are you doing with it? Aren't you a little young to get married?" He chuckles as his thumb brushes over the ring, but I snatch my hand away from him.

"I'm practicing, thank you very much!" I turn back to the mirror running my hands down the soft fabric of the dress.

"Is that right? Well, where is the groom then?" he asks as he goes back to leaning against the wall with his arms crossed.

He's right here, I think to myself. "He doesn't know yet." I mention turning back to Sam.

"Hmm, sounds like he needs to get his head out of his ass and realize what he's missing out on." Laughter erupts from my lips but Sam doesn't laugh. He stands still watching me.

"I might have to tell him that one day."

"I don't think any of these 'boys' are worthy of you."

"Oh stop! You're starting to sound like a big brother and I already have one of those." His face soured when I said brother but he quickly schooled his features.

"Oh! I wanted to thank you for the dance lessons. I've been practicing. Hopefully I don't make a complete idiot out of myself at the dance."

"You don't have to thank me. I'll always be here when you need me." I almost believe him with the amount of sincerity I see in his eyes. I just nod, wringing my hands in front of me.

"Tell mom I'll be down in a minute. I need to change." I turn back to the mirror. Sam hesitates for a moment then turns on his heels, closing the door behind him.

I collapse in a mess of green chiffon on the floor, clutching the ring to my chest. Why does my true love have to be so much older? It's like a sick joke the universe is playing on me. Sam will never see me the same way I see him.

I sigh out of frustration as my back falls to the floor. My ceiling is covered in glow in the dark stars. Every night I wish upon a different one in hopes that one day my dream will come true.

I hold up my hand with the ring and memorize every intimate detail of it. It's what I want my ring to look like someday if I can't have the real thing.

"Marcy!" My mother's voice cuts through my day dreaming.

I close my eyes, holding the ring tightly, "Please, please let him come find me one day," I whisper.

"You found me! Of course I will marry you. It's always been you." I smile up at him. He looks at me questioningly but I shake my head as I lean up to kiss this perfect man. Maybe not perfect but perfect for me. He's beautifully flawed.

I take his hand in mine, joining us forever. I draw a heart on his with my finger then press it into the skin sending it deep into his soul where it will never be replaced.

Twenty Seven

Samuel

"Merry Christmas, sunshine," I whisper into Marcy's ear. She grunts and tries to pull away from me. Someone is grumpy this morning. I guess I had something to do with that since I kept her up most of the night devouring her perfect body. It's an addiction and I can't get enough. I want her more than I've wanted anything in my life.

Marcy covers her head with a pillow, making me chuckle. I pull it from her grasp, tossing it to the end of the bed.

"Five more minutes, please," she whines. I pull her body back against mine, loving the feel of her warmth against me.

"Nope, it's time to get up." Leaning over, I pepper her face with kisses making her giggle and squeal trying to push me away.

"Good, now that you're awake, I have a surprise for you." I can't contain my excitement. I feel like a little boy on Christmas morning.

"Sam," she says groggily, "it's barely even light outside. Are you crazy? This is the kind of thing that pushes wives to kill their husbands on those crime shows." She peeks at me from underneath the curtain of her hair covering her face.

"Aw, you think of me as your husband?" I brush her hair away so she can see..

"That's all you took from that?" She laughs and rolls her eyes.

"Hmm, you know brats get different kinds of presents. I guess I could take this one back since you don't want it."

"Wait!" She sits up quickly looking around for the present. Her messy hair whips around as she glances all over. She looks at me questioningly. "What am I missing?"

"What do you say?" I raise my eyebrow at her.

"Please can I have my present, *sir,*" she emphasized, making me smile at her stubbornness. I open the bedside table drawer to find the box I placed in there last night. She's going to laugh when she sees what it's wrapped in, but in my defense at least it's wrapped.

The shine from the box reflects the sunlight streaming through a crack in the curtains. Marcy's eyes widen first then a smile appears.

"Please tell me you didn't wrap my Christmas present in tin-foil?" she giggles as she takes the box from me and examines it.

"I thought it was a good idea. I mean it's basically wrapping paper, or wrapping foil, same thing. Plus it's shiny."

"Have I told you how much I adore you?" She tangles her hand through the back of my hair then brings me closer for a kiss. My hands cup her face as I take control of the kiss. It's commanding, passionate, everything. This woman has my heart and there's not a damn thing I want to do about it.

"Open it, sunshine," I whisper along her lips as my mouth roams over her jaw then down her neck. I smile at the goosebumps that rise on her skin. My girl loves my warm breath coating her skin.

"I can't if you're doing that..." she breathes.

"Fine, I'll stop." I kiss her forehead then lean back against the headboard waiting on her to open the gift. She shakes it and hears the metal clanking together. Marcy looks at me, her eyes full of questions. She could never guess what it is.

Marcy begins pulling the foil away leaving a white box in her hands. She looks at me for permission before she opens it. I nod with a smile.

She opens the box and is motionless for a moment, taking in what she's seeing. Her hands begin to tremble but she picks up the necklace, dropping the box on the bed. Marcy stares at it with tears in her eyes as she continues holding it up in front of her. I lean up to kiss her shoulder, wrapping my arm around her waist to pull her closer.

"I thought it was time to pass these along," I utter, emotion filling my chest as well.

"They're," she swallows, "they're his." She pulls her gaze away from the gift long enough for me to see the tears falling down her cheeks with a small smile on her face.

"I knew you would want Matt's dog tags. They should have been yours all along." I kiss her temple as she clutches them to her chest.

"Thank you. They're perfect. They're everything. Thank you, Sam," she smiles.

"Now, let's go downstairs so you can tear into all the other things I got you," I insist as I rise from the bed pulling on a pair of red plaid pajama pants that I got just for today. I even got her a matching set. I know it's cheesy but I want all the things with her and I knew she would be ecstatic with matching pajamas. What my baby wants, she gets. She watches me from the bed with a smile.

"You got Christmas pajamas?" she laughs.

"Not just me, princess." I toss her set on the bed. "Now get your ass up so we can go celebrate." she crawls to the end of the bed to grab the clothes, running the soft material under her fingers.

"You're crazy, you know that?" I walk back over to the bed to lean down and whisper in her ear.

"Not as crazy as you for wanting to marry me, princess. What does that say about you?" I chuckle as I turn to head downstairs to start the coffee. A pillow hits the back of my head. So that's how she wants to play it? I slowly turn, then take slow steps back to her.

"Oh, baby. Didn't I say you better be careful or the beast would come out to play?" She nibbles on her bottom lip as she scoots backward on the bed.

"Oops?" She chuckles. I guess her ass isn't sore enough from last night. I can definitely fix that.

"Oh, sunshine..." I tsk as I pounce on the bed, her squeals ringing through the apartment.

"What time are we supposed to be there?" Marcy calls from the bathroom.

"We need to leave here in five minutes."

She steps out of the bathroom in a new dress with her hair and makeup done. She's breathtakingly stunning. I know I won't be able to keep my eye off her tonight. Her green sparkle dress compliments her in all the best ways. I can't wait to show her off. Showing everyone she's mine.

"Well, what do you think?" She twirls around giving me a full view.

I stand, stalking toward her until I can wrap my hands around her waist.

"You are the most captivating, radiant, sexiest woman in the world." I lean down kissing behind her ear. "I want to devour you," I whisper.

"You don't look so bad yourself," she beams up at me.

"Shall we, princess?" I hold my arm out for her to take. She places her hand on my arm and nods.

"Wait, I-uh..." she hesitates, pulling her plump bottom lip into her mouth.

"What is it, sunshine?" I lift her chin, forcing her gaze on me and not at her feet.

"I'm kinda nervous." She shrugs her shoulders like it isn't a big deal then tries to move away from me.

"Hey, where do you think you're going? We're talking and we weren't finished. Don't you know the consequences of that by now?" I chuckle darkly as her eyes flare with desire.

"I just thought we needed to leave," she counters.

"We do but this is more important. I don't want you to be nervous or uncomfortable or anything besides blissfully happy." I pull her back against me looking deeply in her radiant green eyes. "You are my family now and they've basically adopted you as well. There isn't anything to worry about but if at any point during the night you feel uncomfortable just let me know and I'll make some excuse to get us out of there. Okay?"

She nods, whispering, "you would do that?"

"Sunshine, don't you know I would do anything for you? I would strike a match, toss it away then watch as the world burns down around us. I'd even hand you the match for yourself. Anything for you." Marcy dabs the corners of her eyes that glisten with tears.

"Are you trying to ruin my makeup?" she huffs, smiling up at me. Leaning over, I press my lips to her forehead.

"Just telling you the facts. Seemed like you needed a reminder."

"Thank you, babe."

"Oh, 'babe', hmm I like the sound of that. Now, how about we get outta here."

"I'll go anywhere with you." My heart aches from the love I have for this woman.

We arrive at Aunt Amelia's estate right outside the city. Descending through her long winding driveway brings back so many memories from when I was younger and I would come play with Miles and Sebastian. I haven't been here in so long, yet, it still remains familiar like I never really left.

I park beside Miles' gray Aston Martin then race around to the passenger side to help Marcy out. She steps out onto the gravel driveway, her high heels making her stumble. I steady her, my arm around her waist. She leans into me, trusting I'll stay by her side throughout the evening.

"You're not alone. I'll be right here with you." I press my hand against the small of her back as I lead her up the stairs.

Marcy fixes her hair as I knock on the door. She looks delectable. I wish she could see herself the way I see her.

"Samuel, Marcy, I'm so happy you could make it! Merry Christmas!" Aunt Amelia gushes as she ushers us inside then takes us both in a tight embrace. I slip Marcy's jacket from her shoulders and hang it up, along with my own before we continue into the main part of the house.

"Thank you for inviting us, Amelia," Marcy expresses.

"Are you kidding? I've been trying to get this one here for years. Now, thanks to you, he comes." She leans up to kiss Sam's cheek then wipes away the lipstick that she left behind.

"Well, I'm here now. That's all that matters." I remark, wrapping my arm around my girl.

"Is that Sammy I hear coming in?" Sebastian booms from the kitchen. We walk further into Amelia's home, enjoying the wonderful food and smiling faces.

Sebastian and Miles both come to slap me on the back at the same time. Fuckers.

"Nice to see you both," I roll my eyes but smile.

"We're glad you finally grew a pair and went after what you wanted." The three of us look over at the girls catching up with one another. I admit, I missed this. Having people that always have your back. Marcy has opened my eyes to so many things. I feel like we both got a family when she came into my life.

"Yeah, it was inevitable. I think the universe has always been pulling us together," I respond.

"Care for a whiskey?" Miles asks, holding his glass up. Normally I would say yes but I think I've had enough alcohol for two lifetimes. That's not me anymore.

"I'm good, thanks." We stand there watching the girls pass the new babies around. Marcy glances at me as she takes baby River into her arms. Stormy and Sebastian welcomed a beautiful baby girl a few months ago.

Seeing her holding a child in her arms makes me hope that she gets pregnant soon. The possibility of sooner rather than later is real with the way we can't keep our hands off of each other.

Miles comes over holding little Benjamin in his arm.

"Want to meet your smallest cousin?" He hands him over.

"Hey, little fella. I'm your cousin but I'm going to say uncle as well." Miles chuckles but nods.

"I guess that's accurate. We're brothers at heart."

Marcy beams when she sees me holding Ben. I wonder if she's thinking about our future child? She better be because I'm not stopping until she's pregnant. Even then I'll keep going. We can have a whole soccer team as far as I'm concerned. Although, Marcy may have something to say about that. The thought makes me grin.

Marcy

I'm finally home. I found it with the Knights. I never understood the expression "home is where the heart is" but it's true. These people are my family now and forever. They welcomed and embraced me without a second thought. They treat me like I've always been one of their own. I couldn't have asked for a better Christmas. The warmth of being surrounded by caring people makes it truly special. My heart is overflowing. I know Matthew is here with me, he's always with me. Forever in my heart.

"Dessert is up next. Hope you all saved room. I have several pies and sweets for you to choose from," Amelia announces.

"Mother, you really overdid yourself this year. Everything was amazing," Miles praises.

"Oh, hush. I wanted it all to be perfect. It's been so long since we've had everyone here. And now with my new grandbabies, Benjamin and River, it couldn't be any 'ol celebration. I only wish your father was here to see this. He loved his family," she remarks.

"I think we should send a toast up to father. After all, none of us would be here without him," Sebastian resounds.

"I agree," Sam concurs.

Miles pushes his chair out then rises to his feet with a flute of champagne in his hand. "To my father, Benjamin Miles Knight Senior, thank you for showing us the value of family and how it makes the world a better place. You raised us to cherish all the moments, good and bad, because they shape who we are. We miss you, we love you, we'll see you again. Cheers!" He raises his glass in the air as we all join in.

"Cheers!" we all exclaim.

We all retire to the living room while we let the feast settle in our stomachs. I think we all overdid ourselves but it was the best home cooked meal that I've had in a long time. With the exception of Sam's of course.

"So, when are you guys planning on getting married?" Stormy asks as she holds a sleeping River in her arms. Her silver hair cascades down her back in beautiful waves.

"I guess we haven't had much time to talk about it." I look at Sam but he's smiling like he knows a secret. *What has he gotten into this time?* I swear these Knights are trouble.

"Well, I would love to paint a portrait of you in your wedding dress so you can hang it over the mantle." Stormy smiles as she looks down at the sleeping bundle wrapped in her arms.

"Wow, thank you. We would love that, Stormy. Thank you. I will definitely need you girls to go with me to pick the right dress." I look at Amelia and Lizzie to make sure they know I mean them as well.

"Oh dear, we wouldn't miss it. We'll make a day of it after the holidays. I'll make a few calls to ensure we have the shops to ourselves," Amelia chimes in and flurries of excitement roll through me. I can't believe I'm actually going to marry my childhood crush. The man that I've compared every other to. Marcy Knight, I like the sound of that.

"Your love story has sparked an idea for my next book," Lizzie grins." I can't wait to get back to writing, but this one here insists that I rest the appropriate amount of time before I return to work." She rolls her eyes but smiles up at Miles. You can see the love they hold for each other. It's truly magical.

"I'm only taking care of my favorite girl," Miles insists.

"Hey! When did I get replaced?" Amelia chuckles.

"Sorry, mother, no one can compete with my wife."

"Well, that's the way it should be." Amelia smiles at her eldest son.

River begins stirring and whimpering, making Sebastian jump up to come to Stormy's aid. I can't help but to see the crazy transformations these men have undergone since finding their forevers. The once famous playboys of New York City have settled down and are in for the long haul. Maybe my job will be less stressful with these women reeling them in. *Hell, what am I saying?* The

Knights can sneeze and make the front page. My job is never done, but I like it like that.

As the night winds down, we begin our goodbyes. It's a bittersweet moment, saying farewell to the warmth and camaraderie I've found with the Knights this Christmas. But I know that I'll carry these memories with me forever. And this isn't goodbye, *it's a see you later*.

"Come, wife," Sam smirks down at me, holding my jacket in his hands.

"I'm not your wife yet," I retort as he helps me into my coat. Pulling my hair free, I turn to look up at him.

"Sunshine, don't pretend that you didn't always imagine me beside you while twirling around in your dresses. It's been written in the stars forever. You were destined to be my wife once we found our way back to one another."

Sam twirls me around then pulls me in close, our breaths mingling as our eyes dance with desire. In that moment, the world fades away, leaving only the two of us. He softly brushes his lips over mine, igniting a fire within, a longing that transcends time. The air crackles with electricity, and every nerve ending hums with anticipation.

His fingers trace the curve of my jaw, leaving a trail of heat in their wake. Sam's eyes hold mine, a silent promise of forever. As his lips press harder against mine, I yield willingly, lost in the intoxicating feeling of Samuel Knight, my lover, my best friend, my always.

Epilogue

Life isn't always a battle...

Life is a multifaceted journey with moments of joy, challenges, and everything in between. When life leaves you with cracks, those imperfections that make you feel broken, remember that fire can heal. It burns away the old, leaving space for new growth. It's in those moments of vulnerability that you find your strength. Embrace the flames within you, and let them forge resilience. Just like a mosaic, where each broken piece contributes to a beautiful whole, our experiences shape us into something unique and remarkable.

Love doesn't always come easy. For many it's challenging, overcoming obstacles, and fighting to be together. It's holding on so hard that you fear your grip won't be enough. But when it's finally within your reach, you grasp it with both hands because it's impossible to live without.

Remember that even during the fiercest storms, there are oases of calm waiting to be discovered. And when battles arise, may you find the strength within to fight with courage and resilience.

"You know you're in love when you can't fall asleep because reality is finally better than your dreams." *-Dr. Seuss*

Forever was a word for memories, not people.

People are transient beings—wandering souls who touch our lives, leaving imprints like footprints in the sand. They dance into our existence, twirling through chapters, and sometimes, they pirouette away.

So let us cherish the memories—the laughter shared, the tears shed, the whispered promises—as they weave their way into the fabric of our existence. And let us honor the people who color our days, even if their presence is but a fleeting brushstroke on our canvas of life.

*

IN REMEMBRANCE OF

SGT Bob Weaver

K.I.A. 2006

A brother to all

WHY WE DON'T GET OVER GRIEF

Death is a universal experience, this is true. Yet grief isn't something we get over. Getting over it implies it will heal and we'll forget about it, like a hangnail. Grief is a violent eruption. The spewing ash and fiery lava consume our world and reduces our visibility to zero, forcing us into darkness while it destroys everything in its path. We have no choice but to go along wherever it takes us. Years go by before it's cool enough to access the damage. Only then do we begin the reconstruction of self into something meaningful.

-Lynda Cheldelin Fell

Are you a Veteran in crisis or concerned about one?

Find support anytime day or night

To connect with a Veterans Crisis Line responder anytime day or night:

Dial 988 then Press 1.

Start a confidential chat.

Text 838255.

If you have hearing loss, call TTY: 800-799-4889.

https://www.mentalhealth.va.gov/

Mission 22

WHEN THEIR TOUR IS OVER, OUR MISSION BEGINS

Mission 22 provides support to Veterans and their families when they need it most: right now. Through a comprehensive approach of outreach, events, and programs, we're promoting long-term wellness and sustainable growth.

https://mission22.com/

Til Valhalla Project

https://tilvalhallaproject.com/

Mental Health Awareness

Mental health is a crucial aspect of our overall well-being. It includes our emotional, psychological, and social health, and affects how we think, feel, and act. Mental health is important at every stage of life, from childhood and adolescence through adulthood.

Mental health awareness is the ongoing effort to reduce the stigma around mental illness and mental health conditions by sharing personal experiences. It helps people understand that mental illness is not a character flaw but rather an illness like any other.

An increasing awareness of mental health helps society work toward eliminating its stigmas, but it does much more. For instance, developing a greater understanding of mental illness can allow people to recognize those in their lives who may be dealing with anxiety, depression, or other conditions that affect their mental well-being.

If you or someone you know is struggling with mental health, it's important to seek help. The National Alliance on Mental Illness (NAMI) provides resources and support for individuals and families affected by mental illness.

Remember, our mental health journey starts with a single moment. Let's break the stigma together!

Mental Health Foundation

How common are mental illnesses?

Mental illnesses are among the most common health conditions in the United States.

More than 1 in 5 US adults live with a mental illness.

Over 1 in 5 youth (ages 13-18) either currently or at some point during their life, have had a seriously debilitating mental illness.

About 1 in 25 U.S. adults lives with a serious mental illness, such as schizophrenia, bipolar disorder, or major depression.

What causes mental illness?

There is no single cause for mental illness. A number of factors can contribute to risk for mental illness, such as

- Adverse Childhood Experiences, such as trauma or a history of abuse (for example, child abuse, sexual assault, witnessing violence, etc.)
- Experiences related to other ongoing (chronic) medical conditions, such as a traumatic brain injury, cancer, or diabetes
- Biological factors or chemical imbalances in the brain
- Use of alcohol or drugs
- Having feelings of loneliness or isolation

Tools and Resources

The free and confidential resources below can help you or a loved one connect with a skilled, trained mental health professional.

Need Support Now?

If you or someone you know is struggling or in crisis, help is available. Call or text 988 or chat 988lifeline.org

Disaster Distress Helpline

CALL or TEXT 1-800-985-5990 (press 2 for Spanish)

Abuse/Assault/Violence

National Domestic Violence Hotline

1-800-799-7233 or text LOVEIS to 22522

National Child Abuse Hotline

1-800-4AChild (1-800-422-4453) or text 1-800-422-4453

National Sexual Assault Hotline

1-800-656-HOPE (4673) or Online Chat

LGBTQ+

Trans Lifeline

1-877-565-8860 (para español presiona el 2)

The Trevor Project's TrevorLifeline

1-866-488-7386

Older Adults

The Eldercare Locator

1-800-677-1116 – TTY Instructions

Alzheimer's Association Helpline: 1-800-272-3900 (para español presiona el 2)

Veterans/Active-duty Military

Veteran's Crisis Line

988, then select 1, or Crisis Chat

or text: 838255

U.S. Department of Veterans Affairs Mental Health Resources

Help for Military Service Members and Their Families

Finding Treatment

FindTreatment.gov

Find a provider treating substance use disorders, addiction, and mental illness.

American Psychiatric Association Foundation

Find a Psychiatrist

American Academy of Child and Adolescent Psychiatry

Child and Adolescent Psychiatrist Finder

American Psychological Association

Find a Psychologist

Opioid Treatment

Buprenorphine Treatment Practitioner Locator

Opioid Treatment Program Directory by State

More By L.B. Martin

Knight Publishing Series

The Write Knight – *Life isn't always a fairytale*

The Silent Knight – *Life isn't always a holiday*

The Starry Knight – *Life isn't always a work of art*

The Last Knight – *Life isn't always a battle*

Boys of Frampton University

Backstroke – enemies to lovers – *Releasing summer 2024!*

L.B. Martin lives in South Carolina with her husband and two children. She spends her free time reading, writing, and drinking all the coffee. L.B. majored in English literature in college with a minor in British Lit. Her husband is a professional gamer, so when he is playing, she is reading away. She loves writing MCs with mental illness in hopes to shine light on mental health awareness.

"My words spill from my mind to the pages in effort to rid myself of the demons tucked away inside. My hope is that readers will be immersed into my world and come out feeling hopeful and full of purpose."
-L.B. Martin

Linktree https://linktr.ee/lb_martin_author

Made in the USA
Middletown, DE
10 January 2025